APOCALYPSIS

KAHAYATLE

book one

Books by Elle Casey

CONTEMPORARY URBAN FANTASY

War of the Fae (10-book series)
Ten Things You Should Know About Dragons
(short story, The Dragon Chronicles)
My Vampire Summer
Aces High

DYSTOPIAN

Apocalypsis (4-book series)

SCIENCE FICTION

Drifters' Alliance (ongoing series)
Winner Takes All (short story prequel to Drifters' Alliance,
Dark Beyond the Stars Anthology)
The Ivory Tower (short story standalone, Beyond the Stars: A
Planet Too Far Anthology)

ROMANCE

By Degrees
Rebel Wheels (3-book series)
Just One Night (romantic serial)
Just One Week
Love in New York (3-book series)
Shine Not Burn (2-book series)
Bourbon Street Boys (4-book series)
Desperate Measures
Mismatched

ROMANTIC SUSPENSE

*All the Glory: How Jason Bradley Went from
Hero to Zero in Ten Seconds Flat*
Don't Make Me Beautiful
Wrecked (2-book series)

PARANORMAL

Duality (2-book series)
Monkey Business (short story)
Dreampath (short story standalone, The
Telepath Chronicles)
Pocket Full of Sunshine (short story & screenplay)

APOCALYPSIS

KAHAYATLE

book one

ELLE CASEY

DEDICATION

To Aidan "The Executioner" Brindley
Superfan Extraordinaire from Down Under

PROLOGUE

I stuffed the sleeping bag down into my backpack with angry, punching motions, sick and tired of having to be here and doing the same thing over and over again. I hated camping, I hated being organized, and more than anything, I hated what this exercise stood for.

"Don't do it like that. I told you - you have to conserve the room as best you can. You have to travel as efficiently as possible. Take it out and start over."

"I don't see what difference it makes."

"Trust me, it's going to be a really big deal to you in the not so distant future." His voice sounded hollow.

"Says who?" I was being ornery. I knew the answer to the question already.

"Says me, Bryn. And the news. Look around, would you?" He sounded like he was pleading now. "Stop defaulting back to the rebellious young teen act, and get serious. We don't have enough time to play those games anymore."

"They're not games, Dad. I am a teenager. I don't care what the news jerks and the government say." I threw my backpack down on the ground. "And it's not rebellious to not want to play friggin' survivor in the backyard every day."

My dad looked at me with a sad expression and sighed, reaching over to pull me into a tight hug. He dropped his nose to my head and inhaled deeply.

My face was pressed up against his shirt, and I could smell his sweat mixed with the sweet scent of his aftershave. My dad always said he was the last of a dying breed, using that stuff. He couldn't have been more right.

"Maybe it's not going to happen here ... to us." I said it just to hear the words, but I knew it was only wishful thinking.

I could tell he was getting choked up again when he started talking, his voice now hoarse.

"I wish, more than anything else in this world, that you didn't have to be standing here with me in this backyard playing survivor." His whole body started to shake with silent sobs. "Oh, God, Bryn. If I could do anything to change this, anything at all, I would. I swear to God I would. But it's happening. No one can stop it."

I put my arms around his waist, letting go of my earlier stubborn anger, now choking back my own tears. "I know, Dad. I'm sorry. I didn't mean it."

"Yes, you did," he said, sniffing hard and clearing his throat, shifting to hold me at arm's length. He was staring at me while he smiled through his tears, giving me that look. The one that always made me confess.

"Okay, so maybe I did mean it. But I'll shut up about it for a little while."

"Not for too long, though. You wouldn't be my daughter if you weren't complaining about something."

I tried to slap him playfully but he moved too fast for me. My dad is light on his feet, an expert level-one practitioner of krav maga - a certified badass. He'd only recently taken up camping.

"Pick it up," he ordered, now back in control of his emotions. "Do it again. Only this time, get the air out of that bag first, condense it down ..."

I cut him off. "I know, I know ... 'down into the smallest footprint possible.' Geez, Dad, I'm not an idiot."

I shook the sleeping bag out and started rolling it up quickly, using the moves I'd been practicing for four months straight to squeeze it down into a lump the size of a small loaf of bread. I folded the whole thing in half, pushed it to the bottom of the backpack, and then let it unfold itself one time, before putting the other items in on top of it: unbreakable water bottle, half-liter of bleach, square of plastic, cup, hunting knife, and various other tools my father was quite certain I would need ... once all the adults in the world had died off, leaving us kids alone to fend for ourselves.

CHAPTER ONE

I HAD EATEN ALL THE rations that were left in my house, except for five cans of baked beans and two bags of noodles. It's all I'd been eating for a week, and if I had to have another bite of starch I was going to puke. I didn't like the idea of going through my neighbors' houses to find food, but the choice was being made for me now. I was desperate.

Morning would be the best time for me to make my move. I'd heard the sounds of other people - teens like me - moving around in the daytime; but usually it was in the afternoon or at night. Groups of them had gotten together, looking for stuff in the houses that didn't have kids in them. None of the houses had adults in them anymore.

I needed to move without being seen. Leaving my house unprotected would be a very bad idea. I knew that these gangs were soon going to stop showing respect to the houses with kids in them like me. It was only a matter of time before the resources left in these neighborhoods dwindled down to an amount so small, it would no longer be enough to support the number of growling stomachs that roamed the streets; not without the hungry breaking into the occupied places too.

I hadn't heard them hit the house behind me yet, maybe because there was someone living there. I'd never met that neighbor, though, and had never seen any sign of a kid there. There were two other houses on my street that used to have kids my age in them, but they had left - I assume to join one of the roving gangs. I guess they figured they had better chances of surviving in a group.

I didn't feel that way at all. Before the world had gone into the crapper, I'd been pretty much a loner anyway. I liked my music and my books and didn't bother with after-school clubs or hanging out at the local cafe. Besides, my dad had me in martial arts training every weekday and most weekends, practically my whole life; it didn't leave much time for socializing. I'd only moved to this town six months before my dad was suddenly gone. He'd hoped to outrun the apocalypse, but it eventually caught up with him like it did anyone who wasn't going through puberty.

The guys I trained with at various dojos over the years - I was always the only girl - were as serious as my dad about their skills. They lived for the feel of total control and absolute domination, in any situation. I appreciated the power, but it was never really my thing. I did it to make my dad happy. I'd advanced through the ranks, but didn't get as far as he'd wanted me to. Now he wasn't here to help me move forward, and I wished like hell I'd tried harder. For him and for me.

I decided to go to the house behind me to search for food. Maybe there was a kid there, maybe there wasn't. It was worth checking out, at least. I could get there by climbing my backyard fence, and no one who might be out on the street would be able to see me. Up until now, no one had bothered to try and come into my house. I'd put a note on my door that said to stay the hell away and that I had a gun - which was the truth. But in doing that, I'd essentially become a sitting duck. Eventually, they would come for the things they hoped were in my house - food and fresh water. It was going to be time to leave soon. But until that day came, I needed something else to eat. My hunger was gnawing a hole in my stomach.

Two more hours and I'd go over the fence. My hand went nervously to the ring on a chain that hung at my neck - my dad's old wedding ring that he'd given me just before he went away for good.

CHAPTER
TWO

I WALKED OUT INTO MY backyard and closed the door behind me softly. An earlier check of the street in front of my house confirmed it was empty. I'd stayed hidden in my bushes for five full minutes, just to be sure no one was lying low, scoping me out. Five in the morning was apparently still too early for the raiders; it was nice to know that habit hadn't yet changed.

Once I was sure I wasn't being watched here in the backyard either, I went to the fence that separated my yard from the mystery neighbor's place. I peered over the top, my face hidden by high bushes on their side. I could see the back of their house, no movement coming from within.

I used the horizontal board that was about two feet off the ground, holding the vertical fence parts together, as leverage. One foot there gave me the little bit of lift I needed to get my other leg over the top. I used my abs and strong arm muscles to pull myself the rest of the way over. It wasn't pretty, but it did the job, landing me on the ground behind the bushes.

I stayed there for a couple of minutes, calming myself and checking for any signs of having been seen. There was nothing - still no movement from the windows at the back of the house.

I slowly crept from the bushes to the back door, checking the handle to see if it was unlocked. It wasn't. I shook my head at all the people who'd locked their doors to die inside. I hoped these neighbors had done the better thing, and gone to the hospital to do that bit of nasty business, like my dad had.

I was grateful for his final gesture, even though at the time it was the worst day of my life, watching him drive away like that and leave me all by myself. I don't think I could have buried him in the backyard. That would have been too much, and like he had said, I wouldn't have been able to leave him behind when it was time to go. He wanted me to be mobile and flexible - memories shouldn't be tying me down to a sinking ship, he'd said.

I wrapped the hand towel I'd brought with me around my fist and punched the glass panel nearest the door handle to break it, reaching through the hole I'd made to unlock the deadbolt. I opened the door slowly and stepped inside.

I left the door open, tiptoeing through the back hall and into the kitchen. I don't know why I was trying to be so quiet. I guess knowing I was breaking into someone's house made me feel like I should sneak.

I took a whiff of the air, testing it for the smell of rotten flesh. *Nope, no dead bodies in here for sure.* That was a relief. I'd smelled that odor now many times, when the wind blew strongly. Whenever that happened, I wondered how long it would be before that smell stopped being a regular part of my new life.

I found the pantry and opened it, expecting to find it full. But it was nearly empty too.

"What the hell?" I said out into the room. The raiders must have beat me to this place, but it was weird because when they came, they usually made a big mess; and this place was spotless. Everything on the counter was lined up with regimented perfection. Even the hand towels were hanging on the oven door handle as if they'd just been laundered and ironed, put there for the evening's dinner preparation.

I shut the door to the pantry and nearly dropped a doodle in my drawers when I realized I wasn't alone in the house.

CHAPTER THREE

HOLY *SHIT*, DUDE, PUT THAT thing away," I said, feeling my blood pressure shoot up like a rocket and my heart start to beat triple-time. I was staring down the barrel of a big ass handgun. It had to be a .357 Magnum or something. The kid could barely hold it up, it was so heavy.

"What do you think you're doing breaking into my house? You know you're not supposed to do that." His voice sounded like a girl's, it was so soft and high-pitched. *How had he survived if he hadn't entered puberty yet?*

"I didn't know anyone lived here, I swear. I thought I knew all the kids who went to Winter Park High in this neighborhood, but I don't recognize you."

"Yeah, well, I didn't go there. I went to Seminole High. But that doesn't give you the right to break my window and try to steal my stuff."

"I'm sorry, like I said, I didn't know this place was occupied."

I frowned at the kid. His hands were shaking and he was resting his elbows on his stomach to give his arms more support. I guess he wasn't twelve, being in high school, but he sure was small for his age.

"Would you put that stupid thing down before you shoot me, please?"

"Why? So you can eat me and my food?"

I laughed. I couldn't help it. "Eat you? What the hell are you talking about?"

"The canners. You're one of them. Where are your friends?" His eyes darted to the space behind me. I could tell he wanted to turn around and look behind himself too because his eyes kept jerking to the side along with his one shoulder, but he was too afraid to take his eyes off me. He was seriously freaked out.

I shook my head, trying to make any sense at all of what this kid was saying. I looked at him a little closer, trying to figure out if maybe he'd lost his marbles, being alone for these last couple months. But he seemed mostly normal, if not a bit too thin, even for someone who was on a survivor's diet.

"I'm not one of anything. I'm just me, trying to find some food. I'm tired of noodles and beans, that's all. But I'll go back to my house now and leave you alone."

"Ha! So you can come back at night and eat my heart? I don't think so."

I smiled. This kid had no idea who he was messing with. The only reason I hadn't taken that gun away from him and immobilized him with a quick jab to the throat was because I didn't want him freaking out any more than he already was. Plus, I hated hurting people who were nearly half my size and almost that small in weight. "Dude, what are you going to do? Shoot me?"

"Maybe," he said, stubbornly.

"Yeah, right. I don't think so. Not today, anyway." I turned to go.

"Wait!" he said, a desperate tone in his voice.

"What?" I said, half turning.

"Did you say you have noodles?"

"Yeah. So?"

"I have sauce."

My eyes widened. Sauce on noodles sounded like a ten-course meal at the fanciest restaurant in the entire world to me right now.

"You lie," I accused. I wasn't sure what his game was, but I wasn't interested in playing. Who would have spaghetti sauce left in times like these? At this point, the only thing anyone had was the crap no one wanted to eat.

"No. It's back in the other room. I'll show you, if you agree to share your noodles."

I thought about it for a second. Noodles and sauce. It would almost be like a normal meal. My earlier ideas about not eating any more starch seemed not so important anymore. Plus, I could just eat the sauce plain if I didn't feel like having the noodles.

"Fine. I'll trade. No need to show me, I trust you." The kid didn't look like he could hurt a fly, and I had no doubt that I could protect myself against him, gun or no gun. I tried not to think about the man responsible for my confidence because it would only make me upset. He was gone forever and no amount of sadness over it was going to bring him back.

"No, not a trade. We combine."

"Sure, whatever. Where?"

This was the sticky part. If we were going to eat together, one of us would have to abandon our house - which meant it would become a target for one of the gangs. They had too many eyes on the comings and goings of people in the streets to fool for long. I feared leaving my house for anything these days. Even now, for this, I had taken a chance.

"Backyards. At the fence. You cook the noodles and bring them. I'll bring the sauce. We'll divide it in half."

"I should get more than you. I'm taller and heavier," I said. I was guessing this twerp was about twelve, just the age that had saved him - or cursed him, depending on how you looked at it. Anyone not in the middle of puberty was long dead. Those furthest away from it had gone first, the old people and the babies.

"No. Even split, fifty-fifty. I need the calories."

"Fine. Whatever. What time?"

"One hour."

I shrugged. *Dinner for breakfast.* But it was still early enough that I felt relatively safe going out of my house just to my yard.

And at this point, I was no longer recognizing foods as appropriate for certain times of day. I ate when I was hungry, and I ate what was at hand.

"See you then." I left his house without looking back, not really worried that he was going to shoot me in the back. He knew I had pasta now, so I was a valuable friend to have. At least until it was gone.

CHAPTER
FOUR

I COOKED THE PASTA USING the gas stove in my kitchen, using as little water as possible. Since entering survivor mode,
I always drank the pasta water after it was done cooking, even
though it was pretty gross. It was a precious resource I couldn't
afford to dump down the drain. Today I put it into two glasses -
one for me and one for the kid living behind me.

An hour after our meeting, I snuck out my back door, now dou-
bly nervous about being seen. I still wasn't completely convinced
this kid was telling the truth about his sauce, and it was getting
closer to the time that the raiders would be waking up. I had to be
back inside before anyone came looking in my windows.

I got to the fence and whispered, "Are you here?"

"Yes," came his response.

I held up the bowl of rigatoni that I had cooked, bringing it level with the top of the fence. "Here's the pasta. Put the sauce in."

I heard some noise on the other side of the fence and then
something hit the side of the bowl.

A few seconds later he said, "There. I'm done."

I pulled the bowl back down, and sure enough, a big blob of
sauce sat on the top of my sad-looking noodles. I smelled it and

nearly swooned at the tomatoey goodness. I didn't care one bit that it was cold.

"Do you have a bowl?" I asked.

A plastic cereal bowl with a built-in straw on it appeared at the top of the fence. I poured half of the pasta inside it and passed it back over, wondering if he'd slurp the sauce up when he was done with that straw. My dad would have written that off as a germ catcher and something to be avoided. Straws were a bad idea if you were trying not to die of food poisoning and had no way of washing them out well.

"I have water for you too, if you want it. It's kind of starchy since I cooked the noodles in it."

"I'll take it," he said in a quiet voice.

I passed the small plastic cup of water over to him and felt, for the briefest of moments, a tremble in his hands as he took it from me.

"See ya," he said.

"Wait!" I said, not even sure why I wanted him to hang around. Being outside and not inside guarding our houses was risky. If anyone caught a whiff of our meal we'd be toast.

"What? I have to get back inside."

"I know, me too. I just wanted to ask you what your name is."

"Peter. What's yours?"

"Bryn."

"Bryn. Is that short for anything?"

"No. Just Bryn."

"Oh. Okay. See ya, Bryn."

"See ya, Peter."

I returned to my house to eat my breakfast of rigatoni and sauce, scarfing more than half of it down before I'd even reached my back door.

CHAPTER
FIVE

IT WAS FIVE IN THE morning the next day when I happened to look out into my backyard and saw Peter's head at the top of our fence. His eyes had not yet gotten over the edge. Whatever he was standing on wasn't high enough to get him there.

I opened the back door slowly, not ready to let him know he'd been seen. I stayed close to the back of my house and then carefully crept down the side fence that divided my yard from the Slotnik's - my former next door neighbors. Their place was unoccupied and long since emptied. I'd heard it being raided on more than once occasion - the sounds were unmistakable and almost always included breaking glass.

I reached the spot where I'd seen Peter's head and jumped up, grabbing the top of the fence with my hands and lifting myself in one swift motion. I thought a surprise attack might be my best bet.

Peter's face showed a split second of abject fear before he lost his balance and fell backward onto his weedy grass, yelling as he went.

I was surprised at first, then worried. He'd been too loud. Now anyone around would know he wasn't inside.

"Get back into your house, you idiot!" I said in a low but urgent voice.

"I need to talk to you!" he said from his butt on the ground.

"Later. At six. Make sure no one's out first, though." I wanted to be certain no one had heard us and was coming to investigate a possible empty house before we spent too much time outside again.

"Okay," he said, as he got to his feet and scrambled off, disappearing into his back door.

I looked at the vinyl and metal kitchen dining set chair that was lying on its side in the bushes below. The goof was going to totally give us away leaving crap like that lying around. I pulled myself the rest of the way over into his yard, just long enough to grab that chair and wing it over toward his back door, before jumping back over to my side and running to my house.

I got inside and locked the door, breathing heavily. It became clear to me as my chest heaved in and out that I'd lost a little bit of my cardiovascular strength, staying in this house all day all the time; so I made a pact with myself to start doing what I could to rectify that situation.

I looked at my watch. Fifty-one minutes until our meeting. Time to do some pushups and pull-ups, then some basics to keep my krav maga up to par. My dad would have been proud to see me pushing myself like this and that made it easier.

CHAPTER SIX

A T SIX O'CLOCK ON THE dot I went out into my backyard again, only this time I didn't bother with the sneaking stuff. I realized now that surprising Peter had been a bad idea. The doofus had a huge gun and was easily startled. I hated my life, but that didn't mean I wanted another hole put in my head.

Peter was waiting at the fence, this time his head coming up about four inches higher than the last time. I jumped up and pulled myself to the top with my biceps, only shaking a little at the muscle fatigue I'd caused with my hour-long workout. As my eyes cleared the edge of the jagged wood plank, I looked over the edge at his feet.

I was laughing so hard, I had to drop back down. My muscles had turned to jelly.

"Shut up," he said.

"Dude," I gasped, bent over to catch my breath, "you're wearing ladies' heels. What do you expect me to do?"

"It's the only way I could get high enough to see over the fence."

I tried really hard to stop laughing, but I couldn't. I hadn't seen anything that funny in months. They were electric red and about three sizes too big for him. Whoever had owned them had been one hell of a large woman.

"Seriously, shut up. Someone's going to hear you. The canners."

I finally calmed down, that stupid word he kept saying being the thing that got my attention enough to control my hysteria. "Why do you keep saying that? Canners. What the hell is it?"

"You don't know?"

"Obviously not, since I'm asking you." I wondered how much time this guy had spent in the company of others before the end of the world as we knew it had come. He seemed a bit off.

"Kids who eat other kids. Cannibals."

It took my brain a few seconds to process that one. "Say *what* now?"

"You heard me. *Cannibals.*"

"Peter, are you feeling okay? Did you drink some bad water? You know you either have to heat it up or bleach it before you drink it."

He sighed loudly. "Don't believe me if you don't want to, but I know what I know. I've seen things," he said mysteriously. "I just wanted to talk to you about maybe joining forces."

"No," I said immediately. I didn't even have to think about that one. "I'm not into joining gangs." I knew I was much better off with only myself to worry about, especially since this Peter kid was obviously one pork chop shy of a mixed grill.

"I'm not talking about a gang. A gang implies several people. I'm talking about just two: you and me."

"I don't need a gang," I said simply. And it was true. I had never needed much companionship before, and I didn't miss it now. I could run faster than any girl I knew and I could beat down any moron that tried to get a jump on me, thanks to my dad and his passion for krav maga. The last thing I needed was a kid who was afraid of his own shadow hanging around with me, attracting all kinds of unwanted attention.

"You need someone to watch your back. We all do."

"Not me."

"Oh, you don't sleep?" he asked with feigned innocence.

He had me there. That was the one time that I worried for my safety. It had been months since I'd had a good night's sleep. Every little sound made me jump to my feet, thinking someone was coming to take my beans and noodles. Or worse.

"I'll think about it. But tell me why you think I should. I mean, what do you bring to the equation, other than watching my back?"

"I'm smart."

"So am I. Try again."

"I can sing?"

"*Buzz*. Try one more time."

He sighed, his voice wavering now. "I have ten jars of spaghetti sauce, one .357, and ten boxes of bullets. That's it."

I sighed heavily. It wasn't the gun and ammo that got me. Or the sauce. It was the sound of utter defeat in his voice.

"Fine. Pack your crap. I'll help you over the fence tomorrow at five in the morning. Put everything in a backpack. Bring a sleeping bag and any other camping stuff you have."

"Okay," he said, his voice more upbeat now. "See you then. And thanks, Bryn."

"Don't mention it. I'm already kind of regretting my decision."

He didn't say anything in response.

I heard the bushes moving and then the sound of a squeaky door hinge, followed by the too-loud banging of his kitchen chair against the doorframe as he carried it back inside. The last noise to carry across his yard before the door shut was the clop, clop, clopping of his high heels on a tile floor.

I returned to my house, wondering if I'd made the right decision, but knowing I wasn't going to change my mind. My dad had always said, we have to take care of people who can't take care of themselves … and Peter definitely fell into that category.

CHAPTER
SEVEN

I WAS UP BY FOUR o'clock. I tried to tell myself it was the constant little noises that I heard outside my windows that made
me caffeine-eyed before sunrise, but deep down I knew it was
really just me being anxious about Peter coming over to join me.

I'd been alone for four months. It's the longest period of time
I'd ever been without human contact in my life. Now that I'd
found Peter in my backyard, I was craving more time together.

Part of me was disgusted with myself, seeing it as a weakness
- a dangerous one that could put my safety at risk. The other part
of me didn't care what the loner in me thought. People weren't
meant to live in solitude. Before he left, my dad told me I should
find someone to be with - someone I could trust and who could
take care of themselves. I'm pretty sure Peter wasn't the type of
companion he'd had in mind, since he was about as helpless as
a baby bird, but I guess you don't choose your friends when the
world comes to an end; you take what you can get and make do.
Maybe I could teach Peter how to defend himself at least. His bullets weren't going to last forever, and I was pretty sure that when
and if that gun ever went off in his hands, the kick-back would
knock him unconscious.

At five o'clock I went outside, not even bothering to check the front yard first, I was so anxious to get this done. Before I was even to the fence, a backpack came flying over the top. I stepped smoothly to the side to let it drop down beside me, smiling to myself - it was good to know my reflexes were still sharp.

Next came a gigantic sleeping bag - the kind my dad said to avoid using because it wouldn't pack lightly and would stay damp forever. I shook my head, wondering if there was a surplus store that might have some gear left on the shelves.

The next thing I saw was the edge of a bright purple box-type thing at the top of the fence. Peter seemed to be struggling, so I stepped up to help him out.

"What is that?" I asked quietly as I joined him.

"A suitcase," he grunted out.

I grabbed the corner of it and lifted it over the edge, grunting with the effort. "What the heck do you have in here? Bricks?"

"Spaghetti sauce and some other stuff. Don't drop it, there's glass in there."

I managed to get the monstrosity over into my yard, surprised I didn't pull a back muscle doing it. "Wow, you sure know how to travel light," I said, sarcastically. I hoped breaking the news to him that we would be leaving soon and that this elephant wouldn't be coming with us wouldn't make him decide to stay.

Peter's toe came to the top of the fence, his dirty, once white sneakers trying to find purchase on the wood.

I jumped up on the fence a few feet down and climbed over to the other side. While Peter busied himself with getting over, I took the kitchen chair he'd used to boost himself up and brought it to the back door of his house. I laid it on its side and stomped on one of the legs, breaking it off. The last thing I wanted to do was provide some raider a nice ladder to use to get into my yard. I broke off a second leg and then picked them both up, throwing them to separate far corners of the yard, before returning to Peter's struggling form.

I grabbed his flailing foot and pushed on it a little so he'd realize I was there. "Use my hand as leverage," I instructed. As soon as I felt his leg stiffen, I pushed again, giving him a boost that sent him flying over the fence. He was lighter than he even looked, which was saying a lot.

I jumped over to join him, brushing the front of my pants off as I waited for him to get up off the ground.

"You didn't have to push so hard."

"Sorry, I didn't realize you had hollow bird-bones. I expected you to be heavier."

Peter scowled at me and then went to gather his things. He started for the suitcase, but I waved him away.

"You go get the backpack and sponge. I'll get this. I don't want you to break an arm."

"Sponge?"

"That sad excuse for a sleeping bag you have."

Peter went to follow my orders. "Have you always been this anti-social or is it just the apocalypse that's brought out your sunny personality traits?"

I stopped, for a split second offended, but then just happy. *Thank the stars this kid has a sense of humor.* Without it, life was going to be seriously uncomfortable.

"This is me being friendly. Just wait until you piss me off."

"Wow, I'm looking forward to that," he said, dragging his backpack with one hand and his sleeping bag with the other. The bag slowly came out of its rolled-up form to spread out behind him.

"You're sponge is unrolling."

"Whatever."

He got to the door ahead of me because I was trying to carry the suitcase without leaving tracks that were too obvious in the weeds. I didn't want to leave any sign for anyone about what I was doing or who was doing it with me. Trails of heavy things being dragged only awakened curiosity - and when someone was really hungry, the curiosity almost always assumed there was food involved. And in this case, they'd be right.

We got to the back door and I let Peter in. For some reason he'd stopped and waited for me, as if we lived in a world where you didn't just walk into someone's house when you felt like it. It was strange, but nice in a way.

"Here it is. Home sweet home."

He went in ahead of me and I followed with the purple brick.

"Wow. This looks nothing like my place."

"Yeah, well, my dad was kind of hardcore about preparing me for the end of the world." He was staring at the gear I had set up that made my family room look like a camp site. There was only one piece of furniture in the place - a couch.

"It wasn't the end of the world," clarified Peter, "just a restructuring of the world order." He walked over to the table that used to have a TV on it to lift up the picture that was in a frame there. It was taken of my dad and me three years ago, when we took a trip out to the Everglades together.

"Is this your father?"

"Yeah." I pulled Peter's suitcase to the middle of the floor. "Can I open this?"

Peter shrugged, moving on to look at other things in the room. "Sure."

I opened up the case and pulled things out, one by one. There were glass jars of spaghetti sauce stuffed around books and shoes - two pairs of sneakers and a pair of pointy-toed dress shoes - all of them completely useless for any kind of travel. I threw them over my shoulder into a messy pile.

"Hey! Those are my shoes!"

"Garbage. You can't use these to walk any distance in."

"They're all I have."

"You have what's on your feet. We'll find you something else."

"Where?"

"I'm not sure yet." I glanced at his feet. "My dad's feet were bigger than yours, so you can't use his old ones. But we're going to have to leave here soon, so wherever we go, we'll find something on the way."

"Why do you think we have to leave?"

I stopped my unpacking and looked up at him. "Why do you ask like that? As if I have to have a different reason than you?"

"Because you don't know or care about the canners, so you must have other reasons."

I shook my head. *Again with the canners thing.* "We have to leave because the natives are getting restless."

He looked at me, confused.

I went back to the suitcase, pulling out some heavy books and stacking them on the floor. "The gangs. They're starting to get hungrier. Bolder. Eventually they're going to ignore the fact that I have a sign on my door saying to stay the hell away, and they're going to come in and steal my stuff. Plus, I'm almost out of food, so I have to go find more anyway."

"You're right. About the gangs getting hungrier," said Peter, softly.

I looked at him because his tone was kind of freaking me out, and the expression on his face only made me feel more uncomfortable. I stood up, feeling a little pulse of adrenaline enter my system.

I'd learned to be hyper-aware of my body's responses, ready to tune in and use my natural chemicals to enhance my reflexes. At this point I was ready to take Peter down if he so much as made a single move in my direction.

But instead, he started to cry.

CHAPTER EIGHT

I DIDN'T KNOW WHAT TO do with that. I was prepared for a sneak attack, but one of a different kind. Anger, I could deal with. Madness? I could take it out in two seconds flat. But tears? I had no clue what to do with those.

"I'm not from here," he explained, swiping at the tears with the back of his hand. "I snuck down here from Sanford three weeks ago."

"Wow. That's a long distance to walk."

"I didn't walk. I rode my bike."

"Still…"

"I know. But I needed to get away from there. It was life or death."

It seemed like he was being a bit dramatic, but I decided not to give him a hard time about it. He'd stopped crying and I didn't want to start him up again.

"Did you bring all this stuff with you?"

"No, just the shoes. I got the spaghetti sauce and books here."

"Wow, you got lucky."

"Yes and no," he said, giving me a measuring look.

I sighed. "Okay, I'll bite. I can see you want to tell me something. Spit it out."

"It was awful!" he said loudly; then he quickly looked side to side, obviously worried he'd been heard by the wrong sort.

"What was awful?"

"The canners!" he whisper-yelled. "Kids were roaming the streets, attacking other kids and *eating* them!"

I laughed at the outrageousness. I couldn't help it. "Jesus, Peter. Did you eat some mushrooms you found growing on cow pies out in Sanford or what?"

"There are no cows left out there. They've all been eaten too."

I shook my head. "Whatever." I had to get back to going through his stuff, to figure out if we were going to take any of it. I found a jar of pickles wedged in between some books.

"I wasn't an only child, you know. I had a sister."

The words sent chills up my spine. It wasn't so much the words themselves, but the way he said them. I looked up at him slowly, shifting back now to balance on the balls of my feet, but still squatting down near the suitcase. I was so friggin'' confused at that point, I was considering running - and usually in a fight or flight situation, I was all about the fight. But I was coming to the quick realization that Peter was a seriously disturbed individual. And he was standing in my living room.

"They killed my *sister*, Bryn. I couldn't stop them!" He crumpled into a heap on the floor, crying his eyes out. "She was small and couldn't run fast!" he sobbed. "They took her down like an animal! She screamed and screamed and then she didn't make any sounds at all."

I froze in place, no longer thinking about running, as I began to fully understand what he was all about. The kid wasn't a psycho - he'd been traumatized. And if I was hearing him right, he'd actually seen his sister murdered by a group of kids.

"Why would they kill her?" I asked. It didn't make any sense. Nobody was killing anybody - unless maybe they refused to give up their food. I hadn't seen that happen, but I could imagine people being hungry enough to get so angry that they might use too much force to take what they wanted. *But to kill someone?* And besides, it wasn't worth it, losing your life over a jar of spaghetti sauce. "Why didn't she just give them what they wanted?"

"She did!" he screeched.

"Well, why'd they kill her then? Just to be mean?"

He looked at me like I was the biggest idiot left on Earth. "What are you not understanding? Are you a complete *dimwit?!* They killed her because they wanted *her*. They took *her*. She gave them *exactly* what they wanted. *Meat."*

"What the ...?"

"Yeah," he said, nodding his head in quick up and down jerking motions. "Believe me now? They killed her and they ate her, Bryn. They ate my little sister!"

He was telling the truth. No one could lie this convincingly. As realization set in, I felt the bile rising in my throat. I knew I wasn't going to be able to stop this freight train, so I ran to the back door in time to barf out in the weeds, narrowly missing the slate step just by the entrance.

What he was saying couldn't be possible. Rational, normal, sane people did not *eat* other people. That was just ridiculous. The only problem was, my stomach obviously believed Peter's story. And I knew that this meant a part of my brain did too.

I had already been thinking it was time to leave my neighborhood ... and that the resources in my town and all the others probably were getting to very low levels. This story convinced me that the time had definitely come to find a less-populated place to live.

No one had bothered to grow gardens so they could support themselves, especially in the last six months of the time period when all the adults died. Everyone was too busy freaking out. All of the teens in our country had been raised to eat processed foods, put in pretty packages and delivered to our pantries and shelves, courtesy of grocery stores and our parents. They had no clue how to support themselves using the land. At least, none of the kids in this area did. Maybe out in the farmlands it was different. But here? No way. They were desperate and going crazier with the hunger every day.

My dad had shown me the basics of growing tomatoes and beans and stuff, but refused to put a garden in at our house. He'd said hundreds of times before he left that I would need to move away to be safe, and he didn't want me stuck here out of a false sense of comfort. I was starting to suspect in this moment, as I wiped my mouth off with the back of my hand, that my dad had foreseen this problem of savagery taking over the minds of the formerly sane, but had never wanted to speak the actual words to me. Lots of little things he'd said and did took on new meaning for me, telling me he had come to the same conclusion that was now a permanent part of Peter's life: people, when hungry and desperate enough, and without the means or smarts to come up with a better way, would go for the easy kill to survive. Even if it meant eating their own kind.

I vomited again at the idea of a gang chasing down and taking out a child for their dinner.

The door opened and Peter came out, a tissue in his hand. "Here," he said, handing it to me dispassionately.

I took it and stared at it for a second. I hadn't seen a tissue in months. I'd been wiping my butt with leaves and weeds, after doing my business in a hole in the ground in the yard. A week after my dad left, I no longer had running water. It wasn't worth it to waste precious rain or pool water on flushes, so I'd made myself an old-fashioned outhouse out of tarps.

"Thanks," I said, using it to wipe my mouth. "Sorry about that. Lost it a little, I guess."

"Good. Now I know you're not a canner and still human."

"I was kind of worried about you, actually," I admitted. "You seemed a little … off your rocker for a while there. But now I understand."

"Yeah. I guess I have gone a little nuts."

"I would have, too. Probably worse than you." I reached out and punched him lightly on the arm. I meant it as a gesture of friendship, but I felt my fist make contact with bone. He had no body fat on him anywhere.

"Ow!" he said, massaging his arm.

"Dude, why are you so skinny?"

He looked at me like I was crazy. "Maybe because I'm slowly starving to death?"

"What have you been eating?"

"Spaghetti sauce!" he yelled, his face going red with anger and his arms held stiffly at his side.

"Okay, chill, Chef Boyardee. Come on inside. I'll make you some beans and noodles. We need to get some meat on your bones before we head out of here." I tried not to think about the image of meat on a person's bones, but the vision kept assailing my mind. It was awful. I decided then and there that becoming a vegetarian might be a very good idea. I didn't ever want to get so hungry that I'd consider eating my new friend, never mind the fact that he'd make a pretty pitiful meal.

"When are we leaving?"

"I don't know. A few days? We have to make our plan."

Peter followed me inside and then stood at the edge of the kitchen while I added water to the pan from the plastic bottle that stood on the counter. The noodles went in next.

"Where's the water from?"

"It's rainwater. I catch it in a food-safe container outside. A bucket, actually."

"Is it okay to drink?"

"The stuff in this container hasn't been treated, but since I'm heating it to boiling, it doesn't matter. That'll kill any bacteria."

"Yeah. I know that."

I looked at him sideways, not sure why he felt the need to clarify what he knew. Then I continued. "I have another bottle in the cabinet that has water I've treated. I usually just boil it, but I also have bleach."

"Smart."

"My dad's idea. I have enough to last me for years. I hope by the time it runs out, the rain and stream water will be pure enough to drink without it."

"You're thinking without all the factories and other places polluting the atmosphere, there's a chance that the Earth will regenerate itself?"

"That's my hope anyway."

"Mine too. So what about the gas? How do you still have gas working at your house?"

I pulled open the cabinet doors under the stovetop and showed him the propane tanks that sat underneath. "Voilà."

"Wow. Cool. Smart. So where are we going to go? The mountains? I hear there's good fishing there. And streams for water, too."

"I'm not sure. We'll vote."

Peter smiled vaguely. "We're two people. It'll always be a tie or unanimous."

"Until you get above a hundred pounds, you only get half a vote."

Peter looked at me with the most pitiful expression on his face I couldn't stand it.

"I'm just kidding, geez, lighten up." I didn't realize how callous I sounded until he looked down at the ground, overcome by sadness again.

"Shit, I'm sorry. I don't mean to act like I don't care, okay? It's just … I'm not used to such heavy duty emotions."

"You've never lost anyone you cared about? What about your parents?"

"My mom left when I was just a baby. And, yeah, my dad died. But I was prepared for it. And he did it at the hospital. I didn't have to go through … anything like you did." I couldn't even say the words - *I didn't have to see my dad get eaten.* My stomach churned again, but I needed to know more, so I forced the feelings down and continued.

"Tell me about your sister. About Sanford."

"Later. Let me eat and digest before we go there again. It's too upsetting for me right now."

I nodded my head, stirring the pasta that would cook another ten minutes before it was ready. I reached over and pulled a can of beans from the cabinet. "Do you need your beans hot? Or can I give them to you out of the can?"

"Well, I prefer them hot, but I've learned not to be picky anymore."

"Oh, don't worry about it. I can heat them up real quick in the microwave."

I opened up the can and then pushed the button to open up the microwave above my head. I put the can inside, closed the door, and turned the dial to the right, setting it on three minutes.

I turned to look at Peter causally, but he just stood there watching me, saying nothing, his face expressionless.

I waited a few seconds, looking around the kitchen, tapping my foot and humming a little, before turning the dial back to the left, causing the appliance to let out a loud ding! I pulled the can out and handed it to Peter with a spoon.

"There you go. Hot beans, served up nice and cold."

"Thanks," he said, giving me a half-smile before he dug in hungrily, shoving beans into his mouth. He talked around the food and not very prettily. "I thought for a second there you either didn't realize microwaves ran on electricity or that you had some kind of solar power thing going on."

"Slow down, dude. The beans aren't going anywhere."

"Sorry," he mumbled, a bean stuck to the corner of his mouth. "I'm starving."

"I can see that," I said, mostly to myself, as I stirred the pasta some more. I acted like I was checking out the water, but I was really just thinking hard to myself, trying to figure everything out.

Peter was a bit of a mystery. He wasn't from here, but had somehow made it about fifteen miles on his bike without having all his stuff stolen or being attacked by crazy people. And where had he gotten the books and the sauce? Why hadn't the sauce, at least, already been taken? I hadn't looked at the titles of any of the books yet, but none of them were light reading; they were more like encyclopedias. In spite of all the things he'd been through, and the fact that apparently there are monsters living in Sanford, he'd made it to my neighbor's house. *Why that particular one?*

"Why did you pick the house behind mine?" I asked, not looking at him so he'd feel more comfortable answering my questions. I was planning on giving him the third degree, but I wanted to try and be sly about it.

"My aunt lived there. She had these books I needed that she hid in her house and the sauce. She told me where to find them the last time I talked to her."

Well, that explains why this place and the sauce - must have been hidden well.

"I never knew your aunt. Sorry." I looked over in time to see him shrug.

"I didn't know her very well either. She was really an uncle who became an aunt. My parents didn't really get along with her."

"An uncle who became an aunt? How so?"

"Transvestite."

My eyes nearly bugged out of my head. "A transvestite was living behind me this whole time and I didn't even *know* it?"

Peter shook his head at me again, this time more in disgust. "She was a *person*, Bryn. Not a transvestite. You say it like she was a creature."

I instantly felt like an ignorant ass. "Oh, yeah. Of course she was. I didn't mean anything by it."

"My parents weren't the most tolerant people in the world."

There was a world of meaning wrapped up in that simple sentence, and I wondered if I dared to ask for clarification. He was stirring the beans around in his can, but not eating them. It was as if he were waiting for me to say something. So I did.

"Was your uncle gay?"

He shrugged, mumbling, "I don't know. Maybe. Is that a problem?"

"No. Not for me. Was it for you?" My ears burned for some reason. I wasn't sure if I was embarrassed for having asked or just uncomfortable putting him in this position of having to explain himself to me.

He cleared his throat. "No. I'm gay myself, so I don't have a problem with it at all."

I went back to stirring the noodles. "Well, that's good. I didn't want to have to be forced into fending off your advances on my person. A guy could get hurt that way."

Peter laughed. "Nothing to worry about there."

"Hey!" I said, in mock outrage, throwing a dishtowel at him.

He caught it with a surprisingly quick move, pulling it out of the air and tossing it carelessly to the counter.

"Nice reflexes," I said, nodding in appreciation. *Maybe he wouldn't be hopeless to train after all.*

"I used to play a lot of ping pong."

I started laughing so hard, I snorted.

CHAPTER NINE

A FTER PETER HAD EATEN HIS fill of noodles and beans, and I had joined him, indulging in another jar of sauce to boot, we sat down in the living room and took stock of our stuff.

He held up each book from his suitcase in turn. "First, I have a gardening book. My aunt said this one is specifically for Florida."

"Awesome," I said, holding out my hand to take it from him. "This goes in the keeper pile."

"Then, she left me this one. It's an encyclopedia of natural remedies that you can make using herbs and plants and stuff from the things growing in South Florida."

"No way!" I said, taking it from him to read the back. "Wow, this is amazing." My dad and I had talked about me being injured, but not much about me being sick. I guess he'd figured with all the people dying off, there'd probably not be a lot of everyday diseases going around. "I wonder if this has a cure for whatever killed all the adults in it," I said jokingly.

"It doesn't. I already looked."

"Not sure how you could expect to find something when you don't even know what it is," I said sarcastically.

"I have my theories," he said, looking arrogant.

I could totally tell in that moment that he was one of those kids who won the science fair every year with some radical experiment he'd done, looking for cancer cures or whatever. In my old life I would have scoffed at the stupidity of wasting so much time. In my new life, I decided, this guy could be valuable to have around. At least when I got sick. But that didn't mean I wasn't going to give him a hard time about it.

"Oh, you're going to cure the disease that killed ten billion people, when the smartest minds in the world working together weren't enough?"

"No. I don't think I'll need to. The disease died with them."

"You don't think we're all going to die when we reach twenty?" That seemed to be the cut-off age for most of the living.

"No. There are no more hosts. We're all resistant, for whatever reason."

"Our hormones."

"So they said. But no one ever proved it. And people taking hormones at teen levels weren't able to survive."

I shrugged. "It doesn't matter to me. Either I live or I die. I'll do what I can to keep the death part from coming, but when it's my time to go, I'll just go."

"Easy to say when you're healthy."

"Yeah. I know." It was a sobering thought. My dad was the coolest guy I'd ever known, and even he had freaked out in the end when faced with his own mortality. I decided to push those thoughts out of my head and get back to our planning.

"What else do you have?"

"Book on first-aid," he said, handing me a smaller one.

"I have one of those already." I quickly flipped through a few pages. "It's better than this one."

Peter shrugged. "Just toss it then, I don't care."

I threw it into the abandon pile - the stuff we would leave in my house for the raiders to take if they wanted it.

"This is a good one: solar power. It shows how to make an oven and heat water and stuff."

I snatched it from his hand. "This one is *definitely* coming."

I'd been taking infrequent, cold sponge baths without soap for way too long now. The idea that I might actually be able to take a real, and possibly warm shower, sounded like heaven to me - soap or not. A quick flip through the book showed me that we could probably put a list together of things to find along our journey that would make a lot of the items in the book buildable.

"Our load is going to be heavy," he said, looking at the keeper-pile. It was much bigger than the abandon-pile.

"We'll find a way. I want to get a place that's permanent. I don't want to move around all the time. I think we'll be safer if we just take the risk of traveling once."

"So what … are we going to build some kind of fortress or something? Because that's the only way to stay safe that I can think of. And it can't be made of anything that'll burn because the canners like to start fires."

"Well, I'm not really sure. Let's get this stuff sorted out and then we'll talk about it. Maybe with our two half-brains, we can come up with one good idea."

Peter smiled. "Sounds like a plan."

CHAPTER
TEN

W E SAT IN THE LIVING room on the couch that was pushed up against the wall, looking at the neat, orderly piles of things in front of us. The organization was Peter's doing. He seemed to function better when everything was just so, and I didn't care either way.

My dad would have liked Peter. I could still remember how he'd admonish me when we did our survivor training. "Efficiency!" he'd shout, like an overly enthusiastic drill sergeant. "That's going to save your life, Bryn!" I reached up absently to stick my finger through the ring on my necklace, letting it hang there for a second. I'd doubted him before, but I didn't now. We were going to have to be completely anal about using every square inch of space on our backs to haul all this crap to our final destination.

"Okay, so here's what we're taking; now, where are we going?" Peter asked.

"Well, as far as I can see, we have a few choices. We can go to the mountains, the plains, the desert, or the swamps."

"Swamps? No way," said Peter.

"Why not?"

He rolled his eyes. "I can't believe I have to say this ... snakes? Ever heard of them? Gators? I want to run *away* from meat-eaters, not *toward* them."

I jumped up, remembering a book I'd forgotten. "Be right back." I returned in less than a minute and handed Peter the small handbook that had been in my dad's home office.

"Oh, great," he said, in a not-very-happy-sounding voice. "A snake book."

"Yes, and it tells you not only how to identify snakes, but how to treat snake bites, too."

"I'm pretty sure the treatment these days is to bend over and kiss your own ass goodbye."

I laughed. "Don't be so negative. You're a science nerd. Maybe you can figure out how to make anti-venom."

He shrugged. "Maybe."

I looked at him suspiciously. "I think, in a sick way, I just got you to consider living in a swamp."

Peter smiled. "I'm not going to deny it. The idea of being able to do something like that is intriguing."

I shook my head. "You're nuts. You do realize that to make anti-venom, you have to *milk* a friggin'' poisonous snake, right?"

"Yeah, but that's the job for the assistant."

"*Pfft.* Don't tell me, let me guess ... I'm the assistant."

"Well you're definitely not the scientist."

I shoved him with my arm, causing him to tip over sideways. Then I continued, "Anyway, as I was saying, before I was so rudely interrupted, we have some choices. But regardless of where we go, I think our mode of transportation should be mountain bikes."

"Why? I mean, why not motor-scooters or something? They're faster."

"Too noisy. Yes, we could go faster and farther. But if there are actual ... canners or whatever out there, we need to move more quietly. And we need to travel when no one's out."

"What do you mean?"

"I mean, between like four in the morning and seven."

"That's not a lot of traveling time each day."

"Better safe than sorry. And maybe there will be places where we can alter those times a bit, like when we're in the middle of nowhere."

Peter nodded his head. "Okay. I agree to this. So we're going to travel by bike, with backpacks, hauling all this stuff." He looked at me. "Where are we going to go?"

My brain was moving a thousand miles an hour, calculating variables and taking everything I could think of into consideration. My dad had told me to go where no one would find me. He said to make myself safe and find a few friends who'd be there to help me re-build and to watch my back.

"I think we should go to the mountains," I said. I could still remember the trip I'd taken with my dad several years before, up to North Carolina. It was on my list of favorite places ever.

"But it snows there."

"That means there's water."

"It also means frostbite and difficulty finding food."

"Okay, Mr. Voice of Reason, where do you think we should go?"

Peter sighed. "I don't even want to say it."

I quickly flashed my fist and forearms out in a move that was part of my basic warm-ups, finishing with a slow drawing out of my arms to the side. "Say it, or suffer my wrath."

Peter looked at me, completely unimpressed. "What in the hell was that supposed to be? What are you ... a Ninja Turtle?"

I shook my head at him with exaggerated disappointment. "I don't know which is sadder - that you know about Ninja Turtles or that you don't recognize a lethal weapon when you see it."

Peter snorted. He sounded like a total girl. "Lethal weapon? Oh no, whatever am I going to do?" He put his hand to his forehead like he was going to faint, rolled his eyes up into his head, and then fell back into the couch cushions.

I nudged him. "Tell me what you were going to say."

He didn't respond.

"Seriously. Before I have to show you my stuff."

He didn't open his eyes, but he did speak.

"I think we need to go to the Everglades."

CHAPTER ELEVEN

A T FIRST I WAS REALLY resistant to the idea, even though I had suggested it as an alternative. I hated mosquitoes, snakes, and gators … and probably about a thousand other nasties that made their homes there. But Peter made a very convincing point: everyone else hated that stuff too.

"We need to go somewhere no one else wants to go; a place where life would be too hard for most people. And we need a place that has food and water sources."

I nodded my head in resignation. "And nothing beats the Everglades for all of the above."

"Exactly. Sure, the mountains have what we need to survive. But they're also beautiful, hospitable, and very well-known. That's where other people will be going. That's where the canners will be going," said Peter, shifting his voice lower to finish. "It'll be their hunting grounds."

I shivered at the idea of going to live in a place where I would be the prey instead of being the guy at the top of the food chain, hoping in the back of my mind that I would never be okay or blasé about the idea of a person eating another person. I swallowed the sick feeling down, moving my brain to other, less disgusting topics.

"I guess you're right," I said, sighing. "I'll get the map." I went over to our pile of books as we were talking and pulled out the spiral-bound roadmap book. I sat back down next to Peter and flipped through the pages. "Should we stick to highways or back roads?"

"I have no idea."

"Okaaaayyy. Through the middle or down the coast?"

"Your guess is as good as mine."

I smiled, scanning the pages that showed the roads near my house. "We make quite the team, don't we?"

I could hear a smile in Peter's voice when he responded. "The best."

CHAPTER
TWELVE

PETER AND I TOOK TURNS sleeping and staying awake the first night. It was the first time I'd actually been able to sleep deeply and have a dream I remembered. It was of my dad, telling me how to pack my bag, and me complaining about having to play survivor. It made me both happy and sad, glad to re-live the moment but wishing I had appreciated the time spent with him more.

I woke up to relieve Peter on guard duty, and spent the next couple of hours kicking myself mentally for not trying harder with my krav maga training and asking my dad to teach me more things about survival. I should have spent the last few months of our lives together in the library, absorbing information that I could use to rebuild my world into one I could feel happy and safe in. Now that I knew some kids had gone insane - in groups - I didn't feel comfortable at all in my house and in this neighborhood. Peter and I were way too easy to catch here and then … well … be their next meal.

At four in the morning I nudged Peter awake. "Come on. We need to go see what we can find at the neighbors' houses for food before we leave."

"What if someone comes while we're gone?"

"Only one of us is going at a time. The other stays here and guards the house."

"Isn't that dangerous? Being alone?"

"Yes. But we can't risk leaving our books and things for raiders to take."

Peter nodded his head slowly, wiping his face and hair with his hands. "Okay. Who's going out first?"

"I'll go while you wake up." I held out my finger as I stood, warning him, "But no going back to sleep."

Peter slowly got on his feet. "No, I won't. I'm gonna go … pee."

"Out in the back yard. Far right corner. I have a hole in the ground. Just move the board away from it first, please."

"Where are you going?"

"I'm going to start at the corner there, across the street and to the right, and I'll do the first five houses in a row, going that way."

"Okay. Just wait for me to come back, first."

I busied myself with checking my gun and finding more bullets to put in my pocket. I had several boxes of them, but I'd spread them out all over the house, thinking at the time I'd done it that if someone came breaking in, I'd be prepared for a re-load no matter where I was.

Peter came back inside and picked up his gun. "Ready whenever you are."

"I'm taking a potty break and then leaving from the side yard, so just watch for me out the front window. Don't come out though, no matter what, okay?"

"What if someone comes after you?"

"Warn me by ringing that bell on my front porch."

"Bell? Where?"

I brought him to the front door and opened it a crack, showing him the brass decorative bell that had hung in the same place for as long as we'd owned the house.

"What should I ring it with?"

"I don't know. Your gun? A pan? Something metal."

He stepped out on the front porch and raised his gun, ready to bring it crashing down, but I reached out and grabbed his elbow to stop him.

"What the hell are you doing?" I whisper-yelled.

"Testing it," he said, innocently.

"Oh, so you can wake up the raiders and let them know we're open for business?"

Peter grimaced and then whispered, "Oh. Yeah. That was dumb."

I shook my head. "Get back inside, ding-a-ling."

After taking a pee break and brushing my teeth with the tiniest speck of toothpaste I could manage, I left the house, sticking to the edges of abandoned cars and bushes as much as possible. I made it over to the Brown's place without being seen.

I went through their house and the four next to it, checking every cupboard and under every bed and couch I could find. I even went up into their attics, already stiflingly hot. They would have been impossible to go in later in the day when the raiders were normally active, so there was a chance I could find something there that had not yet been discovered.

When I returned to my house a little over an hour later, I had less than half a backpack full of stuff.

"What'd you get?" asked Peter, his eyes gleaming. I couldn't blame him for his excitement - it was kind of like a treasure hunt. Except for the danger of possibly being discovered and attacked, it was fun.

"Well, I got a camping lantern, the oil kind - found it up in an attic. There's lots of oil in it still, plus there was an extra can too."

"Cool."

"I got four cans of mini-ham from the back corner of a cupboard someone had missed."

"Nice," he said, turning one of the cans around to read the ingredients.

I shook my head silently - *as if ingredients even matter anymore.*

"Don't shake your head at me," he said.

"Why not? You're being goofy."

"How do you know it wasn't some weird bio-engineered food that killed all the adults off?"

"Because we ate the same things as them and we're all still here, maybe?" I said in a way that suggested he was the dummy, not me.

"Maybe it's an ingredient that kids are resistant to but adults aren't."

"Whatever. It's only a few cans and we're not likely to find many more of them. Even Costco and Walmart have been cleaned out at this point."

"How do you know?"

I shrugged. "I don't. It's just an educated guess. If I lived closer to one, it's where I would have gone first."

"What else did you get?"

I pulled out a bag of rice and a box of spaghetti. "This is it."

Peter smiled. "A spaghetti dinner."

"I'm so sick of pasta I could puke," I grumbled.

"Well, that's too bad. It's good carbs for when we're riding bikes, and it's easy to make. If we could ever figure out how to make flour, we'd be able to make pasta ourselves. Or something that looked kind of like it."

"I prefer tortillas."

"Whatever. We'll worry about that when we get settled. Now it's my turn to go out." Peter stood up straighter and tucked his gun down the front of his baggy pants. The huge handle hanging over the edge was the only thing keeping it from falling down his pant leg; but it was so heavy, it was pulling his pants down partway.

"You need a holster. Start with the house just on the west side of this one, plus the four next ones. The guy two doors down was a cop. Maybe he has a holster in his bedroom somewhere."

"Okay. Who else lived in those houses? Maybe I can focus on finding certain things."

"I don't know. An old man lived next to him. I never talked to him. He was a little strange. The others? I have no clue. I wasn't the most social of neighbors. Neither was my dad."

Peter said nothing until he got to the front door. "I bet you wish you were more social back then, when you had neighbors to be social with." And then he walked out.

I thought about what he said, moving toward my kitchen window to watch him walk over to the next door neighbor's house. He wasn't trying at all not to be seen. That gun was giving him a false sense of security. I was going to have to remedy that when he got back.

As I waited for him to return, I tried to decide if I was feeling regret over not being more social in the past. Would my outcome be any different now if I'd been friendlier to the neighbors? If I'd gone down and talked to the crazy old guy who was always out in his yard, talking to his fluffy, white toy poodle, Buster, all the time? *No. They would have been just more people to say goodbye to.*

Socializing brought on friendships, and friends were too easily lost to death's whims now. It wasn't worth it. I had to conserve what little sanity I had by making the conscious decision not to drown in misery over the loss of people I'd never get back.

I puttered around the house, nervously checking the windows every five minutes, until I heard a noise at the front door. I ran over and put my ear to the wood, listening for signs that it was Peter.

"Bryn?" he whispered.

"Yeah," I said, getting ready to open the door. But then I hesitated. "Are you alone?" I don't know what I was expecting to hear him say, but it wasn't this.

"Not exactly."

My hand hesitated on the lock, not sure now if I should open it. If there were a canner with him, would he tell me? Or would they somehow force him to get me to open the door without giving away their presence. Or would he even want to warn me? Maybe he was a canner himself, and all of this poor-me routine was just a ruse to get me to lower my guard.

I laughed at my paranoia. As if my one remaining bag of noodles and my starving hundred-pound-body were anything to get excited about. There were much easier meals to find around here.

Everyone from this neighborhood knew I wouldn't go down without a fight. But then again ... Peter wasn't from this area.

"Is it safe to open up?"

Peter huffed out a breath of frustrated air. "Of course it is, you idiot. And hurry up. This guy is heavy."

Guy? I wished like hell I had a peephole. Instead, I got my gun ready, flicking the safety off and bringing it level with the edge of the opening. I unlocked the door and flung it open, holding the gun out in front of me with stiff arms.

"Don't shoot," said Peter in a tired voice, standing on the front stoop holding a dirty, gray-brown mass of tangled cotton that looked like a badly used mop head.

The mop head moved.

It squirmed a little.

And then it barked.

CHAPTER THIRTEEN

O H, *HELL* NO, YOU ARE not bringing that thing in here," I said, as Peter brushed past me to move into the front hall.

"Be quiet and shut the door. You'll wake up the raiders."

I shut the door as I yelled at him in a low tone. "What the hell were you thinking, Peter? We can't take this dog with us! He'll bark his head off!"

"Exactly," said Peter, pulling the backpack off his shoulders. It wasn't totally empty, and had at least one can in it. I could hear it hit the floor as he lost his grip on the strap and let the bag go, reaching down to calm a shivering poodle. "His collar says his name is Buster."

"Yeah, I know his name." I'd heard his crazy owner calling to him many times. I glanced down at the mutt and he looked up at me with his big brown eyes, barely visible behind matted, raggedy hair clumps. I felt my heart start to soften, so I looked away. We couldn't afford to get all mushy over a stupid dog that was only going to get us killed.

"I couldn't just leave him there. He would have died."

"Well, he's managed to survive for months on his own. I hate to think about how he's done that." Visions of my old neighbor being eaten by his poodle made me feel like laughing and barfing at the same time. It was funny in a very, very sick way.

"He wasn't eating his master, if that's what you mean. The old man who lived there had spread about twenty huge bags of dog food out all over the place." Peter rubbed the dog under the chin. "The little guy had managed to dig holes into them and eat the food little by little until most of it was gone." Peter started ba-by-talking then. "He did all his poo-poo and pee-pee in a back bedroom … didn't you, Buster? Didn't you big boy?"

"Was there any left? Dog food, I mean?" I wasn't opposed to eating dog food, even though I knew it was made of pieces parts and probably a healthy dose of horse meat too.

"Not much. I have it in the bag."

I grabbed the backpack, looking inside. There were several canned goods, a plastic bag of what felt like dog food, and a small book. I pulled the book out and turned it over in my hands. It was more a journal than anything, and it had a piece of paper sticking out of it.

"What's this?"

"Open it and see," said Peter, softly. He gently pushed clumps of hair out of Buster's eyes, which went right back to where they had been, despite his efforts.

I walked over to the kitchen, pulling the paper out as I went. I reached into a drawer absently, taking the scissors from inside and walking back to hand them to Peter. "Cut his stupid hair."

The paper was actually an envelope. I turned it over and saw that it had my name on it.

"What the hell?" I said to no one. *Why did that old guy have an envelope with my name on it in his house?* I looked at Peter, suspiciously. "Did you do this? Is this some kind of joke, so I'll agree to keep the dog?"

Peter shook his head, still not meeting my eyes. "No. I found it on his kitchen counter, near the phone. He had a stack of papers there, but this is the only thing that had your name on it."

I turned it over, noticing that it wasn't sealed. The paper inside was crisp and white, the writing done with blue ink, in

old-fashioned script, the careful and precise penmanship making
it seem almost like a work of art. His note took up the entire page.

*Dear Bryn, I wish I could open this letter by saying 'I
hope you are well,' but it seems almost foolish to assume
that this could be the case. If you are reading this, it is
most likely because I have met my end and you are alone
in this world without your father to care for you. I don't
know why God has seen fit to bring this disaster down
upon the heads of our youth, but it is what it is and I can
do nothing to stop it. It is my sincerest wish, however,
that I could do even a little something to make your new
life better for you. You and I never met or talked, but your
loving father came to me before his death to ask that I
watch over you and do what I could to help you. I have
no children of my own, other than Buster, and my lovely
wife died many years ago. I know that when I go, I will
worry very much about Buster, maybe not as much as
your father worries for you, but enough that it causes me
sleepless nights. It is with this in mind that I leave for
you this journal, filled with everything I could remember
of my days in the army, serving in Europe during World
War II. It would be foolish for us to believe that you will
not need to know battle tactics in your new world. I know
your father has prepared you as best he could, to fight and
protect yourself. We've talked many times about you, he
and I, and it is clear, he loves you more than life itself. In
closing, I would ask that if my dear Buster is still alive,
that you do what you can to care for him. He is a sweet
soul and is generous with his love. And I think both you
and he might end up needing each other. One can never
have too many friends nor too many tail wags in her life.
With kindest regards, your neighbor,*

George Winterstone.

I started crying halfway through the letter and had to turn
away from Peter to read the rest. I walked over to the counter
and put the letter and journal down when I was finished reading,

trying to get myself together. But all I could think about was my dad and how he and this neighbor had worked together before they died to try and help me survive. I was overcome with emotion, lost in a dark and deep sea of memories that made me feel like I might drown in despair.

And then I felt something cold and tickly on my ankle. I looked down through my haze of tears and saw a gray mop on the floor with a pink tongue hanging out of it. Buster leaned in and licked my ankle again, looking up at me with brown eyes that were now much easier to see without the clumps of hair hanging in them.

I didn't think about it, I just did it - I scooped him up and held him to my chest, burying my face in his fur for a few seconds while I cried a few more tears.

I abruptly stopped when I realized how awful he smelled, jerking my head back and grimacing while gasping for fresh air. My sadness had evaporated instantly to be replaced by disgust.

"Holy Jesus, what on earth do you smell like, Buster?"

Buster got excited about hearing his name and wiggled like mad, struggling to give me a lick on the face.

"Oh God, no! No kisses to the face, Buster. Oh please, help me, Peter … he stinks to high heaven!"

"I think it's rotten snails," offered Peter. "Dogs like to roll in decomposing things. He had access to his back porch."

"Oh, gag," I said, holding Buster away from me and putting him back on the ground. He was alternately dancing in circles and jumping up on my leg.

"I think he likes you," said Peter, grinning stupidly.

"Stop smiling at me like that. He can't stay." I tried to sound all firm and angry, but it wasn't working. Buster was a complete idiot. He would not quit spinning in circles. "Stop spinning, you jerk."

Peter laughed. "You can't call a dog a jerk."

"Why not? He's acting like one. Getting all smelly like that and tricking me into picking him up."

Peter snapped his fingers to get Buster's attention, successfully convincing him to come over for more grooming. "How did he trick you? He's just a poor little dirty doggy, aren't you Buster? Aren't you? You need a bath. Wanna go in the pool?"

Buster responded by increasing the speed of his tail-wagging by eighty wags a second.

"He tricked me with his eyes," I accused. "Look at them. And that ankle licking thing."

"He's just a doggy woggy, aren't you, Buster? A doggy woggy loggy?" Peter was baby talking again and Buster was eating it up. "Wanna go in the pooley wooley?"

"Stop, Peter, before I come over there and put you both out of your misery."

Peter picked Buster and the scissors up. "I'm going to go give him a good grooming. Be back in an hour."

"Don't make any noise," I grumbled. Now I was going to have to figure out how the hell we were going to make it to safety with a barking spastic poodle as part of our group.

CHAPTER
FOURTEEN

I HAD TO ADMIT. BUSTER looked a hell of a lot better bald. Or nearly so.

"Damn, Peter. You cut so much off, he looks like a newborn mouse. His skin is pink!"

Peter shrugged, obviously unconcerned. "His hair was matted all the way to the roots. I tried to comb it out, but it was hurting him too much. I figured we'd start from scratch and try to keep him brushed out."

I eyed him suspiciously. "What comb did you use?"

"The one in your bathroom."

"Dammit, Peter, you can't use my comb on the dog!"

"Why not?" he asked me, his voice all full of innocence.

"I can't believe I even have to explain this to you ... because I use it on my hair, dummy."

"Your hair isn't any cleaner than his is."

He had a point there.

"I could cut yours if you want," he suggested.

I pointed my finger at him threateningly. "You stay away from me with those things. I like my braid and I'm pretty sure I'd be ugly bald."

"Fine. You should put a feather in it or some beads or something."
I laughed and shook my head at him. "You are so gay."

Peter smiled. "So."

"Hand 'em over, Rover. I don't trust you not to give me a mohawk while I sleep." I held out my hand out for the scissors, which he willingly turned over.

"I'm serious about the feather. We're going to be living off the land and learning how to do what the indians did. You've got the right bone structure to do the whole beads and feather in the braids thing."

"Whatever you say, Peter. I think instead of making fashion decisions for me you should start working on training that dog not to bark."

"Oh, he's already been trained. George left a list of instructions for Buster detailing all the things he can do. Apparently, poodles are one of the smartest breeds there are - for small dogs anyway."

"*Pfft.* I'll believe that when I see it."

"Come on, Buster," said Peter. "Let's go work on your skills. We'll show that meany wienie beanie who's the smart one and who's the ding-dong, won't we? Won't we?" His voice kept getting higher and higher, sending Buster into spasms of delight. "Won't we Buster Wuster Muster? Colonel Mustard in the library? With a rope with a dope? And a board game for doggies! Yes! Yes! You are a handsome boy, aren't you? Aren't you?"

"Dope is right," I said to no one, the two of them already out of earshot. Normally that kind of nonsense baby-talk made me crazy; but hearing it now almost made my life feel normal. Another human being was standing in my house goo-gooing over a silly dog, like I'd seen people do a thousand times in other places.

I picked up George's journal and began reading. Within the first few sentences I was hooked. George could tell one hell of a story. He started out with his recruitment and detailed things he learned in basic training and then things he learned while out in the field. He'd actually been sent overseas and had killed people, nearly dying himself of the cold and starvation before finally being wounded so badly he was sent home.

I went over and put his journal with the other books we'd be taking with us. I had the absurd desire to put it in my pocket instead, but fought against the sentimental feelings. I looked at its smooth leather cover, thinking about the man who'd taken the hours to sit down and hand-write all of that information for me, in exchange for watching out for the little guy he loved. I sighed, knowing that Buster was now a part of my club. Or my group. Or maybe even my family. I really didn't know what we were at this point, but I knew at least that I wasn't alone. And it felt good.

CHAPTER
FIFTEEN

PETER CONVINCED ME THAT WE could both sleep without fear of attack, now that we had Buster with us. He said that all dogs had a natural instinct to protect their pack, and we were now part of Buster's pack. At the time Peter said that, I'd looked down at the fuzzy pink thing that was now defining my place in this world, and laughed.

Pack, my butt, I'd thought. *This is the sorriest pack I've ever seen - a social misfit, a seventy pound fruitcake, and a smelly pink mouse-dog.*

A few hours later, Peter and I were startled awake by the ferocious, pink mouse-dog barking at the front window. I kicked out of my sleeping bag, angry that one of us had failed to stand guard, and grabbed for the gun next to me. I couldn't see anything in the dark.

"What is it?" whispered Peter, panic in his sleepy voice.

"Someone's trying to get in. Stay here!" I found the gun and jumped up, taking off for the front of the house, toward my living room.

As soon as I got there, I saw that someone had broken the window, and was reaching up to unlock it from outside. There was just enough light from the moon and stars to see that the raider's hand had a gardening-type glove on it to protect it from the shards of glass.

I flipped the safety off my gun and yelled, "Get the hell out of my house or I'm going to blow your friggin' head off."

The hand froze. Then I heard whispering. "Shit, man, you said no one was here!" The hand pulled out of the window and some sounds of scrambling around followed.

I could see some forms moving but no faces. Another voice came out of the dark, this one mean and growling.

"All we want is your food. Give it to us and we'll go away."

"No. I don't have any to give. But I do have a gun and I don't mind sharing some of my bullets. I'll put 'em right in your brain, that way they'll be easy for you to carry."

"You think you're funny, bitch? I've got a gun too."

I ducked away from where I'd been standing, taking a spot just behind the edge of the wall. Depending on what kind of gun he had, that bit of wood and drywall might not make any difference, but it made me feel safer.

"Just get the hell out of here," I said loudly, trying to sound tough. The rest of my warning was drowned out by the sounds of Buster barking in another part of the house.

"Bryn! They're at the back door too!" yelled Peter.

I heard glass breaking.

"Shoot their asses!" I yelled.

The figures in my front window took off, yelling and calling out to each other.

A loud *BOOM!* shook the walls of my house and set my eardrums to ringing. The muffled sounds of shattering glass and screams rent the air. They sounded like they were far off, even though I knew they weren't. I shook my head, trying to get the rest of my hearing back.

I quickly gave up trying and left the front of the house to go back to the family room where I had left Peter. I could see him now, in the light of the moon that was shining in through the big hole in my back door - the one that used to be covered in panes of glass but was now just a half door on the bottom with a simple frame on top. He was lying on the ground over our sleeping bags, unconscious.

Buster came trotting over, sitting down next to Peter's face to lick him. I was worried about him, but patting him down all over his chest and neck to see if he'd been shot revealed no blood anywhere but on his forehead; and I was pretty sure it was from his gun hitting him rather than a bullet, since there wasn't any hole. The dummy had knocked himself out with his own weapon.

I got up and walked over to the door, looking tentatively out of the giant hole. There was a kid lying on the ground out in the weeds of my yard. He wasn't moving but a gurgling sound was coming up from his chest. I was kind of bummed to find that my hearing had returned to normal at that point. His death gasps sounded wet and disgusting, continuing for a few seconds before finally stopping with one last, faint wheeze.

"Holy shit," I whispered, "you killed him, Peter."

Peter didn't hear me. He was too busy being unconscious, and I was glad for him. I'm not sure he would have been able to handle this part.

I stepped outside the back door, shoving it hard against the kid's legs to get it open. I crept up to him as quietly as I could, grabbing him by the arms and dragging him over to the side of the house. We weren't going to have time to bury him or do anything else with him for that matter, but I didn't want him blocking access into and out of my house. The idea of eating him flitted through my mind and made me almost vomit onto his bloody chest. No matter how hungry I got, I knew that was never going to be an option for me. There were just too many other things I knew I could find. Hell, I could go live in an orange grove and eat oranges for the rest of my life. Anything but another human being.

I went back inside and locked the door. It seemed silly, now that there was a hole in it so big someone could climb right through, but I felt safer anyway. We had Buster, the wonder dog, watching over his lame-ass pack.

I sat down next to Peter, determined to stay awake until sunrise, watching over him and the hole in my door. I felt his pulse and it was beating nice and strong with a steady rhythm, making me feel a lot better about his prospects.

Buster came over and climbed into my lap, giving me a few licks on the hand before resting his chin on my forearm. I absently petted his fuzzy back as he snored softly, trying to figure out how we were going to get the heck out of there with Peter's injury and our piles of crap, before those raiders came back to finish the job they'd started or get revenge for their fallen comrade.

Lines from George's journal haunted me as I waited for the sun to come up.

CHAPTER
SIXTEEN

I LOOKED UP AT PETER to ask him a question and tried not to laugh at his face. He had a huge bruise on his forehead with a knot the size of a ping pong ball in the center of it.

"Stop laughing at me. It's rude." He was busy pushing things into his backpack.

"No, stop, you're doing it wrong," I said, trying not to sound frustrated. He was useless at this part of our planning. My dad's training was earning huge points from me today. "You have to conserve space. Condense it down into the smallest footprint possible." I got a little choked up at the end, hearing my dad's voice echo in my own words. I used to get so mad at him saying that over and over. *Why did I hate it so much?* I couldn't remember now.

"I'm trying. I just have a monster headache," said Peter, slumping to the ground.

I pushed him gently, easily knocking him over. "Lay down. Take a nap. I'll finish this."

We'd decided that we had to leave later today. This way, Peter would have one day of recuperation and then we could strike out for the Everglades after. Last night's fiasco had pretty much made the decision for us.

"The cop a couple doors down didn't have a holster, but he did have a nice mountain bike. You need to go get it," said Peter, tiredly.

"I will. Soon. Just let me finish this."

"No," said Peter more forcefully. "Go now. The raiders are going to be coming out soon. They were out late last night, but they're not going to sleep forever."

He was right. "Fine." I looked at the dog. "Buster, watch Peter."

Buster responded by doing his doggy dance and wiggling so hard I was afraid he was going to pee.

"God, just *relax*, would you? I'm just talking to you, ding-dong."

Buster made some high pitched whining sounds and then let out a sharp, quick bark.

Peter smiled. "He's telling you to go, that he'll take care of me."

"You talk poodle now. Awesome," I said as I stood. "I think that .357 to the forehead might have caused just a teensy bit of brain damage."

"Just go get the dumb bike. And don't get killed on your way."

"Here," I said, laying his gun on his chest. "Try not to knock yourself out again. I don't think your puny skull could take another hit like that."

"I'll hold it lower next time."

"No, stiffen your arms next time, spaz. We don't need you adding a cracked rib to your list of injuries."

I got up to leave the room and Buster went to follow me.

"No, dummy, stay with him. He needs you more than I do."

Buster looked at Peter and then at me for a second.

I gestured at Peter again. "Stay!"

Buster went back to Peter and laid down next to him.

I nodded in appreciation of the training Buster had apparently not forgotten, and left the room, tucking my own gun in the back of my pants as I walked to the front door.

I waited a few seconds to take two deep breaths and let them out, slowly calming myself before going outside. Everything seemed like it had higher stakes now. People were breaking into my house with guns and threatening to kill me. Peter had put a huge hole in one of them. And one unfortunate soul was currently getting ready to rot on the side of my house because he couldn't take no for an answer or read my note on the front door that said to stay the hell away. This bike was the last thing I was going out to get before I left here for good.

I opened the door and nearly gagged at what I saw there. I took two steps back, forgetting that I shouldn't just be standing there with the door wide open. But I was too stunned to reason properly and do the smart thing.

Sitting on my front porch was a gray skinned, brown-haired *thing*, its eyes open and staring at my knees.

Someone had chopped off the head of the kid Peter had killed and left it for me to find at the front door - a grisly warning that took me less than a second to fully appreciate. It was a promise of retribution staring out at me from the dead eyes of the boy who'd died too young, all because he was hungry and desperate enough to try and steal from me.

I took deep gulping breaths and fought my instincts to slam the door, instead carefully closing it and slowly moving the dead-bolt back into place. I ran back to the living room and dropped down on my knees next to Peter, jiggling his shoulder roughly. Buster just watched me curiously.

"Peter! Get up! We have to leave *now!*"

"What'd you say?" he said, confusion all over his face, his speech sounding slurred. "What time is it? How long have I been sleeping?"

"They friggin'' cut someone's *head* off and put it on the *doorstep!*" I nearly screeched, trying to keep my emotions under control, but losing it anyway. "It's the kid you shot! They cut his head off!"

Peter sat up, now suddenly very wide awake, pressing his hands to his mouth, his eyes looking around the room. When they finally stopped on mine he whispered through his fingers, "That's what they did with my sister. They're eating the rest of him, I guarantee it."

"Wwwhat?!" I whispered, so freaked out I could barely get the word out.

He dropped his hands and used them for leverage to stand. "The canners are here, Bryn. They're here in your neighborhood." His face was white, with probably no more color to it than mine had right now.

"Come on," I said, jumping up, trying to get a handle on myself, even though my ears were ringing from my sky-rocketing blood pressure and my hands and legs were shaking with the adrenaline pumping through my veins to reach my heart and every other part of my body. "Go get your damn bike. Climb over the fence and bring it around back. I'll help you get it over."

Peter stood. "Wouldn't it be easier for me to ride it over on the street?"

I looked at him like he was nuts. "Wouldn't it be easier for them to see you and eat you, you mean?!"

"You have a point there."

"You're damn right I do. Now go. Get. Your. Bike. I'm going to the cop's place to get his. Bring your gun. Shoot anything that moves. Put bullets in your pockets. And Peter," I grabbed his arm and squeezed it hard, "for the love of God. Don't knock yourself out again." I pulled him into a quick hug, not even thinking about it before I did it.

"I'll try not to," he said, patting me on the back and then pulling away to walk out the back door. I watched as he stepped over the pool of gooey dried and stinking blood on the slate step just beyond it. He didn't even look down; he just kept on walking to the fence.

I ran to the front door and swallowed with effort. I was going to have to walk around the head to get out of my yard.

I inched the door open, almost wishing it wouldn't be there anymore, but quickly realizing how stupid that would be - since it would mean the canners were here at this very second, moving severed heads around like chess pieces.

It was still there. Looking at me. Blaming me for its current situation.

I slowly inched out the door, shutting it behind me as quietly as I could. I ducked down, using the bushes to hide my form as much as I could. I looked out and tried to see if there was any movement coming from the houses or yards around me, pulling my gun out of my waistband and taking the safety off as my eyes scanned back and forth. I almost felt sorry for anyone dumb enough to show his face to me right now. I wasn't going to hesitate - my new rule was to shoot first and ask questions later. Or just not ask any questions at all.

After confirming as best I could that I was alone, I snuck two doors down to the cop's house. The front door was wide open and had a big brown X on its inside surface, which had me freaking out all over again. But even the canners had to have enemies - other canners - so I figured if they were here, the door would be shut. I didn't even want to guess what that X meant. I made my way quietly through the kitchen that was in front of the house to the door leading into the garage.

The bike was hanging from hooks in the ceiling. I crept over and grabbed a folding chair on my way; it was too high up for me to reach otherwise. I had to put my gun back in my pants to get the bike down, and panicked the entire time that someone was going to come in while I had that heavy weight in my hand with no way to go for my gun.

As soon as the bike was on the ground, I took my gun out again. I put my two hands on the handlebars, trying to balance the weapon on top. I practiced a few times, moving my first finger from the top of the handlebar to the gun's trigger, seeing if I could do it fast enough to shoot if I were surprised by someone. Once I felt confident that I would be able to, I started wheeling the bike out of the garage and through the house.

I got halfway through the kitchen when I smelled something. Within a split second, my brain processed how very wrong that odor was - wrong because it smelled good, and not like rotting bodies. It was like something from the past. A cookout.

I propped the bike on the edge of the kitchen counter and tiptoed over to the sliding glass doors that led out to the pool area of the house. I could see that the cop had one of those big, stainless steel gas barbecue grills set up in his yard, with a big table and bench seats nearby. It was next to the pool that had several cushioned lounge chairs around it.

The first thing I noticed were the bodies - sleeping ones on the lounge chairs. There were five that I could count, all guys.

The next thing I noticed was the food on the table. It was charred and broken into several pieces, much of it just bones ... but even so, I could see what it was. Or rather, who it had been. I was now willing to bet that the kid with a .357 bullet in his chest was no longer on the side of my house.

I backed away from the glass, trying to keep the bile from rising up into my throat, when I butted up against something. Something warm.

"Well, hello there," said a deep, gravelly voice. I recognized it instantly as the one that had been outside my window the night before.

I swung around, but not in time to keep the guy from taking my gun out of my waistband.

"Going somewhere?" he asked, smiling, holding up the gun and aiming it at my chest.

His teeth were dark yellow with flecks of black things in between, and his hair hadn't been washed in months. A long time ago he might have been handsome, but not anymore. His eyes were way too bright, his skin red and scaley-looking with patches of acne breaking out all over it. And the dried blood all over the front of his clothes told me who had been in charge of the canners' barbecue last night.

"You stay the hell away from me, you friggin'' canner."

"Sorry, but that's not going to be possible. You're being cordially invited to join us for ... breakfast." His smile disappeared and he raised the gun up to my face, turning his hand sideways like some kind of thug gangster did in the movies. "Go outside." He gestured toward the sliding back door with his chin.

My brain did a quick calculation. There were six of them and one of me. I could take this guy, I knew it, but not all of them at once. They'd been eating a lot of protein and I hadn't had much at all in months, except for the few beans I'd eaten. My bodyweight was at an all-time low, and I'd foolishly let my training regimen get too lax.

I was on the balls of my feet, my hands raising of their own accord, my years of training and discipline taking over. My father's voice was in my head now, coaching me as my eyes took in the subtle clues that told me what my enemy was going to do the split second he'd made his decision to do it.

He stepped toward me and I met him quickly and forcefully, giving him no chance to react, kicking my foot out sharply to catch him in the knee. It twisted sideways, just as I had intended, throwing him off balance and hopefully giving him an intense amount of pain. He grunted, loud enough to wake his friends, so I knew I only had a few seconds to end this game.

Before he could get fully upright, I kicked the gun out of his hand, sending it across the room. It hit the wall with a loud thud.

He tried to swing out at me with a sloppy punch, but his knee put him off balance and he lacked all but the most primitive fighting skills, making him an easy take-down. I gave him a harsh jab to the larynx, collapsing his throat and causing him to reach up to try and help himself breathe. I took the opportunity to kick him square in the balls as hard as I could. Practitioners of krav maga know one thing: you do what you need to do to win. Nothing is tabu and there is no mercy for the enemy.

He fell down right where he stood, completely immobilized and unable to breathe. I kicked him hard in the temple to send him into temporary oblivion so he wouldn't be able to call out to his friends any more than he already had. I stopped short of killing him because I wasn't comfortable with it when he hadn't actually tried to kill *me* yet. I was okay with murder in self-defense, but right now, it didn't feel right to go that far. I looked up quickly on my way to retrieve my gun to check on the status of the other canners and saw that they were all still sleeping. For the first time I also noticed that there were empty liquor bottles and beer cans all over the place. The idiots were sleeping off a drunken night of partying and friend-eating.

Good. Gives me time to get the hell out of here. I looked down at the guy I'd knocked out, deciding that he might not be immobilized long enough with a ball shot and a kick to the temple. I ran over to the television and grabbed the cord that was plugged into the wall and two other cords that hooked the DVR to the TV and some other device. Leaning over, I felt my dad's ring hit me in the chin. It made me feel stronger, less a victim.

I used one set of cords to tie his hands, one for his feet and one for his mouth, which I secured after shoving one of his dirty socks in first. I nearly gagged at the smell of it, but didn't doubt for one second that I was doing the right thing. This guy would have raped me and possibly eaten me if he could have. The fact that he'd eaten one of his own friends told me he was no longer human. "A bunch of friggin'" zombies is what you guys are," I said to the unconscious scumbag.

After I tested the knots and decided they were tight enough, I left, grabbing the bike and running it out of there as fast as I could without tripping. I didn't bother checking for onlookers or people spying, only worried about getting the hell out of this neighborhood now overrun with cannibals.

I kicked the disgusting head out of the way and burst through the front door, sending Buster into fits of barking. I dropped to my knees gathering him in my arms, whispering, "*Shhhhhh,* you idiot! It's just me!"

Peter came over quickly, saying, "I got the bike to the edge, but I can't lift it!"

"Come on," I said loudly, grabbing his elbow as I jumped up to run to the back of the house.

"What happened?" he asked, already out of breath from me rushing him out on his bike retrieval mission.

"The canners are at the cop's house, and they ate that guy you shot. We have to get the hell out of here *now.*"

"What?!" yelled Peter.

I swung around and frowned at him, whispering, "Shut up, you idiot! Do you want them to hear you?"

Peter clamped his hand over his mouth, shaking his head silently.

I grabbed the top of the fence and vaulted myself over it, giving hardly any thought to the nearly super-human strength I'd just displayed. I grabbed the bike that was waiting on the other side and threw it over the fence in the spot I prayed Peter wasn't standing. Then I launched myself back over one more time.

"Holy crap, Bryn. Are you Wonder Woman now, too?"

"Adrenaline. It's not going to last forever. Come on, let's go!"

I grabbed the bike and ran it into the house, its wheels barely touching the ground.

I fast-packed our backpacks with Peter working as my assistant. I shouted out items and he handed them to me, rushing around the room to grab things as fast as he could. I had both backpacks done in less than three minutes.

"Try it on," I said.

Peter couldn't even get it on his back himself. I stood behind him and lifted it up, waiting for him to get the straps over before letting go. He nearly collapsed under its weight.

"Try this one instead," I said.

I'd thought they were the same weight but for some reason this second pack didn't have the same effect on him. It was mine, and made for long distance hiking.

"It's better," he assured me. "I'll take this one. After I put on more weight, we can switch."

"Don't worry about it, Lancelot," I said. "Just get your bike and let's go."

"But what about Buster?" he asked.

We both looked down at the fuzzy pink thing who was looking up at us with the happiest face a dog could possibly have. He'd just heard his name, and apparently to Buster, that always meant good things. His tail was wagging like mad, making his whole butt wiggle.

"Hold on," I said, letting a frustrated sigh escape me. I rushed to my bedroom and rummaged around in an old toy box my dad had bought for me when I was five. I grabbed the bag that was in there and came out, dropping down to squat near Buster.

"A *Hello Kitty* backpack?"

"Shut up. It's old. It's all I have."

"You're going to carry Buster around in a Hello Kitty backpack," he said. "Why can't I have a camera for things like this?" he asked the air around him.

I shoved Buster into the bag when he refused to go willingly. He poked his head out of the top as I buckled it down and strapped it to the front of me. While my hands were busy, Buster took the opportunity to lick my lips.

"Buster, no lip licking!" I growled as I wiped his dog saliva off with the back of my hand. "Gross."

"He's kissing you ... awwww, that's so sweet! He likes Hello Kitty as much as you do."

I gave Peter the stink-eye. "Keep it up and you're going to be the Hello Kitty commando, got it?"

"Yes, Sir!" he saluted. "I mean, Ma'am!"

I grabbed the heavier backpack and put it on, grunting with the weight, fearing I wasn't going to get very far with this thing on. It's a good thing we only planned to move a few hours a day.

"Ready?" asked Peter.

I looked around at my family room, taking in all the things around me. My eye landed on the photo of me and my dad in the Everglades. I walked over and slammed the frame down on the edge of the table, breaking the glass. I pulled the picture out and folded it up, sticking it in the pocket of my jeans.

"Now I am."

I paid little attention to the blue stain that was left behind on the frame's backing piece. It had rubbed off of the picture that was now in my pocket. It briefly reminded me how my dad liked to put details on the back of every photo he developed, so we'd remember when and where it was taken - as if I'd ever forget.

We wheeled our bikes out the door, avoiding looking at the severed head as best we could. We climbed onto our bikes once we were on the sidewalk and took off, pedaling as fast as we could, heading out of the neighborhood to parts yet unknown.

I couldn't help but look at the cop's house as we rode by. The brown X, which I now knew to be the canner's invitation to a barbecue, was still on the door, looking so innocent and yet so sinister at the same time. I wondered if I'd ever get the image of that monster looking at me out of my mind, praying I'd never see him again.

CHAPTER
SEVENTEEN

ICOULD HEAR PETER PANTING behind me.
"Are we there yet?" he gasped out.

"If you ask me again, I'm going to speed up and leave you behind."

Buster reached up to lick me again - for the hundredth time in the last half hour that we'd been riding. My chin was totally sticky with dog drool. I tried not to get mad about it since I knew he thought he was doing me a favor.

"Can we just stop for a minute?" he pleaded.

"No. We're almost there."

"Where's there?"

"The army-navy surplus store. They might have something we can use."

"Ha!" yelled Peter. "As if we could carry more things."

He had a point, but I had to try. If nothing else, Peter needed replacement shoes. His weren't going to last very long. They were the kind of sneakers cheerleaders wore, not the kind you could use for walking and hiking any distance.

We rolled into the parking lot a few minutes later. The store was actually just a small warehouse, back in the middle of a bunch of them in a commercial section of town. I could see already that someone had been there before us; the glass of the front window was broken and things were strewn out on the ground in front.

I got off my bike and motioned for Peter to do the same. I put Buster's bag down on the ground and he ran out of it, dancing around a few seconds before going to lift his leg on a nearby plant.

"I'll go check it out. You stay out here. Give that fuzzy pink thing some water while you're at it." I looked at Peter's bright red face and heaving chest. "Get your breath back while you wait too, would ya?"

He lifted his hand weakly in agreement, but didn't say anything.

I was pretty sure he wasn't even capable at this point. I needed to find some food for him in here if at all possible. The kid had almost zero stamina and definitely no body fat to fuel his exercise.

I picked my way over the rubble, Buster following me closely for a while before running off to check things out on his own. I ignored him and instead focused on finding stuff we might need.

I found some foil packed, dried meals behind the counter - they looked like damaged merchandise or maybe stuff someone had returned. I guess none of the raiders had bothered to look back there, which is why there were still around … lucky for us. I also found mini fishing poles and line and hooks, so I grabbed those. There were three poles, four spools of line and a box of hooks. But I really hit the jackpot when I got to the back part of the store. This place apparently also did some sales in mountain bike and camping supplies.

Buster must have sensed my excitement because he came running back to me all hyper, bouncing around while I worked to drag the thing I'd found to the front of the store.

I got to the glass door and said, "Get off your butt and help me."

Peter jumped up and ran over. "What the heck? … What is that thing?"

"It's a mini trailer. You attach it to the back of a bike and put your crap in it."

"Oh my goodness," he said, jumping up and down and clapping, "it's like we won the lottery or something!" He couldn't have looked more gay if he'd tried.

I smiled at his happiness. "Seriously, I think we did hit the lottery. Now put your damn bag in here. Make a spot for Buster Brown too."

"He's not Buster Brown. He's Buster Pink."

I rolled my eyes. "Whatever."

I went back into the store and grabbed the few other things that had caught my eye on the way out, making two trips to get it all. I took a pair of military-style boots for Peter in his size, four pairs of work pants - two for him and two for me, socks, camouflage t-shirts, the last six pairs of work gloves they had, the fishing stuff, the damaged meals, a tiny single-burner camp stove with ten containers of fuel, one frying pan and a pair of tongs. With the things my dad had already made sure I had and this stuff, we were all set.

"Who's going to tow the trailer?" Peter asked.

"Me for now. When you get more fluffed out, maybe we can trade off."

"How do we hook it to the bike?"

"I'm not sure. But there are some tools behind the counter and the instructions are here, so we can figure it out. Hurry up, go get them. I don't want to hang out here any longer than we have to."

An hour later we finally had the thing hooked up. Peter and I made a good team. He read the directions and handed me tools while I did the work. I'd never really considered myself a handy person before, but doing this made me feel confident. Not only can I escape the clutches of cannibals bent on my destruction, I can also do mechanic-type work. Next project: building a house in the swamp.

"Come on," I said, dropping the tools into the small trailer. "Let's go." I looked at the dog. "Buster, get up in the trailer."

He just looked at me.

"Get in the trailer, Buster."

"You have to use hand motions. Show him what you mean," suggested Peter.

I pointed to the spot in the trailer that had been left empty for him. "Get in there, you stupid, fuzzy, pink thing!"

He jumped into the trailer and wagged his tail at me.

"I swear to God, he's smiling at me." I stared at the dog, frowning, worried for my sanity.

"He is. I can see it," agreed a delighted-sounding Peter.

"Stupid dog."

"He's not stupid," insisted Peter as he climbed on his bike. "He's brilliant. And brave. Without him we'd be ... "

He didn't say the rest of his sentence but I knew what he was thinking, so I finished it for him. "We would have been cooked."

"Exactly," said Peter quietly, as he rode past me.

I got on my bike and took a few tentative pedals forward and found the trailer surprisingly easy to pull behind me. I turned a few circles around the parking lot and it just followed behind, bumping very little over the cracks and dips in the asphalt.

Peter began talking to the dog again, using his higher-pitched voice. "You like that, don't you Buster Wuster? Pinky dinky? Doggy woggy loggy?"

"Stop, you're making me sick to my stomach," I said, as we wheeled out of the parking lot and back to the road.

"What's the matter? Is Brynnie winnnie getting angry wangry?"

I aimed my bike for him, narrowly missing and sending him nearly into the ditch.

"Hey! Watch it, lunatic driver!"

"Don't baby talk at me or I'll be forced to put you down."

"You heard that, Buster! She just threatened me with euthanasia!"

Just my luck. I've hooked myself to a nutcase poodle-lover who thinks he can talk to dogs.

I shook my head, ignoring his blather in favor of watching road signs, looking for the one that would direct us over to Interstate 95.

It was time to head south.

CHAPTER
EIGHTEEN

W E GOT TO THE HIGHWAY forty-five minutes later. We would have gotten there sooner but we mis-read the map twice.

"Finally!" shouted Peter. "We made it!" He was so full of glee, it was hard not to smile.

We took the on-ramp up to the highway surface. I was nervous about being out there this exposed, but it was still relatively early in the day and there was plenty of room to make evasive maneuvers if we were seen by anyone. Plus, there were lots of abandoned cars to hide behind.

Peter came up beside me. "Why are all these cars here? They don't have bodies in them."

We passed by an older Honda, its driver-side door open. "I was wondering the same thing, but then I decided it wasn't adults who were driving them and just died at the wheel. I think these are cars that kids were driving when they ran out of gas."

"Ohhhh," said Peter. "That makes sense. I wonder where they are now. The kids, I mean."

"Who knows? I just hope they stay the hell away from us."

"Would it be so bad to have others join our pack?" he asked, looking over at me.

"Yes. No. I don't know." It was a tough question I didn't have a ready answer for. "If they're cannibals? Yes, obviously it would be bad. But anybody we add is another mouth to feed, another person who could blow our cover ... it's probably not worth it, even if they aren't canners."

"But what about ... for companionship?" Peter said more softly.

"You're all the companion I need. You and Buster." I looked back at the little guy who was now curled in a ball, his head tucked into his side with his eyes closed. The wind ruffled his fuzz a little, making him twitch an ear. I turned back to watch where I was going, swerving to miss a chunk of tire in the road and causing the trailer to rock a little.

"Yeah," said Peter, "but just me and Buster won't be enough ... not forever. I mean, at some point you'll want ... someone else."

"Do you mean like for sex?"

Peter's face turned pink. "Maybe. Or whatever. Kissing. Talking to. Cuddling."

"God, you are such a chick sometimes," I teased.

"Shut up. Everyone needs to be cuddled once in a while."

I wanted to say that I was pretty sure those canners didn't need to cuddle anymore, but I kept my mouth shut. I didn't want to spoil the moment.

"Yeah. Maybe," I agreed. "But right now, all I care about is finding a place where we can settle down."

"Me too," said Peter. "And Bryn ...," he cleared his throat, and glanced at me a couple times before continuing. "I just want to say ... thanks. Thanks for taking me in and bringing me with you too. I'm really glad we're together."

"You don't want to cuddle now, do you?"

Peter laughed. "Heck no," he squeaked. "Not with you."

"Phew. Good. You had me scared for a second there."

Peter reached out to slap me but I easily swerved out of his reach.

"Hands to yourself there ... stop trying to flirt with me."

"Ew. Like I'd flirt with a girl."

I chuckled and kept peddling. I was damn glad I'd taken Peter in too, but I wasn't going to tell him that. It was more fun to let him stew and wonder. He made me wish I hadn't been an only child. I never realized teasing could be this much fun.

CHAPTER
NINETEEN

IT WAS STARTING TO GET hot outside; and hot in Central Florida is its own kind of special misery. Pretty soon we were going to be sweating so much, we'd be unable to keep up with it and fully hydrate ourselves with the few bottles of water we had.

"We need to find somewhere to stop," I said over my shoulder.

Peter was pumping away at his pedals, his face looking too red for my comfort.

"Good. I'm planning on dropping dead in the first spot of shade we see … it was nice … knowing you," he huffed out.

"Come on," I said, smiling at his morbid humor. "Don't be such a wuss." All morning long he'd been giving out these one liners that had me laughing. He was good company. "There's an exit ramp just up there. We can stay under the overpass." I checked Buster and he seemed happy, his chin hanging over the edge of the trailer and his ears flicking forward and back from time to time as he caught sounds coming from birds or the wind in power lines or palms. We had rigged a tarp to give him shelter from the sun. Peter had been afraid Buster would get a sunburn - I was just worried about him having a sun stroke. I refused to let Peter put any of our sunscreen on the dog, though.

We had to conserve it for ourselves. Buster was just going to have to deal.

We got off the highway that seemed to stretch out forever in front of us and turned around to go under the overpass. The temperature was markedly cooler there in the shade, and the steep, ramped edges gave me a sense of security. If someone wanted to come get us, it was going to be an uphill battle - literally.

We perched the bikes up there on their sides along with the trailer. I wedged the bike pedal making contact with the ramped surface into a small hole, keeping the trailer from being able to drag the bike down to the bottom.

"Now what?" asked Peter.

"Now we cover ourselves. Or our bikes anyway."

"What do you mean?" he asked, sitting down and taking a swig from his water bottle. We had three that were full of drinkable water. The other one we planned to use for cooking only.

"Just watch and learn." I went into one of the backpacks and pulled the large tarp from inside. One side of the tarp was a dull gray and the other various shades of green. I opened it up and put it on top of our bikes and most of the trailer, green side down. I pointed to the corner nearest Peter. "Put your foot on that side."

He did as instructed.

I walked down the ramp with Buster following me. He looked so funny walking down at such a steep incline, I felt sorry for him, so I picked him up to carry him the rest of the way down. He had looked like he was afraid he was going to tumble ass over teakettle as my grandma used to say, but it hadn't stopped him from going with me anyway. He was nothing if not loyal.

Once we got to the bottom, I put him back on his feet and went in search of some rocks. I found four pretty decent sized ones and returned to Peter, leaning into the slope to make my climb with the extra weight easier. Buster was much happier going uphill than he had been going down.

I stretched the tarp back out and placed rocks down on the corners to hold it in place.

"Voilà," I said when I finished. "Done. Now no one will see us hanging out up here."

Peter looked down at his red t-shirt. "Uhhhh, yeah."

"Oh, right. Hold on a sec." I lifted up the tarp to reach into the backpack one more time. I had seen this t-shirt on the floor in the army-navy store, so I had shoved it in the bag for later. I pulled it out and threw it to him. "Put this one on. Take the other one off. We'll use it for ... bullfighting or something later."

Peter slowly opened up the camouflage shirt, his eyes taking in the printed slogan on the front of it.

"No way. I am not wearing this."

I frowned at him. "Listen, life isn't a fashion show anymore. You can't afford to be picky. Just put it on. You're going to call attention to us with that friggin' siren of a shirt on."

"But come on, Bryn. *This* shirt?" He looked at me, a pained expression on his face.

I shrugged. "It was the only one left. And it's your size. Just put it on backward if you can't handle the words."

I turned so he could have a little privacy. When I looked back a few seconds later he was pulling it over his head. He had the skinniest chest I'd ever seen. It prompted me to go over to the bags and try to find some food for him. I pulled out one of the damaged meals and walked over, handing it to him. "Eat this. You're so skinny it gives me a headache."

He took the food without saying anything, handing me the red shirt in exchange. I quickly folded it up and shoved it into one of the bags. It reminded me that we'd have to find a way to wash our clothes when we got to our destination. If anyone got downwind of either of us they'd smell us coming from a mile away.

I took out a can of beans and popped the top open, tipping the can to my mouth to let a few beans fall in. After I'd had three mouths-full, I handed it over to Peter. "You finish these. I've had enough."

"You have to keep your strength up, Bryn. You can't give me all the food."

"I don't plan to. But that was good enough for me. I think we're going to go past some orange groves on our way. Maybe we'll be able to find some trees with fruit on them tonight." I seemed to remember smelling orange blossoms on our way down, when I went to the Everglades with my dad.

"I think orange season is over."

I shrugged. "I don't mind eating overripe fruit."

Peter didn't argue. He ate everything I gave him and then drank half his water. "I'm going to take a nap," he said.

"Good. Me too." I motioned for Buster to come sit next to me. He climbed up in my lap instead. "Hey, dog. How am I supposed to sleep if you're in my lap?"

He jumped up a few inches to lick my chin.

"Come here, you goofy mess," I said, resting on my side and putting him on the ground near my stomach. I brought my knees up to shelter him a little. "No more licking. Just go to sleep."

Peter and I were back to back now, each of us facing out to one side of the overpass. From my vantage point, all I could see was scrubland and some short trees off in the distance.

"You got your gun?" I asked Peter.

"Yep."

"Shoot anyone who looks dangerous."

"Okay," he said, yawning.

"Buster, you make sure no one gets near us, okay?" I said in a low tone.

Buster took that as in invitation to get up and dance, so I pushed my hand down on his back. "No, sit, you dummy. Stop dancing around."

"Would you two be quiet? People are trying to sleep over here."

I bumped Peter's butt with mine. "Shush. You're going to blow our cover."

That was the last thing I remember saying before drifting off into an uncomfortable sleep, tiny pieces of gravel digging into the skin of my arm.

CHAPTER
TWENTY

A LOUD CLAP OF THUNDER woke me from the bad dream I was having of the canner who'd grabbed me, chasing us down on a motorcycle. The thunder had taken on the ominous tones of war drums, beating as he got closer and closer. I woke startled, sitting up so fast I almost slid down the ramp.

I looked at our bikes and noticed that the tarp had come up on one side. Peter was still asleep and I decided to leave him that way as long as possible. The kid was obviously exhausted.

As the first drops of rain fell, inspiration struck. I quickly got under the tarp and took out the square of plastic and small bucket my dad had bought for me before he left. Buster followed me over to the edge of the overpass, where I proceeded to try and rig up a water catcher.

I gave up after a few minutes and just sat there in the rain, holding the plastic up and slightly folded, on a diagonal, so the water hitting it would drain into the bucket I was holding steady with the insides of my feet. The shower was over in less than an hour, but it had come down hard enough to give me enough water to fill all three bottles with some left over. I poured the extra into the bowl with the straw on it for Buster, who eagerly drank it all up.

I sat there thinking about our next move as Peter slept on, waiting for the humid air to dry me off. It wasn't working so well. By the time he got up an hour later, I'd mapped out the next couple days of riding but was still pretty damp.

"Hey," he said, sitting up and stretching. He looked around and then over at me. "What the heck happened to you?"

"I got us some more water."

"Did you get it from a drainage ditch?"

"Ha, ha, very funny. It rained. I filled up our water bottles. Here." I handed him a full one.

"Awesome. Thanks."

I watched him drink half of it in seconds and made a mental note to be sure to get more in the bucket next time. I was feeling better and better about going toward the Everglades. We'd never run out of water or food there. The key would be figuring out how to catch the food. I wasn't even sure if the fish we'd get there were edible. I wished we had a book about the animals in the swamps - other than just the one we had on snakes.

"So what's the plan?" asked Peter, his thirst now satisfied. He handed me his bottle and I put it back in the trailer.

"Well, if we move from four in the morning until nine, we'll be able to get about fifty miles a day. And we're about two hundred and fifty miles from where I think we need to be."

"So about five days of traveling, you think?"

"Something like that. I don't remember much about the area; I've only been there once. I figure we'll get down there and stop when we find a place that looks good. Maybe once we get closer we can go into a tourist shop with some books that have info or a map of the whole place."

"The Everglades are pretty big," said Peter, sounding skeptical.

"I know. But we need to find a specific spot. One that's hard to reach and has trees to hide a shelter in."

"How are *we* going to get into it if it's hard to reach?"

"Boat?" I suggested.

"I can see you've put a lot of time into this plan," he said sarcastically.

"Yeah, well, how much time have you put into it, smartass?"

"None." He held up his hand for a high-five. "You're right. I'm sorry. I appreciate you doing all this for us."

I begrudgingly slapped his hand back. "The plan is flexible. We'll just figure it out as we go along. It's better that way, anyway - if one of us gets caught, we won't be able to divulge any secrets."

"Since we don't have any."

"Exactly." I smiled at my unintentional genius.

"Let's just pray we don't get taken captive, because the only reason someone would do that would be to ... well, you know."

"Invite you to dinner," I said.

"Yeah."

"Do you want to tell me about your sister now?" I tried not to cringe at the fact that I'd just brought up his sister while we were on the topic of being eaten for dinner, but it was impossible. Sometimes my mouth got away from me before I could stop it. "Sorry. That wasn't cool."

Peter didn't seem to mind. His eyes got a far off look to them as he stared off into the distance. "She was twelve. Really small for her age, though. She looked about ten or so. We used to fight all the time. She was always getting into my stuff and I hated it."

I had no experience with siblings invading my territory, but I could see how it might be irritating.

"We were in Sanford, in our house. We had to bury both of our parents in the back yard. They died on the same day."

"That's awful," I said, meaning it. I had only lost one parent and that was bad enough.

"My sister and I had a hard time moving them out into the yard. We couldn't stop crying, because we kept worrying that we were hurting them. Isn't that stupid? I mean, they were already dead. We checked their pulses like a hundred times to be sure."

I shook my head but said nothing. Even when bodies were dead, if they belonged to people you loved in life, they seemed sacred. I was once again reminded of how grateful I was to my father for doing his dying elsewhere.

Buster went over and sat in Peter's lap. Tears were going down his cheeks and Buster kept trying to jump up and lick them. Peter kept him contained by playing with and petting his ears absently as he continued his story.

"After we got them buried, we stayed in the house, living off the things left in the pantry. My mom always made spaghetti on Sundays, just like my aunt, so she had about fifty jars of sauce in the garage. She bought them in bulk at Costco."

"I loved Costco," I said wistfully.

"Me too. What I wouldn't give right now to just live in one. They even have mattresses there." He sighed and cleared his throat, continuing in a stronger voice now. "Anyway, one day we decided to take a walk down to the convenience store that was near our house, just a few blocks away. We were joking around about getting a slushy, I remember, when we first saw them."

"Them?" I asked, to fill the silence. Peter was lost in the memories somewhere, and I knew it wasn't a good place to be. I scooted over and put my hand on his back. "You don't have to tell me if you don't want to."

"No, I do," he said sternly. "Someone else besides me should know what they did to her. To Lily." His voice broke at her name.

Buster tried to get up to come over to me, but I pushed him away, sending him back to Peter. He needed the dog more than I did right now.

"As soon as we saw the group of them, we knew they were trouble. They walked in a big group, right down the middle of the street, not caring who saw them. Some of them had baseball bats. One had a gun."

"Was it the same guys we saw?"

"I don't know. I doubt it." He looked at me, fear in his eyes. "I mean, what are the chances they would have taken the same route as me to get to my aunt's house?"

"Not good," I assured him. "Practically impossible."

"Yeah. You're right." He stared straight ahead again. "It means there's more than one gang of them out there, though. Not exactly good news."

I shook my head in disgust. "They're like packs of wild animals. Zombies."

"I used to read zombie books and go to those movies, laughing at the gore." He smiled bitterly.

"Me too." I reached over to pet Buster with him. "So what happened then?"

"We took off running. It's like all they needed to see - it got them all excited. They were hollering and cheering, like they were egging each other on. It was a sick game to them. I've never been so friggin' scared in my entire life."

Peter grabbed my hand that was petting Buster's head. I just sat there and let him squeeze it, saying nothing, just listening.

Peter's voice was wavering badly now. "Lily took my hand and I saw her face. She was super scared too. And then as we were cutting through one of our neighbor's yards, she tripped on one of the roots that was sticking up out of the ground and landed on her knees. I tried to help her get up but she'd twisted her ankle. She couldn't move."

I put my other hand on top of his, squeezing now too. I could totally picture the scene, his poor little sister on the ground and the pack of wolves closing in.

"She yelled at me to keep going, but I didn't want to leave her there."

"There was nothing else you could do," I said, firmly. "You had to save yourself."

"I know," he said, putting his head down. "But I couldn't just leave her."

"What'd you do?" I asked softly.

"I stood there over her, waiting for them to come. She kept grabbing my pant leg, pushing me, screaming at me to leave, but I couldn't." He started crying again. "I just couldn't."

"How did you live?" I asked. I knew those canners had no souls left. They wouldn't have just let him go.

"They came and took her from me, dragging her away while she screamed my name over and over and over. One of them punched me in the face and knocked me down, saying I was too skinny to bother with."

ELLE CASEY

"That's kind of rude," I said, without thinking. "Sorry."

"No. Don't worry about it. Anyway, they took her away, and I tried to follow, but one of them came back with the baseball bat and swung it at me. So I dropped far behind, following them from a distance. I saw where they took her and then ran back to my house to get my gun."

"You were going to kick some ass, weren't you?"

"You're damn straight I was," he said bitterly. "I took a whole box of bullets in my pockets and went back to their house."

He was crying again, more intensely now, small sobs bursting out between the words. "When I got there, though, it was too late. I went around to the back where I could hear their voices ..."

I didn't want to hear the rest of the story. I knew pretty much how it ended and I knew the details were only going to make the knowing worse. But Peter needed to tell someone, and Buster wasn't exactly in a position to appreciate its awfulness enough to help Peter feel like he wasn't alone.

"What did you see?"

"Oh, God. It was awful. My worst nightmare come to life. I saw my sister's head. On the ground. They were ... they were ..." His shoulders were quaking now, tears and snot dripping off of his face. "They were cutting her up ... and putting her body parts on a big grill! There was blood everywhere!"

I felt the vomit coming up again and swallowed three times in quick succession to keep it down. My salivary glands were working like mad, telling me to get moving, so I wouldn't barf on my friend.

But I couldn't leave him. I knew he didn't want to be alone right now - couldn't be alone right now. He'd seen pretty much the most horrific thing I could possibly imagine a person having to endure. And it had happened to his baby sister.

I put my arm across his back and pulled him in tight to me. "Shhhh, I know it's awful. I know it's terrible. Evil stuff. Evil. They're going to pay." I had no idea how that was going to happen, but prayed karma might take care of some of it.

"Oh, they did. Believe me."

I stopped squeezing him for a minute. "What'd you do?"

"I shot four of them. One right in the face."

I hugged him again. "*Good* for you, Peter. I don't know how you did that without knocking yourself out, but I wish you'd shot all of them in the face. In the nuts too."

Peter agreed angrily. "Me too. I think I got lucky with not hitting myself. The gun kicked more up instead of back for some reason. I think Lily's spirit was there helping me."

"I'll bet she was too. How'd you get away?"

"I ran like hell while they all ran around screaming … got back to my house, threw my stuff in a bag and took off on my bike."

"And ended up in my back yard."

"Yeah. I ended up in your back yard."

"In your Aunt-who-wasn't-really-an-aunt's house."

He smiled, now a little less angrily. "Yes. In my aunt's house."

"The one with the bright red pumps."

He giggled and sniffed hard, shoving me off of him. "Yes, the one with the pumps."

I stood up and brushed myself off. "Well, I wish I could say something to make it better for you, Peter, but I just can't think of anything. If I could, I'd go kill them all for you."

"I know you would. And for some strange reason, that makes me feel just a tiny bit better." He looked up at me, his eyes all red and puffy but no longer leaking.

I continued. "All I know is, they'd better never show their ugly canner faces in my Everglades, or they're going to go down … and it won't be pretty."

"Yeah," said Peter. "Damn straight."

"Gator bait."

"I like it," he said.

"Snakebite victims."

"Another good idea," encouraged Peter.

"I'm out of good ideas now, though," I said, smiling at Peter's slightly uplifted mood.

"That's okay, I'm good with those." He stood up. "I'm gonna go pee."

"Okay. Stay out of sight."

"Who's going to see us out here in the middle of nowhere?" he asked.

I shook my head slowly. "Do we really want to know the answer to that question?"

"No," he agreed, sad once again. "Probably not."

I felt bad about reminding him of our precarious position, but it wouldn't do to go around with a false sense of security, just because we had a couple of guns and a fuzzy pink watchdog.

Buster followed along next to Peter, both of them stopping just at the edge of our ramp to pee out into the bushes. It was comical watching them do it together - Buster with his tiny leg lifted and Peter with his cammo shirt on backward. I could read the bright white words on it from here: *Guns don't kill people. People kill people.*

CHAPTER
TWENTY-ONE

WE PASSED THE REST OF the day talking about our schools, our friends, and the things we had liked to do before the world started falling apart. It turned out Peter didn't have a whole lot of friends, nor did he do much outside of school, other than sing and play video games. We had a lot in common - more than we had thought we would.

"I don't understand why you didn't have any friends. That's just ridiculous," I said, now angry at the unfairness of a world that was supposed to have been functioning just fine, before it all went to hell in a hand basket.

"I've been bullied pretty much since kindergarten. No one likes to be friends with a victim."

"Why didn't your parents do something about it?"

"They didn't know. I lied about a lot of things."

"Why'd you do that? Why not let them stick up for you?"

"Because I didn't want them to find out," he said, his wispy voice going even softer than normal.

"Find out what? That you're a serial killer?"

"No, jerk. That I'm gay."

"Why not? Being gay's not a death sentence anymore. The world has changed."

"Easy for you to say."

I shrugged. "I guess."

"I had a theory that most of the guys who picked on me did it because they were attracted to me and hated themselves for it." He smiled briefly, almost sadly.

"Interesting. Sick and a little twisted, but interesting."

"Seriously. I mean, don't we usually hate things that we recognize in ourselves?"

"I think you've wasted a lot of time reading self-help books."

"Yeah, I probably did. But sometimes thinking that made it easier for me."

"Didn't teachers or other students notice?"

"Probably."

"Why didn't they do anything about it?"

"I don't know. I guess they were too busy with their own lives."

"*Pfft.* No wonder the world came to an end. Everyone living in it was a bunch of assholes."

Peter laughed. "I've thought that more than once. Like this disease or virus was a giant cleansing of the planet."

"Yeah, well, it wasn't a very efficient method. It got rid of the good guys, too. My dad was a good guy."

"I can tell ... by the way you talk about him. You really loved him."

"I still do. He's still alive in my head. I hear his voice all the time, telling me to be smart and to practice my martial arts."

Peter smiled. "I wouldn't tell too many people that, if I were you."

"Why," I scoffed. "What are they going to do? Lock me away? I can do whatever I want without consequences now. I'm totally free." I gave him a cocky look which I immediately lost at his next statement.

"Be careful. That's what the canners say to themselves every night before they go hunting."

I sat down, totally deflated. "Thanks a lot, killjoy, for bringing me back down to our crappy reality." I stuck my tongue out at him and gave him a raspberry.

"Well, we are going to start a new world out here, a new country or whatever, and we have to hold onto our moral fiber as best we can."

"Okay, Father Jim."

"Who's Father Jim?"

"A guy at this church I went to a couple times. My dad said I should try to experience organized religion in several forms, so I could make an educated choice about whether I wanted to join a church or whatever."

"What'd you decide?"

"I decided I didn't like some guy with a big red nose telling me what I was supposed to be thinking and believing. Especially since right after services he went on to break all the rules he'd just laid down for everyone else. They always say not to judge in the sermons and then they go ahead and judge anyway."

"I was never that thrilled with church either. The one my parents went to didn't believe gays were born this way. They were big on conversions or whatever."

"Conversions?"

"Getting gay men to go straight through therapy."

"A-holes."

"Yeah. Pretty much."

"No wonder you didn't tell your parents."

Peter shrugged but said nothing.

I guessed from his reaction that I probably should avoid the topic of parents being jerks. Not just now but forever. We were bound to run into other kids eventually, and we all had our baggage - things tied up in the way we had lived with our families and the things we'd seen and done since they'd died and left us here. It was safer to just talk about the future.

"So once we get to our final spot, what do you think we should do?" I asked.

"Well, get shelter for one. Food and water sources. Supplies for contingencies. You do realize we have potential hurricanes to deal with, right?"

"Yeah, don't remind me. Hurricanes here, tornadoes in the other states, mudslides, avalanches, floods. Nowhere is safe."

"I guess we need to take a look at our environment and design our lives around it. Then maybe we could risk finding others to join us."

I fixed him with a stare. "You're really set on this cuddling thing, aren't you?"

Peter sighed at me and said, "Shut. Up."

I smiled evilly at him. "Make me."

Peter reached out to slap me, but I grabbed his arm and twisted it lightly.

"Wrong answer. Try again."

He whipped his other hand out, faster this time, but I caught it anyway, twisting it up with the other one. "Buzzy buzz buzz. Try again."

His right foot came next, which I easily blocked with a kick of my own.

"Ow. Watch it, lady. I have a delicate constitution."

I let his hands go. "You need some training. You're soft, slow, and obvious. That makes you easy to kill."

"Yeah, well not everyone can be a kung-fu master like you."

"I'm not into kung-fu. It's call krav maga."

"What's that supposed to be? Something you made up?"

"No. It's been around for a long time. The Israeli Special Forces use it and so do lots of police departments around the United States and some other countries too."

"How'd you learn it?"

"My dad was an expert. I've been doing it since I was little."

"So you have like a black belt or something?"

"No. They have a different system, at least in the dojos where I worked out. I'm an E1 level."

"Is that the highest?"

"No way. But it's not the lowest either." I smiled in self-satisfaction. I'd worked hard to get where I was, even though I could have gotten further with more work.

"Do you think you could teach me?"

"Yes. I could. And I think I *should*. It will help you not only survive, but also it'll improve your general fitness level, which to be honest, pretty much sucks right now."

Peter stood up, acting all miffed. "Yeah, well, like I said. I have a delicate constitution." He faced down the ramp, looking at nothing.

"Just because you're gay doesn't mean you have to be all weak," I said.

Peter whipped around to face me. "Me being gay has *nothing* to do with my strength, *okay?* I happen to be very strong, just not in the ways that you are!"

"Wow, geez, I'm sorry. I didn't mean to offend you. I'm just saying … you can be delicate and still know how to kick ass when need be."

Peter shrugged, sniffing lightly. "That would be fine with me. Just so long as you don't expect me to get all kinds of muscley. I don't know if that would look so good on me."

"Are you kidding? You'd look great with some definition in your arms and legs. Guys go crazy for that stuff." I really had no idea what I was talking about, but it sounded good and he need-ed some inspiration to fatten up a little.

"Do you think so?"

"Sure. But don't you know that? I mean, haven't you ever had a … boyfriend or whatever?"

"No. Like I said. I didn't have many friends growing up."

"Well friends and boyfriends are different things."

"Have you had any? Boyfriends I mean?"

"No. Not really. I've had guys I liked before, but none of them ever asked me out."

"Why?"

"I don't know," I said annoyed. "How would I know that?"

"You could guess. Who were they?"

"You want names?"

"No, but tell me how you knew them."

I rolled my eyes, convinced this was a fruitless exercise. "They were usually guys I was training with."

"Well, that's your problem," he said, matter-of-factly.

"How so?"

"They saw you as a training partner, another one of the *guys*. I'll bet you were one of the only girls there, right?"

"Yes. Always."

"And your dad was involved in the training?"

"Very much."

"And if this training was all hard-core like that other martial arts stuff, that meant there was a ton of, like, discipline and stuff going on?"

"Yeeesss ..."

Peter threw up his hands. "Well, there you go! Mystery solved!" He seemed very proud of himself.

"I don't get it. How did you solve the mystery?"

"Don't be dense. You were one of the guys. The only ones who might have been attracted to you would have been gay guys, looking for a friend."

"Seriously?"

"Seriously. Did any of the guys act all nice to you all the time without ever acting sexually attracted to you?"

"Yeah, there was this one ... "

"Gay. I guarantee it."

"Holy crap. I can't believe Bobby was gay. Actually, no, I *can* believe it. He was always staring at the guy I had a crush on too. At the time I thought he was just taking a lot of interest in his techniques."

Peter snorted. "Yeah. I'll bet he was."

"Oh, man. That sucks. I'm like ... neuter gender or something."

Peter laughed. "You're not neuter. You just need to hang out in environments that support women like you."

"Women like me," I said flatly. "That could get you on your back on the ground in less than two seconds, you know."

"Stop flirting with me. I told you, I'm gay. No, what I mean is, you're strong and feminine at the same time. But in the dojo or whatever it's called, you're just another one of the guys. But see them at a dance or a place with make-up on and a skirt, maybe ... then they'll see you in another way - not as one of the guys."

"So that's the key? Makeup and a skirt?"

"Well, in an over-simplified way of speaking, yes."

I shook my head. "Guys are so stupid."

"You won't get any arguments from me there."

"You're a guy."

"Not really. Not like you're saying. I'm more in touch with my feminine side than the guys you're used to."

I nodded my head. *That was for damn sure.* "Well, this has all been very enlightening," I said, yawning, "but now it's time for us to go to sleep so we can get up at four or so and get our fifty miles in."

"Okay. I have to go … um … do something first."

"A doodle?"

Peter looked at me aghast. "What did you just say?"

"A doodle. You have to go do a doodle, right? Or did you mean something else? Did you mean you have to go rub one out? I hope that's not what you meant, because seriously, I think that kind of thing can wait."

Peter's expression was priceless - kind of a cross between incredulity and disgust. He just shook his head, mumbling as he walked away. "As if I'm going to share my bathroom habits with her …"

Buster went to follow him, so I yelled out, "Buster, stay! Peter has to go do a doodle. No poodles allowed during doodle time." I giggled at Peter throwing his hands up in defeat.

By the time we got to the Everglades, I was going to be an expert teaser.

I waited for Peter to be out of sight before I went and took care of my own doodle business. Togetherness was one thing - but certain stuff was better kept private, and this was one thing I knew I never needed to share. Not even with Buster.

"Buster, stay!" I commanded, pointing at the wagon.

He happily jumped in, wagging his behind like crazy.

"Watch our stuff. Bite anyone who tries to touch anything."

I left, wondering if Buster would ever actually be any use to us as a guard dog that did anything but bark and lick people to death.

CHAPTER
TWENTY-TWO

I GOT MY ANSWER AS I was zipping up my pants. Buster began barking his fuzzy head off, and shortly thereafter, I heard
the sounds of somebody yelling. It was a male voice, but too deep
to be Peter's.

I ran back to the bikes, praying I wasn't going to have to fight
off a canner. I had my gun in my hand, where it had been the entire time I'd been taking care of business. I was leaving nothing to
chance, and literally refused to be caught unarmed with my pants
down. All these weird expressions my dad used to use were totally taking on new meaning for me.

I arrived at the ramp in time to see a big guy holding his hands
up in surrender, while a ferocious-looking Buster held him at bay
a few feet away from the trailer.

"Who the hell are you?!" I yelled, striding over awkwardly on
the steep slope.

"I'm just a guy!" he yelled, but he had an accent. It sounded
like he said, "I'm chust a guy."

"You're not just a guy, you're a thief. And a dirty cannibal too,
probably!"

I had arrived at the trailer, stopping next to Buster. I bent down without taking my eyes off the guy in front of us to pet him and murmur, "Good boy, Killer, good doggy."

"He bit my ankle. I hope he hass hiss rabiess shots." The guy's speech was very clipped as he pronounced every letter, just so and very precisely.

"What's up with the accent?" I asked.

"H-what accent. I don't haff an accent."

"Yes, you do. It's not 'h-what'. It's just 'what'. And you're putting too many esses on the ends of your words."

"I'm Hamerican."

I laughed. "Try again, liar."

"Fine. What are you, da immigration police or something? I'm Cherman."

"German?"

"Yes. Dat's what I said."

"What's your name and why are you messing with our stuff?"

He smiled. "You talk about your dok like he'ss a person."

"She's not talking about the dog," said Peter from behind me. "She's talking about me."

"And the dog," I corrected.

"And Buster," said Peter, standing next to me, holding his gun down at his side. I was glad he decided to do that. It looked a lot more intimidating when his hands weren't shaking.

"Okay, fine. You are a party of three. My name iss Bodo. I am from Chermany. I came here for an exchange program last year and den the family I was staying with, dey all died. Now de Internet iss down and I cannot reach my family. I do not even know if dey are alife."

I leaned over to Peter and said in a loud whisper, "He means 'alive'."

"Dat's what I said," clarified Bodo. "Alife."

Peter shook his head. "Stop harassing the poor guy, Bryn. He's German. But he speaks pretty good English, actually." Peter turned his attention back to Bodo, addressing him directly. "Hello, Bodo. Welcome to the United States. I'm sorry you got stuck here, but you should probably know that anyone in your country over the age of twenty and under the age of ten is dead now. You're probably stuck here for life unless you know how to sail."

"Wow. Way to break it to him easy," I said, chuckling. Mr. Sensitive was getting tougher by the minute.

"I know dis. Efreyone is dead now. I haff been on dis highway for days, looking for someone. Anyone. It wass crazy in my town, so I left it."

"Yeah, well, I don't advise heading north. There are cannibals up there."

"I call dem zombies," said Bodo. "Dey haff dem in my old town, too. I was living in West Palm Beach."

Peter and I exchanged a look, smiling.

"You like zombies?" said Bodo. Then he took a step back. "If you are thinking about killing me and eating me, I will tell you dat it would be a mistake. I am a lethal weapon." He held up his hands in a poor approximation of a karate stance.

I couldn't help but snigger at him. He was absolutely adorable, but so full of crap it wasn't even funny. I could have been wrong, but I felt like to be a canner, you had to totally lose your sense of humor. And this guy still had his, whether he realized it or not.

"We don't eat people," said Peter. "But we don't have enough food to share right now."

"Oh, dat's not a problem," said Bodo, sliding his backpack off his shoulder.

I held up my gun. "Not too fast, there, Bodo. We've already killed some guys who messed with us before."

He held up his hands, palms out. "I'm chust going to show you my food. So you can see I did not come here to take your thingks."

He pulled can after can of raviolis and tuna out. The last thing he took out was a tall container of Pringles.

"Holy crap. You have *Pringles*," I said, in a daze. I hadn't had a Pringle in over a year. Normally, that wouldn't be a big deal for me. But right now, it seemed like a crying shame.

"I eat one per day. I haff enough Pringkles for a few more months. Unless I share. Den a little bit less." He smiled, revealing straight, white teeth. They were so not like the canner's teeth I had seen.

"Bodo, I have to warn you," said Peter, his voice sounding very serious and mature. "Bryn here really is a lethal weapon, so if you try anything funny, she will snap your neck. She was trained by the Israeli Special Forces. Do you agree not to steal any of our food or things if we let you stay with us tonight?"

Bodo nodded his head quickly. "Oh yes, definitely. Wow, dat's impressif. The Issraeli Special Forcess. I will not touch anything. And if you vant, *oops*, I mean want, I can play you my harmonica. My family used to tell me dat I am very good." He smiled and said, "I'm trying to improof my accent so I can blend in better. For me, it's da double youss dat get me efreytime."

"Dude, trust me when I say, it's not just the double yous that are getting you, but it doesn't matter to us if you have an accent. And no, thanks, we don't need to hear your harmonica. We don't want to attract any attention with music. Maybe some other time."

"Yeah, sure. No problem. Chust tell me when you want to hear it and I will play it for you." He put all the cans back in his bag.

"You stay over there," I said, directing Bodo to a spot about ten feet below us.

"Okay, dat's not a problem."

I leaned in and whispered to Peter. "Did you hear that? It's not a problem."

Peter rolled his eyes and whispered back. "You are so mean. He's foreign. He can't help it if he repeats the phrases he knows."

"I'm just goofing around. His accent is cute."

"I know. It totally is," said Peter, his voice taking on a dreamy quality.

I nudged him. "I'm pretty sure he's not your type."

"A boy can fantasize," he said nudging me back.

Bodo went down the ramp and sat down, reaching into his sack. "Do you guyss want some Pringkles? I am happy to share." He held the can up behind his head.

Peter looked at me nervously. "Do you trust him?"

I shook my head. "No. The only ones I trust are you and Buster. How do we know he doesn't have a gun or something else in that bag?"

Peter walked down to where Bodo was sitting. "We want to search your bag."

Bodo shrugged, handing it over. "Go ahead. It's not a problem at all."

Peter brought it back and went through it, while I kept my gun trained on Bodo's back.

Bodo took the plastic lid off the Pringles can and took out a chip, turning sideways so we could watch him put it in his mouth.

I felt myself start to salivate, watching that chip go in; and I didn't know whether it was the food or his cute face that was causing it to happen. He was tall, broad-shouldered, and blue-eyed. The stereotypical Aryan European man. *Wowza.*

"He's clean," said Peter. "He doesn't even have a gun or a knife. Just a can opener."

Peter took a few steps toward Bodo and tossed the backpack to him.

Bodo held up the can of chips and shook it a little. "I'll chrade you … one chip each for something you have."

I took four long steps down the slope and snatched the can out of his hand.

"Hey," he said, half standing, "dat's not fair."

"You want to join this crew? You sacrifice everything. Pringles and all."

Bodo thought for a second and then looked up, his crystal blue eyes boring into mine. "You are offering me a place with you? In your family?"

I looked back at Peter who shrugged in return.

I turned my gaze back to Bodo and said, "It's more like a tribe than a family, but yeah. There's a place for you here if you agree to share with us, protect us, and not give us away to any canners … zombies."

"I will like dat. To be with your … tribe you call it. And I will share my food with you. I am sorry it is not much. And I will pro-tect you. I think I can do dat pretty good, anyway."

I stared at him intently, wishing I could read his mind. "I swear to God, Bodo, if you're lying to me, and you try to hurt any of us,

I'll kill you with my bare hands. Do you understand? I promise you, I will do that. *That's not a problem.*" And I meant it with all my heart and soul. I hadn't been able to protect my last family from the death and destruction that had raged over the Earth, but I could protect my new family from the dangers that lurked out there in the night for us. And I'd do whatever it took, even if it meant taking someone's life - even a cute guy's life.

He nodded his head. "I gif you my promise. It is true. We are family now, see? You have the Pringkles. Eat dem all if you want, even dough dey are my favorite American snack. I will not hurt anyone." He sat back down on the slope and drew his knees up to his chest, resting his forearms on them as he stared down the incline.

I walked slowly backward to join Peter and Buster, motioning for Peter to walk up higher with me. Once we were near the top, so much that we had to bend down to avoid hitting our heads, I said, "So. What do you think?"

"Well, he doesn't seem crazy. Just funny."

"Yeah, that's what I was thinking."

"Okay, then, I guess we let him stay. But at the first sign of something being off, we cut him loose," said Peter.

I smiled. "Well that's not a good criteria."

"Criterium."

"Whatever. I mean, you're off all the time, but I don't cut you out."

Peter shoved me. "Get away from me, you rude beast."

"Come on. Let's go eat dinner and then we'll go to bed. We'll make him sleep away from us the first night." I pointed my finger at Peter. "And no cuddling, you hear me?"

Peter ignored me, instead going to the trailer to find some of the dried military meals. He quickly whipped up a meal and invited Bodo to join us for dinner.

Bodo ate his own stuff, but was generous enough to give us each two of his precious 'Pringkles'. It felt like a picnic, and I decided after Bodo's third ridiculous story of his horrible mishaps he'd endured trying to find travel partners, that he was going to fit in just fine. As long as he didn't try to kill us or steal from us while we slept.

CHAPTER
TWENTY-THREE

I WOKE UP TO THE beeping of the alarm on my watch. It was three thirty in the morning and time to get on the road. The first thing that came to mind was the fact that Bodo was really going to slow us down until we found him a bike.

I sat up and nudged Peter awake. "Time to get up, sleepy head." I looked down to where Bodo had gone to sleep and saw nothing. He was gone. I shoved Peter harder and then got on my feet. "Get up, Peter. Bodo's gone."

"What'd you say?" mumbled Peter, rolling over onto his back. "Oh, God, this ground is so friggin' hard." He paused for a couple seconds and then sat up all of a sudden. "Did you say Bodo's gone?" Peter looked down to where Bodo had been sleeping. "Crap. That's weird."

I had a small panic attack when I thought about our supplies. I rushed over to the trailer and lifted up the tarp. My eyes scanned the contents, taking in our backpacks that still looked full, the tools, the square of plastic, the bucket. All of our food seemed to be there, too. I pulled the last item I noticed out of the trailer and held it up.

"What do you suppose this means?"

Peter squinted his eyes and then they opened wider. "He left us his Pringles?"

"Yes, he left us his 'Pringkles'. And he didn't take anything else that I can see."

"You still have your gun?"

"Yeah. Do you?"

"Yeah. What about the bullets?" asked Peter.

I grabbed the bottom of the backpack where we kept the bullets and shook the boxes that I felt there. They sounded full. "Still here."

"What should we do? Wait for him? Maybe he's ... doing his business or something."

"Yeah, but why would he take his backpack if he was doodling?"

"God, I wish you'd stop saying that," said Peter, standing up and scrubbing his face a few times. "I'm going to go pee. I'll be back with better answers."

Buster and I went to go pee behind a bush, and we got back after Peter, who was drinking some water and eating a chip. We sat around for a few minutes, but then decided to just leave.

"For whatever reason, he's gone, but we can't wait around anymore. We have to get to the Everglades."

"Did we ever tell him yesterday what our plans are?" asked Peter.

"No. I didn't. And I don't remember you telling him. Why? Are you worried about him ratting us out?"

"No. Actually, I was hoping maybe he could eventually catch up with us. But I know that's not very realistic, since the Everglades is kind of huge and we don't even know exactly where we're going."

"Well, I'm not going to worry about it. Maybe we'll see him again some day. It was nice of him to leave us his Pringkles though."

"You can stop calling them Pringkles now," laughed Peter.

"I kind of prefer it that way, actually. Pringkles. It has a nice ring to it."

"Come on," said Peter, grabbing the handlebars of his bike and wrestling it down the slope. "We need to get fifty miles today at least."

I had a hell of a time getting my bike down the hill without crashing it and mangling the trailer, but somehow I got it done without damaging myself or the equipment. Buster wisely stayed far away until I was on flat ground again, but as soon as the bike was upright, he ran and jumped into the trailer, turning a few circles on his Hello Kitty backpack before lying down. He rested one paw over the edge of the trailer and then looked at me expectantly. Sometimes he was so humanlike, it was scary. It was easy to see why George had been so attached to him. I was really glad Peter had brought him along, even though having a dog wasn't necessarily the smartest choice we'd made. He ate some of our food and he did bark occasionally when he shouldn't - but I guess I couldn't argue about his watchdog skills. He'd alerted us twice already, and one of those times he'd been a life saver.

"Good dog, Buster Pink. Good boy."

I was rewarded with a doggy grin and a tail wag.

Peter led the way up the ramp, heading south on the highway again. I drew up parallel to him so we could chat. It was still dark, but the sky was light enough that we could make out the hulking forms of cars along the way.

"I was kind of excited about having a third person in our tribe," said Peter wistfully.

"Yeah. Me too, actually, which surprises me. I honestly was fine with it being just us. But having Bodo there with his goofy accent and way of saying things was entertaining."

"I'm sure we'll meet some other fun people on our way or once we get there."

"I doubt it. Maybe on our way, but I kind of hope not. I think we got lucky finding one good guy when we could have found a lot of bad ones. I'm starting to think the bad ones are the majority now."

"Yeah, like a gang mentality kind of a thing," suggested Peter.

"Exactly. I mean, maybe one person alone wouldn't say, 'Oh, I'm going to eat a person for dinner tonight', but when a group of people are together and they get each other all wound up, I guess it's different." I was trying to figure out how a civilized society could degenerate so far and as quickly as ours had.

"I think it's more like you have a group led by someone who's either very charismatic or very vicious, someone with a screw loose obviously, and he decides for everyone that cannibalism is a valid way to exist. And the rest of the group goes along either because they're just as crazy, or brainwashed, or just afraid to go against him."

I laughed. "Yeah, can you imagine? You're at the barbecue and you say, 'Oh, no thanks. I'm a vegetarian.'"

Peter got silent all of a sudden and I wanted to smash myself in the face with something.

"Jesus, Peter, I am such a jerk. I'm sorry. I don't mean to be so flippant about that stuff."

Peter shook his head. "No, don't apologize. I know you don't mean anything by it." He started to cry, using an arm to try and hide his face while he kept riding.

I held my hand out to him to get him to stop moving forward. "Stop for second." I got off my bike and went over to where Peter was standing, straddling his bike. "Time for cuddles," I said, pulling him into a hug. "Don't cry, please. I'll never say anything about the stupid canners again. I'll try harder to be more sensitive."

"No, don't change. I like the way you are just fine." He sniffed hard and cleared his throat. "What happened to my sister wasn't funny, but if we can't laugh about the terrible things happening in our world right now, I'm afraid we'll eventually go insane. And that's what led to Lily's death, so we need to avoid that."

"Okay, avoid insanity. Check. I'm down with that plan."

Peter rested his head on my shoulder for a minute. "You know, for a girl who mocks the cuddle, you're pretty good at it."

"Yeah, well, my dad taught me. He was a great hugger."

"Um, Bryn?" Peter picked his head up.

"Yeah?"

"I think we have company."

I stiffened, standing up straight and releasing Peter, turning to see what he was looking at.

Off in the distance, in the dawning light of the day, I could just barely make out a bright orange, wiggling flag coming down the highway toward us. "What the hell?"

CHAPTER
TWENTY-FOUR

THE ORANGE FLAG GOT CLOSER and closer, and as it did, I finally realized what I was looking at. Bodo was on a bike - a beach cruiser with a basket on the front of it and a flag on the back - riding as hard and as fast as he could up the highway toward us.

He pulled up all red-faced and smiling. "Hi, guyss. Vhat'ss up?"

I shook my head slowly, laughing. "What in the hell are you riding?"

"It's a bike. What doess it look like? See? It even hass a fleg."

"It's a flag, goof, not a fleg."

"Dat's what I said. Da bike hass a fleg. Anyway, it's not a problem. I found it so I can ride with you and not slow you down. Isn't that a faboolus idea?" He smiled at both of us, back and forth, nodding his head in apparent agreement with himself. "Oh, und, it hass a basket on da front for da little doggy." He looked down at Buster and nodded some more. "Do you want to ride in da little basket, little doggy?"

Buster looked at him and then at me, crouching lower on his Hello Kitty backpack.

"I think he wants to stay with me," I said, kind of hoping Bodo's feelings wouldn't be hurt, being rejected by a naked poodle. He seemed to be trying really hard.

"Well, dat's perfect, becauss I got dis bike really for you. See? It hass a big seat on it. It's made for people with bigger rear ends dan men." He had moved his butt off the seat and was pointing to it.

Now I could care less whether Buster had hurt his feelings. "Are you saying I have a fat ass?"

"A fat ass?" Bodo looked confused for a second and then shocked. "Oh, no, dat's not at all what I am saying. No, your butt isn't big. Actually, I do not know if you're butt is big or not, I haven't looked. But da rest of you is quite small, so I expect your butt is too."

Peter was laughing so hard he was bent over holding his stomach.

"Stop laughing, you idiot," I said.

"Oh, God," he moaned, giggling in between words, "I can't help it. It's so funny. He got you a big butt bike!"

"No, Peter, don't say dat," chided Bodo. "I just got dis kind of seat because it's good for girls. And da basket is for her little doggy." He looked at me with a sad frown on his face. "I will ride dis bike. It is okay for me. It is not a problem at all. I am sorry about your butt."

That sent Peter off into more gales of laughter.

"Don't apologize for my ass, Bodo. My ass is just fine, thank you very much." I hated to admit it at this point, but that seat did look a heck of a lot more comfortable than my current seat did. And my butt was sore from riding on the small, hard surface for so many hours the day before.

"Okay. I'm ssorry. My English is not good. I offended you and dat is my mistake."

"No," I waved him off, "it's fine. Really. I see what you were trying to do and I appreciate it. But before we go any farther, we need to get that flag off of there. You're alerting every canner within a one-mile radius that we're coming."

"Yes, I liked the fleg, but I can see how it might be a problem."

Peter giggled some more, but went over to the trailer to get the tools. "What do we need?" he asked me.

I went over to take a look, bending down to see what type of screw or nut was holding the flag in place. That was when I felt Bodo's hand grab the back of my neck.

In two seconds flat, I had spun around, grabbed Bodo's hand, wrenched it from my neck and pulled him off the bike.

The bike clattered to the ground and Bodo went tumbling after it, his hand now bent at an extreme angle and in danger of being snapped by me as I stood over him, legs spread apart, ready to smash his face in with my foot at any second. I was pissed, but he just laughed.

"Dat was *amaszing!* Did you see dat, Peter? She *iss* a lethal weapon. It wass like a movie or somesing." Then he got a frown on his face. "Actually, dat kind of hurts right now."

I was sweating and my heart was pounding a thousand beats a minute. "What the hell was that all about?" I demanded.

"Nothing. I was chust testing your reflexes. Dey're pretty good, by da way."

I shook my head and looked over at Peter. "Did you see what he did?"

"No, but I saw what you did. Impressive." He was nodding his head in appreciation.

"He grabbed me by the back of the neck!" I was still pissed. I couldn't tell if the guy was just messing with me or if he'd really tried to do something and now was trying to play it off.

"Can I haff my hand back, please? I don't think it's going to bend any more dan dat before it breaks."

I slowly let him go, watching him warily as he stood, shaking his hand a little and massaging it with the other.

He was smiling his stupid head off. "I love dis. You are halff my size and probably no more dan fifty-fife kilos ... but den you take me down like Triple H in da ring. You are one hell of a woman, you know dat? I loff American girls."

Peter came walking up and put his arm around me. "Yeah, Bryn is one hell of an American girl, I can agree with you there."

I nudged him in the ribs and he flinched, but he didn't let me go and he didn't shut up.

"But she's not tough all the time. Inside she's like a … marshmallow. All soft and sweet."

"Oh, really? Iss dat so?" said Bodo, smiling conspiratorially with Peter. "What doess your boyfriend think about you spending all dis time with Peter, eh?" He pointed to the ring on the necklace around my neck.

I wiggled out of Peter's grasp and moved away. "You guys are a couple of idiots, you know that? And I don't have a boyfriend. The ring was my dad's." I bent down by the bike and turned to look up at Bodo. "Touch me again and I'll break your wrist next time. Or kick you in the nuts so hard, you won't feel them for a month. Now hand me the adjustable wrench."

Bodo's eyes widened and he slowly reached down to cup his sensitive parts, speaking to Peter but looking at me. "Wow. She doesn't mess around."

"No. She doesn't," agreed Peter, handing me the wrench. "Just try to stay on her good side, would you? She can get cranky sometimes."

I worked at getting the small nut off that was holding the flag in place. "If you guys don't stop talking about me, I'm going to leave you both behind and go to the Everglades by myself. With Buster."

"Oh, we're going to da Everglades?" asked Bodo. "Did choo know dare are alligators dare? And lots of snakes?"

"Yeah," said Peter wryly. "We're aware."

"Okay, well if dat's not a problem for you, den it's not a problem for me."

I couldn't help but giggle at that, my anger over his need to test my skills evaporating. I wondered if I went to Germany and learned some German whether I would say one stupid phrase over and over like that. I'd have to get Bodo to teach me one so I could use it and make him crazy with it.

I finally got the nut off and wiggled the flag off the back wheel. "Done." I threw it over to the edge of the highway.

"Can't we keep it?" asked Bodo.

"Why would we do that?"

He shrugged. "I don't know. I chust kind of like it."

"Well if you want to figure out how to hide it in the trailer so no one can see it, I don't care."

"Good!" he said, jogging over to pick it up. He came back and rummaged around in the trailer to bend it around the inside walls, and managed to get it in there without too much trouble. "Dare. You see? Not a problem."

I went to climb on my bike, and Bodo came up next to me, making me instantly wary.

"You want to trade bikes with me? I swear, it's not because of your butt."

I rolled my eyes. "Yes. I'll trade bikes with you. Just wait a minute."

I went to the trailer and reached down for Buster. "Come on, Buster, come ride with me." He hopped out and I took the Hello Kitty backpack to put it in the basket of the bike, lifting Buster up to sit on top of it. He rested his chin on the edge, his eyebrows moving as he watched me only with his eyes. It was pretty comical, how he just settled in so easily like that. He was as goofy as the rest of us.

"Okay. Now I'm ready."

Bodo got up on my bike and Peter got on his, and we pedaled down the highway. My butt felt a hundred times better.

CHAPTER
TWENTY-FIVE

"So, HOW FAR DO WE go today?" asked Bodo. We'd been going for about an hour, making small talk along the way in places and sometimes just riding in quiet companionship.

"Our goal is fifty miles, but it's not set in stone," answered Peter. "We want to get there as soon as we can."

"But we want to avoid the canners."

"Canners. You use dis word for da cannibals?"

"It's Peter's word."

"It means something else in English?"

"It could mean someone who puts things in cans, I guess," said Peter. "But obviously that's not what I mean when I say it."

"I was chust wondering. I like it. It sounds more normal den zombies. Dey are not undead, after all."

"As far as I'm concerned they are," I said bitterly. "They're going to ruin our world ... what's left of it, anyway. They're ghouls."

"Maybe someone will stop dem," suggested Bodo. "Like dee army or something."

"There is no army left."

"Yes, but dare is army eqvipment left. And veapons … I mean, *weapons*."

"With our luck it'll be the canners that get to that stuff first." I shivered, considering the ramifications. "I don't even want to think about it, really. Can we move on to other topics?"

"How about food?" suggested Bodo. "My favorite American food besides da Pringkles is peanut butter."

I laughed. "You and every kid under the age of nine."

"Really? It's a food for da little kids?"

"No. I like peanut butter, too," said Peter. "It's not just for kids. But lots of people feed their kids peanut butter and jelly when they're little, so we kind of get hooked on it."

"In my country it was Nutella. I used to have it on toast in da morning when I wass a little boy."

"We have that here now, too."

"I know. But it's old newss for me. I prefer da peanut butter. Dat is my dream now, to find a peanut butter factory where I can take a hundret jars of it."

"We'll keep our eyes open," said Peter.

I looked over at him to catch him rolling his eyes.

"What food do you like da most, Bryn?"

"Hmmm, that's a tough one. I think … I miss Doritos most."

"Oh, dat's a good choice. I like dem too. Da ones dat make your fingers orangch."

"Yeah, that's my favorite flavor, too," said Peter. "But the food I miss the most is pizza."

"Oh, yeah, pizza. I forgot about that. Put pizza on my list," I said. I shook my head to get it out of pizza land. "We have to stop talking about this stuff. I'm getting seriously hungry and it's not time to stop and eat yet."

"What I want to know is when you are going to teach us your moofs. I need to get very tricky da way dat you are, so if someone tries to come in and take our stuff, I can show him who is da boss and break some of hiss bones maybe."

"Maybe when we get to our new place, we can get lessons from Bryn," said Peter. "I wouldn't mind that either."

"We'll be like dose Special Forccess guys, jah? ... I mean, yes?"

I shook my head. "I don't know if I'll be a very good teacher, but I will try."

We kept riding along, but I noticed a change in the looks of the cars we were passing. It was kind of spooky in a way.

"Do you guys notice anything different around here?"

"Yeah," said Peter.

"No, not really," said Bodo.

"What do you see, Peter?"

"Well, some of the glass on the cars is broken. And look! That car over there looks like it was burned."

"Yeah. The cars farther north were all normal. I mean, they had doors and windows open, but none of this vandalism I'm seeing here."

The sun was now fully up. I looked at my watch. "It's almost ten o'clock. Maybe we should stop now." I looked off the side of the highway and saw a group of short trees in the distance. "Are those orange trees?"

"Yes, dey are."

"Are you thinking we should sleep there?" asked Peter.

"Yeah. We can hide the bikes and ourselves pretty easily, and maybe there'll be some fruit.

Bodo headed for the edge of the road and we followed him.

Buster woke up when I went over the bumpy grass. I decided to get off and walk the bike. I didn't need some big thorn getting pushed into the tire with my heavy weight on it. I had very little in the way of spare tubes and patch kits.

"Wait up, guys!" I called out. "I need to walk the bike."

Peter and Bodo got off and waited for me to catch up. We crossed over a shallow canal and walked across a wide open field before reaching the orange grove ten minutes later, all of us sweating after battling patches of sand that the bikes liked to get bogged down in, especially Peter's. His bike had the thinnest tires of the three.

"So where to now?" asked Peter, looking around.

"I'd like go in deep enough that we can't be seen from the road. But not too deep. I want to be able to sneak over and watch the highway without having to go too far."

"Go four rows in," suggested Peter. "I'll stay here and tell you if I can see you from outside the grove."

"Okay. Come on, Bodo. Let's go find a spot."

"Okay. You're da boss. Show me da way."

I wheeled the bike in deeper, looking up at the trees as we went, hoping to see some fruit. I saw a few oranges up in the higher branches, which meant I'd have to climb to reach any of them. There were plenty of rotted ones on the ground, but they didn't look edible. The earth smelled wet and almost sour as our feet trod across it and stirred up the scents.

We stopped four rows in and waited for a few minutes. Eventually Buster let out a small half-bark, letting us know that Peter was coming; he broke through the trees in front of us a few seconds later.

"This is perfect. I couldn't see you at all after the third row."

We set up camp, using the tarp to cover our bikes and the trailer, and I dug out another one to sit on so we wouldn't get wet on the damp ground. We were under a tree that had the highest branches, hoping it would not only block us from sight but also shade us from the worst of the sun.

"So, what do we do now?" asked Bodo.

"Find some fruit, take naps, make plans. Whatever," I said.

"Let's go deeper in the groves for the fruit," said Peter. "I don't want anyone seeing us up in the trees near the highway."

"Agreed," I said. "And someone has to stay here by the stuff at all times. And not just Buster."

Buster looked up at me upon hearing his name and came over, dancing around in circles by my feet. I bent down and picked him up to give him a squeeze. I put my face in his little shoulder, inhaling his doggy smell. It was starting to grow on me - part Buster, part fresh air, and kind of comforting in a way. I wished I'd had a dog before. Hugging this furry pink thing now, I realized I had probably missed out on a special kind of love in my life not ever having one. Buster must have been feeling the love too, because he squirmed all over trying to get into a better position to lick my face.

"Cut it out, you mangy mutt."

"He's no mangy mutt. He's a purebred," insisted Peter. "Come over here, Buster, where your pedigree can be better appreciated."

I was only bent over halfway before Buster leapt from my arms to go collect his cuddles from Peter. He jumped up over and over, trying to get a lick in on Peter's chin, eventually knocking Peter backward and taking total advantage of the situation by attack-licking him all over the face. He darted in left and then right, licking when he was close, barking when he wasn't, lunging whenever he could for a piece of exposed skin to drool on.

Peter rolled around trying to get away, covering his face and yelling, "Get away, get away! Ew! Stop licking me!" But he wasn't trying very hard.

Buster was having the time of his life. Eventually he ran out of gas, though, and sat in the grass, panting away in the shade of the tree with his little legs stuck out straight behind him, his tongue hanging out and a big doggy smile on his face.

Peter sat up and rummaged around in the trailer, getting out the water and the bowl for Buster, filling it and setting it in front of him.

"I'll stay with the stuff and Buster. You guys go find us some oranges. I'm hungry." He reached over and petted the dog's ears, causing him to flip over on his back for a belly rub. Buster had no shame in his game at all and Peter seemed happy to oblige.

Bodo and I headed off into the trees. It felt weird being alone with him. I wasn't worried about him attacking me or anything - neither for purposes of overwhelming me or for testing my skills. It's just that he was a good-looking, straight guy who had a quirky sense of humor and seemed to appreciate 'girls like me', as Peter would say. It made me nervous and self-conscious.

"You don't need to be nerfous arount me. I'm not going to hurt you."

I tried to act like I wasn't a little freaked out by him reading my body language so well. "You couldn't hurt me if you tried."

"Well, I don't know if dat is true or not, but I'm not gonna try it anytime soon, I can tell you dat. I need my hands to ride dat bike."

I laughed.

"How about dat one?" He stopped and pointed to a tree that had several bright orange fruits almost at the top.

"Can you climb trees?" I asked, my eyebrow raised. "Because I can't climb that high. Not in those kinds of trees."

"I can try. But really it should be you. You are more little dan me. Dese branches aren't very big."

We walked over to the tree and looked up. There was one fruit that was hanging low enough that Bodo could almost reach it - almost, but not quite. He jumped up several times and only barely missed it.

He crouched down. "Here. Get on my choulders. Den you can get it."

My eyes widened. All I could think about was how bad I smelled. I really didn't want my body parts being that close to his nose until I'd had a shower. Or two.

"Uh, no thanks."

He looked up at me from his position near the ground. "Why not? Are you afraid of heights dat small?"

"No."

"Okay, den. What's da problem?"

"There's no problem."

"Hey," he smiled. "Dat's my line."

I smiled back. "Never mind. Let's just go back."

He shook his head, sticking his lips out in a pout. "No. I'm not going anywhere. Get on my shoulders and get dat fruit. Don't be afraid of da little tree."

"I'm not afraid of the tree, idiot."

"What are you afraid of, den? Me?" He pointed to his back, his face looking at the ground now. "No. You're not afraid of Bodo. Come on, den. Get up dare."

"No," I said, getting frustrated now. He just wouldn't take no for an answer and I didn't have a good explanation to give him that didn't involve divulging my hangups.

He stood up and walked over closer to me, forcing me to take a step back to maintain a comfortable distance between us.

"We're a family now. You can tell me what da problem is."

"We're not family ... we're maybe in a tribe together, but you have to do more than go on a half-day bike ride with me to earn family status."

He raised his eyebrows up and down a few times at me and smiled. "Yes, but I got you dat big butt seat with da bike, right? Dat was something special, I think."

I laughed. "Yeah, that was good. My butt's not nearly as sore now."

"See? Bodo's a good guy. Climb up, okay? Let's get dat skinny guy Peter some fruit. He's gonna starve to death soon."

That was like driving a knife in my heart for some reason. "Wow, you play dirty, don't you?"

He shrugged, unapologetically. "I'm Cherman. We're tough people. We suffer and we get up and we keep going. I have been told dat I am very methodical and persistent."

"Are all Germans like you?"

"I don't know. All da ones I know are like me. But not as good in da face or da body as me."

"Of course not," I said, laughing. He was probably right, but there was no way in hell I was going to admit that now or ever.

"So. You're getting up now, right?"

"As long as you don't mind the fact that I stink to high heaven."

"What is high heaven? Is dat your ... you know ... private placess?"

I nearly gagged, accidentally inhaling some drool. I tried to correct him before his brain could wander any farther down that lane. *"Gah*, no! Holy ... *Kack!* ... No. Shit. *Jesus*, Bodo, it's an expression. Stink to high heaven means you smell bad. Everywhere, not any particular part of you."

"Ooooh, I see." His face turned a little red. "Well, dat's embarrassing, isn't it? I'm sorry. You can slap me if you want. I deserve it." He held out his cheek for me.

"No, never mind. You didn't know." The truth was, my high heavens did stink, and I was pretty sure I wanted to be the only one who knew that.

"Okay, I can solve dis problem. I will get on *your* shoulders," he suggested.

"Are you nuts? You must weight one-seventy or one-eighty."

"Maybe. But you don't want to get on my choulders and Peter is slowly starving to death right now, so it's da only way."

I rolled my eyes. "Fine! Bend over, stupid. And hold your breath so you don't smell my stink."

Bodo pinched his nose and squatted down so I could climb up, which I did while trying to ignore the bright red heat of embarrassment that climbed up my neck and reached my ears and face.

I grabbed the orange and one other that was nearby. "Okay, put me down."

"Wait, dare's anudder one over dare!" he said, jogging off to another tree.

"Oh my *god*, you're going to *drop* me!" I screeched, grabbing his hair and holding onto the oranges with my forearm against my stomach.

"Get it. Dare's tree of dem."

I made a sling out of my shirt and dropped all the oranges in, glancing down and noticing for the first time he had stopped plugging his nose. "Plug your nose!"

"Oh, sorry!" he said, reaching up to pinch his nostrils again. "Anudder one!" he said, starting to run again.

I held onto his hair at first but it wasn't working, so I reached under his head and grabbed his chin. I could feel stubble there and it reminded me of my dad. It was strange to have a memory of my dad wrapped up in this moment with Bodo. It made it easier for me to laugh along with his teasing, which I was finally realizing this was. He wasn't just a dopey German guy. He was a dopey, silly, *fun* German guy.

"Get dem. One, two, tree, four. Now we have a picnic."

"Fine. I have them all. Now put me *down*."

"Okay," he said cheerily, headed back toward Peter, taking long strides that reminded me of riding a horse. He was really tall.

"Any day now…"

"Okay!"

We came through the last row and arrived back at our bikes and Peter. Buster was barking and running around.

"Put me down before Buster tells every canner within five miles we're here."

"Okay, you asked for it!" said Bodo, before he reached up and put his hands under my thighs.

I only had enough time to yell, "What the hell are you...!" before I was launched up into the air above Bodo's head.

The oranges went flying in every direction as my arms and legs sprang out, trying to find purchase with something solid and only meeting air. And then a split second later, I landed, cradled in Bodo's arms. He'd thrown me up above him and caught me like a baby.

"Uh *huh!* How about *dat* move? You like dat one, yes? Like da circus!"

"Bodo, put me down, you ass."

He inhaled strongly and made a confused face. Then a face like he smelled something distasteful. "You are right. You do smell."

I started hitting and kicking him in a flurry of fists and feet, no finesse to my moves at all. I just wanted to get him the hell away from me and my smelly self.

He dropped my legs so I was standing and then released me the rest of the way, ducking away from me and putting his arms and hands up to protect his face and head. Once far enough away that I couldn't reach him anymore, he went running away into the trees, laughing hysterically the whole way.

Peter was dying - curled up on the tarp and holding Buster to him, laughing and snorting so hard I thought he was going to vomit. Then he farted and laughed all over again.

"Holy shit, you guys have problems," I yelled, stalking off with a beet red face to find a private place to pee and bake in my humiliation.

CHAPTER
TWENTY-SIX

BY THE TIME I GOT back to the tarp, Peter and Bodo had calmed down and set out a lunch for us. We each got a bottle of water, a chip, two oranges, and a dried hunk of beef from one of the army-navy meals. It looked like a feast.

"Wow, Peter, this looks awesome."

"Yeah, it's like a real meal almost," he agreed.

"I put my food in da trailer too. You can give it whenever you want. I leave it for you," Bodo said to Peter.

I was too embarrassed to look at Bodo, so I looked at Buster instead, giving him a small chunk of my meat. I noticed the guys did the same thing. Buster also didn't mind oranges, apparently.

When I finished I got up and found the square of plastic and the water bucket. "I'm going to set up the water catcher. I'm sure it'll rain later." The clouds were already coming in from far off. Florida could be counted on for rain every day in the afternoon during this time of year. "Peter, show Bodo the bleach and the cooking water so he doesn't accidentally drink those."

"Okay."

My water catcher was nothing sophisticated. I just took the plastic square and hooked two corners to two sticks stuck in the ground, using clips that my dad had given me from his desk - binder clips - and then put the other end of the plastic in the bucket on a slant. The rain hit the plastic and ran down into the container. It was big enough to catch a volume of water that filled our bottles each day, which was convenient. Less than a drop of bleach, just a finger-dab really, was enough to sterilize any-thing that might be wrong with the bucket or the clouds above our heads, germ-wise. I still wasn't convinced there wasn't some weird form of pollution going on.

I went back to join the guys and found them already sleep-ing under the tree. It was hot and muggy as hell, so the shade made for the most decent napping situation we could hope for. The rows of trees caused a slight wind tunnel effect, which was slightly cooling on my sweaty skin.

I figured Buster would wake us up if anyone came around, and our stuff was camouflaged with the green tarp, so I laid down next to Peter and fell asleep without worrying overly much about being attacked. Having Bodo there, even though he wasn't a skilled fighter, made me feel better. Our numbers were grow-ing, and so were our odds for survival.

CHAPTER
TWENTY-SEVEN

ONCE AGAIN I WAS AWAKENED by booms, only this time it wasn't thunder. The rain had already come and gone. The noise I heard was the sound of exploding cars.

"What the ...," I started to say, but Peter's hand on my arm stopped me in mid-sentence.

"Shhhh. Someone's blowing up the cars," he whispered.

Another big explosion sounded in the distance, and then a fireball burst up from the highway somewhere.

"Dare are some craaazy people out dare tonight," whispered Bodo. He'd moved over to my other side, kneeling and trying to peer through the trees.

"What should we do?" whispered Peter.

I looked at their two faces, barely able to see them in the dark. My watch said it was around midnight. "I'm not sure. Stay put, probably. I'm afraid if we move they might see us."

"What if they decide to come into the groves?" said Peter, his fear almost palpable.

"We'll need to hide. We can take the tarp off the ground and get under it. Or we could climb up into the trees."

"I don't think we should leafe da bikes and da trailer alone."

"I agree," said Peter.

The sounds of shouting, yelling, and occasional singing greeted our ears. Flashes of memory hit me, visions of the beer cans and liquor bottles spread around the pool area of the cop's house - where the canners were having their barbecue.

"I think they're canners," I said.

"Me too," said Bodo.

Peter grabbed my arm, squeezing it. "Bryn, I'm not afraid to admit that I'm scared out of my wits right now."

I patted his hand. "Me too. Don't worry about it. They're not going to come out here."

"How do you know?" he whispered, panic lacing his words.

"I don't. I'm just hoping." But really, I was thinking that it was very likely they'd come out here. Someone had been picking these oranges, and it was probably someone coming from the highway. We'd already seen some burned cars, so that told me the canners lived nearby.

"I think we better get ready to hide," said Bodo. "The sounds are getting closser."

I didn't waste any time arguing. "Okay. Let's do this. Peter, your job is to keep Buster quiet. So far he's only let out one of those muffled woof things, but all we need is one of his barking frenzies to grab the canners' attention."

"Okay. I'll do my best."

"Bodo, you and I will get the bikes pulled in closer to this tree, take down the water collector, and then cover everything up ... including us."

"Are we all going to be under the tarp?" asked Peter, gripping Buster now like his life depended on it.

"No. Just you and Buster. I'm going up in the tree. Bodo, you're going to get in that tree over there, next to us. Take my gun."

"No! You keep your gun," he insisted.

"No. I can fight. You can't. You need it more than I do."

"Hey. Dat's not ... very ... I don't know. Right or something."

"Take it, Bodo. She is right. I need a gun too. It's the only way I was able to save us last time."

"Oh, so I'm like da protector of da family over dare in dat tree?"

"Yes, if that makes you happy," I said sarcastically. I guess even German guys had their egos.

"Okay. I'll do it. What are da rules? I kill anyone I see? Or just anyone who is trying to kill us?"

"We don't know how many there are, so only shoot if there's no other way to survive. I'd rather they just left without knowing we were here."

"What if only one of dem is a problem? If we shoot him and make dat loud noise, everyone will come."

"Which is why I won't be under that tarp. I can take anyone out who bothers us, without making any noise."

I could see Bodo nodding his head. "Uh-huh, like da Special Forcess. I like dat idea." He stood up. "Okay, I will see you later den. Hug for good luck?" he said holding out his arms.

"Maybe another time," I said, standing so I could pick up the edge of the tarp.

"Okay. Anudder time. Dat is not a problem." He pulled his bike in closer to Peter, covering it better with the tarp and then walked away. A few seconds later, I heard the leaves of the nearby tree rustling.

"I'm going to cover you up, Peter. You got your gun and bullets?"

"Yes. And Bryn, be careful, please. Don't do anything unless it's totally necessary, okay?"

"You got it," I said, as I pulled the tarp up over his head.

"You should have hugged him," came his muffled voice from underneath.

"Shut up, you idiot," I mumbled as I jogged over to get the water collector and bring it back to set on the ground near the base of the tree hiding Peter.

Once all our stuff was hidden, I stepped up to the lowest branch, just above where Peter and Buster were sitting, putting the toe of my sneaker on it and grabbing a higher branch to lift myself up. The leaves were quaking, sounding like they were making enough noise to be heard all over the grove. I got into the best position I could as quickly as possible, to be able to see what was going on below with Peter and across the way with Bodo. The darkness made it impossible for me to be able to pick out his actual form, but I knew he was there somewhere and that he had a gun to watch my back with. I just prayed he knew how to use it and that I wouldn't get shot in any crossfire.

Minutes crawled by like hours, and I felt the sweat trickling down my back. Every time another car exploded, I jumped. They must have been adding their own gas to the flames, because those cars couldn't have had much fuel left in them to cause such big explosions. Maybe they had grenades or something. It made me think about what Bodo had said earlier, about armies and their equipment. There were all kinds of weapons caches around these towns, and it didn't take a rocket scientist to figure out it would be the canners who would focus their energies on finding them. Normal people like me and Peter and Bodo were just trying to find a home and a way to survive peacefully. Weapons and bombs shouldn't have to be a part of our lives anymore. *friggin' canner zombie jerks.* I was going to have to consult George's journal when we got up the next day. Maybe he had something to say about setting up a good place to survive in a world that had become a battleground.

My mind had strayed far afield, but strange voices coming from the open space between the highway and the grove brought it zooming back to the present. I couldn't hear what they were saying, but I could tell they were drunk. They were being loud and their speech was slurred. When they got closer I realized why I hadn't been able to understand them - they were speaking Spanish.

My legs had fallen asleep, being stuck bent up in the tree, so I slowly moved one and then the other, to get the circulation going again. I wouldn't be of any use to anyone if I fell to the ground on my butt when I got out of my hiding spot. The sharp tingles I felt in my legs told me the blood was moving again. I slowly lowered myself out of the branches, keeping my body as close to the trunk as possible, trying to blend in with its form.

The voices seemed to split apart. One was heading over to where Bodo and I had gotten our oranges and one was coming this way. I couldn't see him yet, but I could hear him. He was singing something and occasionally laughed and burped. He stopped moving all of a sudden and I almost moved away from the tree to see why, but then I heard the sound of liquid hitting the ground and realized the guy was peeing. Thank god, he hadn't decided to do it ten feet farther in - he probably would have peed right on Peter's head.

I could hear the slight sounds of a struggle going on under the tarp and then very muted sounds of Peter shushing the dog. I hoped like crazy that he had his hand over that dog's muzzle or he was going to give us all away.

I heard a zipper go up and then the sounds of footsteps headed away. The guy was leaving and I was just getting ready to breathe a sigh of relief when Buster let out a bark that was unmistakeable.

"Eh?" said the drunken voice.

I heard his footsteps slow, stop, and then start moving in our direction again.

Buster barked a second time.

Dammit, Peter, shut that dog up! I yelled in my mind. But I couldn't do anything except wait until the guy got closer.

"Oh, peeerrroo, ven aquí, peeerrrooo," he slurred and then laughed. He hiccuped once and then burped loudly and disgustingly.

I prayed he didn't have a gun. A drunk guy with a knife I could handle. One with a gun ... ? Not as easily.

He got close enough that I could see him now. He was fat - a lot bigger than me. It pissed me off that he was overweight in times like these. It meant he was eating people who weren't fast enough to get away from him and his friends. A lot of them. Any feelings of mercy I might have had left my heart and my head in that moment, and all I could think about was stopping the madness that this idiot represented.

He was just about to reach the spot where Peter and the now struggling Buster were, when I separated myself from the tree and stood just three feet away from him. From here I could both strike and evade. I was in perfect position. I could hear my dad's voice in my head. "Read the body language. Find his vulnerabilities and exploit them. Speed. Finesse. Conserve your energy. Strike fast and strike hard."

"Qué ... ?" he said, struggling backward two steps. "Dios mío," he huffed out, putting his hand on his heart. "Oi, mi corazón."

I took two steps forward, maintaining the distance between us.

"You need to leave, canner," I said.

"You speak ... English," he said.

"Of course I speak English, asshole, this is the United States."

"Not anymore it's not," he said lazily. He took a step toward me. "We haven't seen any girls in a while. No new ones anyway," he said, laughing at something he found amusing - something I'm sure I didn't want to know the details of. "You're comin' with me," he said, taking another step toward me and reaching his hand out as if to take my elbow.

I easily side-stepped him. "No, actually, I'm not. I'm not going anywhere and neither are you." He needed to be immobilized, one way or another. We couldn't travel while they were still out, and I couldn't let him go back to tell his friends where we were. I was counting on the fact that their loyalty to this guy was as weak as the last canner gang's was to their fallen comrade. If he never came back they wouldn't bother looking for him - except maybe to come eat him later.

"You think you can take me down?" he said incredulously. "Go ahead, white girl, take your bes' shot."

I decided that a surprise attack was my best bet. I looked off in the distance, putting my fingernail to my mouth, pretending to bite it, as if I were scared and contemplating giving up - and then I jumped at him, slamming him in the nose and shattering the bone with the heel of my hand. Blood spurted out everywhere and he stumbled back, yelling. I cut the sound off by coming after him and sending a roundhouse kick into his temple, knocking him down to his side and stunning him temporarily.

His head was so damn fat that my roundhouse didn't send him as far into never-never land as I had intended. I ran over and kicked him hard in the face with the toe of my shoe, snapping his head back - and yet, still, he was moving. I knew his next move was going to be to scream for his friends, so I leaned in and punched him hard in the jaw, bringing the power from my back and shoulder into the movement, knowing I was going to pay for it later with bruised knuckles. I should have used the heel of my hand, but I just wasn't sure I could get enough force that way.

That small bit of concentration loss on my part was all he needed. He grabbed my ankle and pulled me down, rolling over part way to trap me under his fat girth. I had only one alternative left to me, since one of my arms was trapped along with my lower body under his chest. I closed my eyes and jammed my face into his crotch, biting down on the nearest bit of soft flesh I could find.

A high pitched squeal came from his mouth which quickly turned into just a loud bit of air wheezing out from his lungs. I had one of his testicles on lockdown and was using every bit of willpower I owned in my body not to gag at the smells that were assailing my nostrils.

His body curled in on itself as it tried to salvage what little bit of his man parts might still be in one piece. I knew whatever I was biting was done for, the blood from it seeping through his pants now.

I let go when I knew it was over for him, spitting and retching as I struggled to get him off me. Suddenly I was freed of his weight and looked up to see the large, dark figure of Bodo pulling him off of me. He dumped the pudgy body, still writhing in silent screams of pain, off to the side and reached down to help me up, saying nothing.

I couldn't stand all the way up, my retching now turning into full-blown vomiting. Bodo stood over me and rubbed my back, then took my braid in his hand to keep it out of the mess. He secured it under my shirt and left, coming back a few seconds later with a water bottle in his hand.

Part of me wished it was the one full of bleach, the smell and taste in my mouth was so bad.

"Thanks," I whispered, my voice shaking. Being so close to death like that had amped up my senses to near super power proportions. I felt like I could punch a hole in the tree truck. Or cave that canner's skull in with my fist. Part of me really wanted to do it, too. *How dare he have such a stinky crotch.*

"We have to kill him," said Bodo, softly.

I shook my head. "Just hit him really hard in the temple with the butt of the gun and knock him out. We'll decide what to do with him later."

"Okay. Dat's not a problem."

Bodo left me and I heard the sick sound of metal hitting bone, and then a grunt followed by silence. Bodo was at my side again within seconds to rub my back some more. I was finally able to stand and shrugged him off.

"Thanks."

"Yes, of course," he whispered. "Can I do anything else for you?"

"No. Just make sure that other guy doesn't find his friend." I walked over to sit by Peter and Buster, who were now out from under the tarp. I couldn't hear the other guy at all anymore.

"Sorry," whispered Peter. I could tell he was crying. "I tried to keep him quiet, but he wouldn't stop."

"Shhh, don't worry about it. Buster's a dog. That's what dogs do. When we get to the Everglades it won't matter."

"You're not going to kill Buster?"

"Are you nuts? Of course I'm not going to hurt Buster. He's part of the tribe, stupid."

"What happened?" said Peter, sniffing, apparently over his biggest fear of losing his fuzzy pink friend.

"I don't want to talk about the details right now. I'm trying not to vomit again. We just need to lie low and wait for them to move on. They're already going away. I can hear them farther down."

"You smell funny," he said.

"Yeah. Excuse me while I go bleach my face." I crawled over to the trailer, my stomach feeling sick all over again. I pulled out the bleach and put a half-capful in the cooking water by the light of the stars. Then I used that water to scrub my face as best I could. I even rinsed my mouth out with some of it before swishing regular water around to get the bleach taste out. I found that I much prefer the smell of bleach to canner crotch.

CHAPTER
TWENTY-EIGHT

THE CANNERS WHO WERE BLOWING up cars moved on and none of them had come back to look for their friend. At least not yet.

"It's time to go, Bryn. Or do you think we should stay longer?" asked Peter.

"No, we need to go, definitely. They're going to eventually wonder what happened with Bigboy over there."

"What should we do with him, den?" Bodo was squatting down, tapping the side of the gun against his palm, looking very serious.

My lip curled in distaste. Part of me wanted to kill the canner, but the years of morality I'd learned from my dad and the discipline of my training won out. "We can't kill him. Then we're little better than those idiots out there."

"But he will come after us, won't he?" asked Bodo. "Why giff him a chance to kill us again?"

"He doesn't know we're *going north to Orlando*, does he?" I gave the guys looks that said not to contradict me. "So we'll just knock him out again and leave. He won't know where to look." I didn't know if the canner could hear me or not. He hadn't moved since Bodo had smashed him one, but I'd heard once that people picked things up when they were unconscious, and I wasn't taking any chances.

"Oh, dats riiiight. He doesn't know about our trip to Orlando. I want to go liff in Dissney World."

"Alright, Peter, get these tarps put away and put the water from that bucket into our bottles, while I go see if the coast is clear. And Bodo, you go give Smelly Pants another crack in the head for good measure so he doesn't wake up for a while. Unless you want me to do it."

"No, diss iss a chob for a man. I will do it, it's not a problem."

"Is *anything* ever a problem for you, Bodo?"

"Rarely. One time maybe I can remember I had a problem."

I laughed. "Good. I like a guy I can depend on."

"Yess, und I like a girl who can kick a guy's ass when she needs to protect her family."

He walked away to do the dirty work and I walked out toward the edge of the trees to see where the enemy was, my face burning with the flattery.

CHAPTER
TWENTY-NINE

IT WAS STILL DARK WHEN we got back on the highway, but we could see small flames here and there, coming from cars that had not completely burned out yet.

"All they do is destroy things," said Peter, sounding depressed.

"Yeah. They're animals. They don't care about this world anymore. They've given up," I said.

"How many miless do you think we should go today?" asked Bodo, pedaling away and dragging the trailer behind him. I had the big butt seat bike again with Buster riding shotgun in the basket.

"As many as possible. We originally said fifty a day, but I don't want any of those guys coming after us. I think we should go at least until eleven today, as long as we aren't too hot or tired."

"Yes, let's not add sun stroke to our list of woes," said Peter wryly.

"We need hets," said Bodo.

"What's a het?" I asked.

"A het. You know, you put it on your head. A het."

"Oooh, a hat. Yeah. We do need hats," I agreed.

"Dat's what I said. A het." He looked over at Peter who I could see was smiling in the bare light of the pre-dawn. "It's my accent again, issn't it? I try so hard to sound Hamerican but I keep failing."

"No, you're doing just fine," said Peter. "Sometimes you do better than others. Your accent comes and goes."

"When I'm tired or freaking out, den I know, it is stronger. I can't concentrate so much in dose situations."

"Well, I don't think you should lose all of it. It's kind of cool if you ask me," I said.

"Really? Do you think so?"

"Yeah. Hasn't anyone ever told you that before?"

"I don't think so."

"She's right. Accents are cool."

"You would haff an accent in Cherman, I know dat. I hear American accents all de time. Or I used to, when I was at home in Frankfurt."

"I wish I spoke another language," said Peter wistfully. "All I was ever able to take was Latin. What a bunch of garbage that turned out to be for me."

"No one knew the world was going to end. Latin would have been great for the S.A.T."

"Oh it was. I scored a 2250."

"What? That's ... amazing," I said, seriously impressed. I'd taken it twice and hadn't done nearly that well.

"A lot of good it does me now."

"Hey, dis new worlt needs smart guys like you to start things up again. We need people with good minds in math and mechanics. I think dat is where you will find me most helpful. I am an enchineering student. I can build thingks. My parents were both enchineers."

"That's good to know. You can be in charge of that," I said, glad to be rid of a responsibility. "You will direct the building of our shelter, wherever it happens to be."

"Maybe we can findt a shelter dat is already built."

"In the swamp? Not likely," I said, scoffing at the idea.

"Dare are lots of places already in de Everglades. I haff seen dem. Hamerican indians haff lifft dare for a long time. Two or three tribes if I remember correctly."

"Yeah, but isn't that all just touristy stuff?" asked Peter. "I don't know if they've actually lived there since the eighteen hundreds or whatever."

"I guess we'll find out when we get there," I said, my mind wandering to the idea that living in the swamp might not be as inhospitable as we had originally thought. In a way that made me happy because, well, obviously I didn't like the idea of sharing a bed with a cottonmouth. But on the other hand, if it was hospitable to me, it would be to canners too. And eventually they'd get all the easy prey and it would be next on their lists to find the harder stuff. Like us in the indian villages of the swamps.

"Wherever we end up, it has to be hard to get to and hard to find."

"Agreed," said Peter. "I'm glad we don't have to worry about planes or things coming overhead."

"Yeah, I guess there are a few benefits to the lack of fuel in the world. But I wouldn't have minded being able to run a generator and have some electricity or warm water again. I'm not even going to dream about air conditioning."

"We have that solar power book. Maybe once we're settled we can go out on some scouting missions and find things to do some of that."

"I dit a project last year in school with a solar cell. It was very interesting. I would like to see dis book of yours."

"When we stop today, I'll get it out for you," said Peter.

We passed the rest of the morning talking about potential inventions we could manage to make with the limited supplies we imagined might be in the towns skirting the edge of the Everglades. The canals running down the sides of the highways got wider, deeper, and more wild-looking. More than once we saw gators out on their banks, lying immobile, sunning themselves. I tried not to feel intimidated by them since they'd soon be my permanent neighbors, but it was impossible. They were like prehistoric creatures who had survived the last cataclysmic Earth event and now this one too. They were indestructible, but we definitely weren't.

The deepest part of me was feeling desperate, thinking that we might not be at the top of the food chain anymore. Living the life of hunted prey was definitely stressful and unhealthy. Humans had become lax and bloated in their sense of superiority. I'd been raised to believe in my natural supremacy, and I wasn't accustomed to this knowledge that I was vulnerable and weak, at the mercy of the elements and those of a baser nature than I.

My stomach was hurting again. I had to find a way around this fear, or it was going to eat me up from the inside out. If the canners didn't get me, I was going to get myself with the stress. In that moment, as I contemplated my own place in the cycle of life, I could see what might drive a canner to do the crazy things they do. It was an affirmation, in a way, of their spot at the top. A sick, insane, and delusional one, but an affirmation nonetheless.

CHAPTER THIRTY

T HE SUN ROSE HIGH IN the sky and the day got hotter and more humid than the one before had been. I prayed for rain, but the heavens didn't cooperate. There was blue sky for as far as the eye could see.

"We'd better stop," said Peter. "I'm getting too hot. My body can't cool itself down anymore and my legs are cramping."

"Dats not a good sign. You are dehydrated."

"Alright. There's an overpass up ahead." We'd passed a town a while back, but now we were out in the middle of nowhere again. There were fewer cars on the road and none of them were burned.

"Are you sure it's safe?" asked Peter.

"No," I laughed, not quite believing he'd just asked me that. "Do you have any better ideas?"

"No," he said weakly. "Sorry."

"Don't worry about it." Now I felt bad for making him feel stupid. "I wish I could offer us something better, but I just don't see anything; and I haven't in a while. I thought the grove was safe, but it obviously wasn't."

"I think it's good. Let's go dare," said Bodo, pedaling harder now. He pulled ahead of us and I just let him go. I was anxious to get off the highway too, but I didn't want to leave Peter behind. He was visibly flagging now that he'd seen his goal. It was like he'd lost the will to press on.

"Don't give up, we're almost there."

"I know," he said breathlessly. "I'm coming."

We made it to the exit and got off the highway, coasting down the slope all the way to the bottom of the big concrete incline below. Off in the distance there were two gas stations on opposite sides of the street from one another and a giant sign that said 'Cracker Barrel'. Back in the day, that chain of restaurants had been one of my favorite places to eat when my dad and I took road trips. They had the best candy store attached to the restaurant.

Bodo was waiting down at the bottom. "Do you want me to bring da bike up dare again? Or are we staying down here?"

I looked up at the slope and then off at the service stations, gently lifting Buster from the basket at the front of my handlebars. "I don't know. I was originally thinking go up, but now … I feel like I want to be able to just take off without worrying about getting bikes down. Just in case."

"I agree," said Peter, sitting down on the ground. "Let's stay down here tonight. Can we eat now? I'm starving." He tipped his water bottle up and almost drained it, putting the remaining bit in the bowl for Buster who wasted no time drinking every last drop.

I walked over and handed Peter my bottle. He looked like he needed it more than me.

"I can't take yours," he said, trying to push it away.

"I can make more. We have cooking water and bleach. But I'm sure it'll rain later, so don't worry about it. Drink. You don't look so hot."

"I don't feel so hot, either," he said, no longer arguing. He finished my bottle and then laid back, right on the gravel. Buster laid down in between his legs, resting his head on Peter's thigh. Peter didn't move a muscle.

I gestured silently at Peter so Bodo would see, and he nodded.

"I will get da camp site set up for sleeping if you want."

"Yeah, go ahead. The sun's moving over there, so do your best to find a spot that will still be in the shade in a few hours."

"Of course, yes, I will do dat," he said, digging out the tarps.

I got out the parts for the water catcher and set it up just outside the shelter of the highway overhead. I knew that even with blue skies now, the clouds could come in quickly and bring the rain with them. We were lower on water than I liked to be, especially since I was planning to make pasta with sauce tonight. Peter really looked like he needed the calories and I had a terrible craving for tomatoes that was getting harder and harder to ignore.

I went back to the site that Bodo had set up, and sat down. "Bodo, have you ever had a garden?"

"Yes. My mudder always had one when I was growing up. I had to pull da weeds all da time. Dat was my chob. One of many."

"I want tomatoes. Real ones, not the kind from a can."

"Dey are easy to grow. I can do dat for you."

Hearing him say that warmed my heart. I'd been taking care of my own survival for so long, and now Peter's, it was nice to hear that someone was going to do something for me for a change.

Bodo looked up from his organizing and smiled at me. "You look happy about dat."

"I am." He had the nicest blue eyes I'd ever seen on a guy. I'd noticed them before, but for some reason, they looked even bluer today.

"Goot ... I mean, good. You are very pretty, but especially when you smile."

I looked down at my dirty, raggedy fingernails and laughed. "Wow, Bodo, you don't set the bar very high, do you?"

"What does dat mean?" he said, a confused expression on his face. "Set da bar?"

"Never mind."

"You think I am making a lie, don't you?"

"Not necessarily. But I haven't had a shower in weeks and I've probably never looked worse in my entire seventeen years of life." I looked up and smiled at him anyway, happy with his effort, even if it wasn't true. "So I find it hard to believe you can see beneath the grime to anything that looks appealing, but I appreciate the gesture."

"Well, what I see looks pretty good to me. Plus, you are very strong, like my mudder was. She loved me a lot and I loved her too ... but I also atmired her. No matter what, she always did the best she could. Efen when my fadder left, she always worked very hard to make sure dat I could do thingks. Like come to the Unitet States for example."

I lifted an eyebrow. "Well, that sure worked out well for you."

"It did." He shrugged, ignoring my sarcasm. "The worlt that we knew is ofer. Not just here, but efreywhere. Apart from my mom, dare was no one dare in Chermany dat I cared about so much. I'm okay with being stuck here. With you and Peter and da little doggy."

I was impressed with his positive outlook. Germans were tough, there was no doubt about that.

"Bodo, what's your last name?"

"Ruster."

I giggled. "Your last name is *Rooster*? As in cock-a-doodle-doo?"

He smiled. "What dit you just say? Cock-a- ... *what?*"

We were both grinning like idiots at each other. "I said, 'cock-a-doodle-doo'. That's what roosters say. You know? Male chickens?" I put my hands in my armpits and did a few chicken wing-flaps for effect.

"Ohhhh, I ssee. No, not a rooster. Spelled like R-U-S-T-E-R. See?"

I laughed some more. "Okay. I would have pronounced that *ruster*, like the word 'rust'."

"You can say it however you want. I don't care, really. It's not a problem."

"No, I like rooster. That's cool. I can see that," I said, pretending to look him over.

"What do you mean? Like I am a proud bird who walks around a bunch of girl chickens and tells all de udder boy chickens to go away?"

"Maybe." He did seem to be perfectly at ease around me. Either that meant he was supremely confident or he didn't consider me to be a member of his henhouse.

"No. I am not dat proud. Plus I am a one-chicken kindt of guy. I don't think I could manatch more den one chicken at a time."

I don't know why that made me so happy, but it did. It's not like there was a lot of competition around here or that I'd decided that I wanted him to be my boyfriend. But still … he was funny and cute and didn't seem stuck-up at all.

"Is it possible to be conceited anymore?" I voiced my thoughts aloud without even realizing I was doing it. But it was out there now and I was curious to know what Bodo thought, so I waited for his answer.

Peter spoke up before he did, though. "No."

"Oh, it's possible, I think, but it wouldn't do any good," disagreed Bodo. "Not unless dare was a group of guys around and just a few girlss."

"Does it ever do any good?" I asked.

"Sure. Women go for dat."

I frowned at him. "Whaaat? You're nuts. Girls don't like conceited guys."

"Yes they do," agreed Peter.

"You guys are nuts."

"Then why do all the conceited guys have girlfriends and all the nice ones don't?"

He had a point there. *Maybe.* "But which came first? The girlfriend or the conceit?"

Peter sat up slowly and tried to reach around to brush his back off. I leaned in to help him as he explained himself.

"Try to imagine back to when you were in like third or fourth grade. Which boys did you have a crush on?"

"None of them."

"Come on. Don't lie. Okay, which ones stood out to you, then?"

Bodo was watching us intensely, looking very interested in our discussion.

"I guess the ones who stood out were the ones looking for the most attention."

"Were they just loud or showing off?"

"Showing off, mostly."

"And when they did that, did they get positive reinforcement or negative?"

"It depended."

"On what?"

I tried to think of the few boys I could recall from my much younger days as being kind of loud and in-your-face types, and remembered three of them. Two cute ones and one not so cute. I realized that the cute ones were seen as cocky, as if they had something to crow about, and the not so cute one just seemed obnoxious.

I sighed. "It depended on what they looked like."

"Explain dat part," said Bodo, leaning in and studying my face.

"Well, I hate to say it because it sounds so shallow, but the ones that were good-looking were encouraged, and the ones who weren't, were looked at as obnoxious and shunned."

"So you encouraged the conceit of the good-looking guys and told the ugly ones to stay in the background, essentially," said Peter.

"God, that's terrible when you put it like that," I said, a little disgusted with myself. "Man, was I shallow or what? I helped perpetuate the problem from the time I was like, ten or something."

"Don't feel bad about it. We all did. It's how we were raised."

"It's dat theory of efolution. The handsome specimens survive to make babies. De ugly ones dat have less desirable thingks die off. Nobody wants to make babies with dem."

"So your theory that women like conceit is true to some degree. That's sad."

"Yes, but it is good for the survifal of de human race. You want to make babies with de ones who are strong and bold and fearless. Dey are de ones dat will make it through the tough times."

I didn't want to look at Peter because by Bodo's definition, he was going to survive and Peter wasn't. Or at least, Bodo had better chances than Peter did.

"Well, I'm not worried about making any babies," said Peter, lying back down.

"Yeah, he just wants someone to cuddle with," I teased, nudging his leg.

"What about you, Bryn. Where is your boyfriend? Why issn't he with you and Peter and Buster."

"I don't have one."

"I don't belief dat," said Bodo, smiling at me.

"She's telling the truth," said Peter. "I never saw one."

"What do you mean, you never saw one?" I demanded.

"In the couple weeks I spied on you. I never saw anyone at your house but you."

"You jerk," I said nudging him with my foot. "You didn't tell me you were spying on me."

"Well, I had to make sure I wasn't living behind a canner, didn't I?"

I obviously hadn't given Peter enough credit. The kid was sneaky. I'd never seen or heard anything. "That kind of makes me nervous that you were able to do that without me knowing. It makes me wonder how many other people managed it."

"I never saw anyone spying on you, other than me, if that makes you feel any better."

"I'm not sure if it does or not."

Bodo was looking off over toward the gas stations. "Dare's a Cracker Barrel over dare."

"I saw that. I used to love that place," I said wistfully.

"They have cool candy," said Peter.

"That's exactly what I was thinking," I said, smiling. "I haven't had any candy in ages."

"Do you want to go over dare and see if dey haff any?"

I shook my head. "Too risky. It's not worth getting shot or eaten over some jaw breakers."

Bodo shrugged, but I saw him stealing glances over at it from time to time for the next few hours. The sun was high and sapping the rest of my strength away. Peter had fallen asleep and was snoring lightly, Buster sound asleep in his legs.

"Don't even think about it, Bodo," I said, lying down, joining Peter. "I don't want you getting killed or captured."

"You don't haff to worry about me."

"Whatever. If you go over there and get caught, I'm not coming for you."

He didn't answer and I fell asleep before I could bother to worry about it anymore.

CHAPTER
THIRTY-ONE

THE CANNERS HAD ME IN their grip, pulling me by the shoulders toward their fire pit area. I was struggling, but they had ropes around me and I couldn't get free.

"Bryn! Bryn!" yelled Peter.

"Peter? Where are you?" I couldn't see him anywhere. It was too dark.

"Bryn!" came his voice, bouncing painfully off my eardrum and startling me out of my nightmare.

I sat bolt upright, looking around me in a panic, trying to figure out for a second where I was. It was dark for some reason. I saw our trailer and Peter and Buster looking up at me curiously, their faces lit by the moonlight shining in sideways from the far horizon. "What the hell?" I said, rubbing my face, my brain now coming into focus. "Holy crap, I was having a *terrible* dream. How long was I out?"

"I know. You woke me up talking in your sleep. And it's late. Like after dinner time. We all slept right through it. Bodo's not here. "

I sighed heavily, knowing exactly where he was. "*Dammit, Bodo.*"

"Do you know where he is?"

"Yes. He went to that friggin' Cracker Barrel."

"Did you tell him to go there?" asked Peter, obvious disapproval in his voice.

"No, of course I didn't. In fact, I specifically told him *not* to go there."

Peter chuckled. "He only listens to your orders when he feels like listening to them."

"I don't give orders, Peter. I'm not General Custer or whatever."

"Well, you're our leader, like it or not. And leaders give orders."

"I give suggestions. And I strongly *suggested* that he not go there earlier today. I told him we weren't going to rescue his ass if he got in trouble, too."

"Did you mean it?"

"No!" I said angrily.

"Why are you mad at me? I'm not at the Cracker Barrel."

I ran my hand over my face again. "I'm not mad at you. I'm just frustrated. Now we have to go over there, risk our own butts, and possibly lose time on the road. Actually, that would be the best case scenario."

"The worst case scenario being that we get eaten."

"Yeah. That would be the worst thing I can think of."

"Can you do me a favor and not tempt fate with statements like that?" said Peter, sounding like he was only half joking.

"Yeah, you're right. Things can always, always be worse." I reached down and grabbed my gun from the ground where I'd been sleeping. "Just stay here. I'm going to go see what he's gotten himself into."

"Huh-uh, no way am I staying here alone. I'm coming with you."

"Well get on your damn bike, then, because we can't leave our stuff here."

"What are we going to do with Bodo's bike?"

"We'll leave the big butt bike here and if he comes back while we're gone he can get it. I don't want to leave the trailer unattended."

"Okay. Good idea. Maybe we should leave Buster here with Bodo's bike."

"Fine. Use that bungee cord in the trailer to tie him to the frame. He has a hook you can use on his collar."

Peter got Buster all tied up and we got on our bikes to head over to the restaurant.

We'd gotten all of ten feet before Buster started barking.

"What the hell is his problem?" I hissed.

Peter turned around and went back, saying, "Shhh! Buster! No!"

But Buster wasn't having any of that being left behind stuff. He was whining and dancing around, making it very clear that if we tried to leave him again, he was going to call all the canners from the nearby towns to come to dinner.

"friggin' dog," I growled, turning around and waiting for Peter to untie him. I got off my bike and snatched the Hello Kitty backpack out of the trailer. "Get in here, you stupid mutt. I'm not going to risk you running around like an idiot, waking up all the canners. You're riding with me."

He got in the bag without fighting me on it, and I zipped it almost all the way up. I left a space at the top that he poked his head out of. This time I put him on my back so I wouldn't have to take a Buster tongue bath on the way over to the Cracker Barrel.

We left the highway underpass and Peter started giggling.

"Shut up, Peter." I was still grouchy.

"I ... I ... can't. You have no idea ... how ridiculous you look ... with a poodle in a Hello Kitty backpack on your back."

"I can imagine, trust me." I shook my head. *Stupid Bodo is going to pay for this.*

We pulled up into the parking lot of the Cracker Barrel. It was completely dark. My watch showed eleven o'clock - prime canner partying time - but so far, I'd heard no sounds; and it seemed like the canners were partial to shouting and making loud asses of themselves, so I was hoping this meant this was a canner-free zone.

I stopped near the front porch of the restaurant. Cracker Barrels were all designed the same way, with a large open area in front that held rocking chairs for sale and big chess games set up in between them. I guess it was supposed to resemble an old trading post from the Wild West.

Peter pulled up next to me. "Do you see anything?" he whispered.

"No," I whispered back. "Let's go around back ... make a loop."

Peter followed behind me as I went counter clock-wise around the building.

Everything was black. And silent. There was no sign of Bodo or anyone else for that matter. In fact, all the windows of the place were still intact and there was no sign of vandalism anywhere. I was getting totally creeped out by the perfectness of it all.

"There's something really wrong about this place," whispered Peter loudly. "It looks like no one's been here yet. Like it's frozen in time!"

We drew up to the front of the building again and I stopped, getting off my bike.

"What are you doing?" asked Peter, panic in his voice.

"I'm just going to look in the window. I'll be right back." I walked over to Peter, sliding the backpack off my arms. "Take Buster and keep him quiet. If I see anything disturbing, I'll let you know. Be ready to ride like hell out of here."

I crept up to the porch of the restaurant, headed not for the front doors, but for a small window that I knew looked into the gift shop area. All these places were the same, with a gift shop in front that you had to walk through to get to the dining room.

As soon as I got to the window and looked in, I knew why we weren't seeing Bodo anywhere. He was sitting in a chair in the middle of the room, tied to it with zip ties, and a small girl was pointing a rifle at his head from just a few feet away.

My heart fell down to my feet. I could see he was talking fast, probably trying to convince the girl not to shoot him in the face. She kept glancing behind her as if there were another person in the room, but I couldn't see him. There were still some racks of shirts there, and whoever he was, he was behind one of them. He must have been pretty short, too, because the displays were only about four feet high.

I left the porch and ran around the back, gesturing to Peter to stay put. I found the back door I had seen on my earlier trip around and tested it. It was locked, but I decided not to let that stop me. I searched the nearby ground and found a piece of old rusted rebar. I jammed it into the space between the door and frame and pulled on it as hard as I could. I felt the frame bending a little, and encouraged by my little success, put more of my back into it. I could feel my shoulder muscles nearly popping with the effort, but I was rewarded by the metal giving a little bit more. I stopped to check my progress and saw that I'd moved the frame enough to the side that the lock was no longer holding the door closed. I pulled the rebar out and held it in my hand. It wasn't brass knuckles or a knife, but I felt a little less guilty using it as a potential weapon than the gun. I had to conserve my bullets anyway.

I eased the door open, praying they hadn't heard me breaking the lock. The only sounds that had reached my ears were those of my grunting, so hopefully that meant they'd heard nothing inside.

I found myself in a kitchen. I tiptoed around the stainless steel prep tables and over to a door that had a round window on it. I could see into the dining room from there but not the gift shop.

I slowly pushed the door out, watching through the window as I did, making sure no one was coming. I slipped through the crack, entering the dining room as silently as I could, my sneakers making slight squeaking sounds on the dirty tile floor. I took two steps out into a narrow hallway that had coffee machines and racks of glasses set up on a long counter. *This must be where the waitresses poured the orange juice.* I went to the end of the hallway and found myself at the spot where the gift shop met the dining room. I had a perfect view into the room where Bodo was being held captive, and now I knew why I couldn't see the person who'd been standing behind the girl before.

It was a guy in a wheelchair, his head below the level of the rack of t-shirts.

I found myself facing a moral dilemma. All my life I'd been told to take special care with handicapped people. I never used the handicapped bathroom, even when it was the only one available and I had to pee really bad, just in case someone in a wheelchair might come in and need it. I offered to push people in chairs up ramps. I took things down off high shelves in the grocery store for ladies using canes or walkers.

But now a guy in a wheelchair and his girlfriend or sister or whatever, were holding my friend hostage. Did I sneak up behind him and put a gun to his head, taking advantage of his obviously inferior position of strength? How could I live with myself if I did something like that?

I heard his casual-sounding voice from across the fifteen-foot space.

"Just shoot him in the face and be done with it."

Moral dilemma solved. I snuck out and flicked the safety off my weapon, coming up slowly behind the guy, my gun raised level with his chair.

As soon as I reached him, I put the metal barrel to the back of his head, pushing it forward ever so slightly. "Don't fucking move or I'll blow your stupid head off."

The girl with the rifle spun around and I ducked behind the wheelchair, keeping the guy between us. "Shoot me or my friend, and I'll kill this asshole right here in his chair. I don't give a crap if he's paralyzed or whatever."

"Go ahead and shoot me," he said, nonchalantly. "I don't give a rat's ass." He put his hands on the wheels of his chair and started to turn it around.

I panicked. I didn't really want to shoot him, but I needed to use him as my shield. I grabbed the handle of the chair with the gun in my hand and pulled him back, jamming the rebar into his wheel spokes with the other. "You're not going anywhere, dick."

"Hey! What'd you put in my wheel! Take that out!"

"Jimmy, just shut up and let me handle this!" shouted the girl.

I turned my attentions from Jimmy to his protector. "All you have to do is let my friend go, and I'll leave you two alone. But if you try anything funny, we'll take this place down to the ground. I have friends outside who are waiting for me to get back."

She narrowed her eyes at me. "I don't believe you."

I could see her strength was waning. The rifle was pointed more toward the ground now, even though she kept trying to hitch it up, using her elbows braced against her sides.

"I don't care if you believe me or not. Let my friend go, or you and your boyfriend here are going to have an extra hole in your heads."

"Good!" yelled Jimmy. "Shoot me!"

"Shut up, Jimmy!" both the girl and I screamed at the same time. Both of us were startled at first and then I smiled.

She smiled back, a little sadly. "He don't wanna live," she said with a heavy southern accent.

"Who does?" I said. "The world sucks right now. I just want to get my friend and go."

"Bryn, she has dose jaw breakers you were talking about. I was just trying to get you some and dey jumped me."

I shook my head. "You got jumped by a ten year old and a gimp. I'm so proud right now, Bodo."

"I ain't ten. I'm fifteen. And that ain't very polite, callin' a guy in a wheelchair a gimp. And he's my brother by the way."

"You got pregnant with your brudder?" asked Bodo, the look on his face not hiding his disgust.

"Pregnant?" I said, noticing for the first time that she did look a little round in the middle.

"My brother? Oh gawd, that's disgustin'. No, it wasn't my brother, you idget. It was one o' them wild boys runnin' around out there in the night. Attacked me when I was out gettin' water from the well. But Jimmy killed 'im right where he stood when he was done hurtin' me. But it was too late. I got knocked up."

"Holy *crap*, that sucks," I said, before I could stop myself.

"Yeah," she sighed. "Tell me about it. Havin' a baby in the middle o' this mess. And with the father bein' all crazy an' such."

The father being a cannibal rapist, you mean. I thought it but I didn't say it. Poor girl had enough on her plate to deal with. "Well, at least you have this nice place to live."

"Yeah, well, we got weapons. And we've killed enough of 'em that they stay away. Only you two dummies have come here in the last couple weeks."

"Well, we're not bad people and we don't mean to cause you any harm or any ... stress. We'll just leave you alone if you let us go."

"I've a mind to let you go," she said as if measuring her options. "Where'd you say you was headin'?"

"Orlando," I said, at the exact same time Bodo said, "The Everglades."

I shook my head. "Bodo, do you not listen to *anything* I say?"

"Hey, dey're nice people. Dis iss like a place people can go for information. Maybe one day dey can sendt people to where we liff so we can grow our community."

"Or maybe they'll tell the canners who we are and where we're going so they can all show up and eat us!"

"Oh, *hell* no," said Jimmy, struggling to turn around. "Them freaks done ate our dog and raped my sister! You think we'd help them sons-a-bitches? Sissy, gimme that gun so I can shoot this girl and her foreigner friend."

"Shut up, Jimmy. You don't need a gun right now. You're talkin' crazy."

She walked over to Bodo and flicked out the blade from a knife she'd taken out of the pocket of her pants. I tensed up for second and pushed the gun harder against Jimmy's head before I realized she was just cutting the zip ties off Bodo's wrists and ankles. She grunted with the effort of bending over.

When she stood up her face was all red. She blew the straggly pieces of hair off her forehead before she said, "There you go, Bodo. Take your jaw breakers and get the hell out."

I stood up, thanking her and her brother profusely, still pointing the gun casually at his head. "Listen, guys, seriously, thank you so much for letting him go. I'm really sorry to have caused you this trouble."

"How'd you get in anyway?" asked Jimmy.

I'd come around to face him and saw his suspicion.

"Uhhhh, you left the back door unlocked." I prayed we'd be long gone before they discovered that little lie.

"Uh-huh," he said, squinting at me, obviously not believing a word I'd said. "I don't believe I left that door open, actually. I guess I'll just have to go back there and check."

He tried to turn around to wheel away, but the rebar was still in his spokes.

"Okay, well, we'll just be going now. It was nice meeting you, Sissy ... Jimmy." I backed up, heading in Bodo's direction.

Bodo was standing in front of a jar on the counter, pulling out jawbreakers and stuffing them into his pants pockets. He looked over his shoulder at Sissy. "If you see any good people who want to start a new life, you send dem to de Everglades. Dat's where we are going."

"Yeah, and any bad people? Tell them we went to Orlando," I added, grabbing Bodo's elbow. "Time to go," I urged under my breath.

"But I need to get da candies for you."

"Not now," I said, pulling on him harder.

Jimmy had reached around and pulled the rebar free and was turning to head back to the kitchen.

I took off running. "Bye, Sissy! Good luck with the baby!"

"Bye, Sissy!" said Bodo, as he ran alongside me.

We burst through the front door and I yelled as quietly as I could, "Go! Go! Go! before he realizes I broke their door!"

Peter quickly turned around and headed out of the parking lot, his legs pumping furiously. I saw the Hello Kitty backpack with Buster's head coming out of the top, bouncing around on his back. Buster let out an excited bark when he saw us running.

I went to jump on the bike but Bodo beat me to it. "Bodo, get *off!*" I yelled, panicked that he was going to leave me behind to get shot.

"Get on da handlebars, quick!"

I didn't bother to question his orders. I jumped on and grabbed the handles just inside the grips, finding a spot on either side of the front forks to rest my sneakers.

Bodo started pedaling and the bike slowly pulled away. The combined weight of him, me, and the trailer was making it hard for him to pick up speed.

I heard yelling back at the Cracker Barrel, and we weren't yet out of the parking lot. "Hurry, Bodo! Hurry! Pedal faster!"

I felt his breath on my neck and realized he was standing up now, grinding out the rotations on the gears as fast as his thigh muscles were capable. We were at the road when I heard a shot ring out and the voice coming from the store.

"You broke our dooooor!! Get *back* here!!

Bodo was now laughing while he was pedaling and I just shook my head. I was using every abdominal muscle I had to hold onto my spot on the top of those handlebars, my heart going too fast and too wild for my brain. I was seeing auras around the stars above our heads. How Bodo had the strength to pedal three hundred and fifty pounds of us and laugh at the same time, I'll never know. *friggin' Germans.*

Within a few seconds we were back under the overpass. I jumped off the handlebars and got onto the other bike, immediately going to join Peter at the bottom of the exit ramp.

"Come on!" I shouted as I zoomed past him, Bodo right behind me.

"I guess we're leaving now?" asked Peter, pumping hard to catch up to me.

I didn't slow down enough to talk until we were about a mile away.

CHAPTER THIRTY-TWO

I WAS PEDALING STEADILY, KEEPING my eyes forward.
"You're mad aren't you?" asked Bodo, coming up next to me.

"Ya think?" I said sarcastically.

"I got da jawbreakers, dough."

"You almost got killed, you stupid jerk."

"What happened back there?" asked Peter, coming up to ride on my other side. "One minute I was standing there in a totally silent parking lot, and the next thing I knew you two were running out, yelling, and someone was shooting a gun."

I was still angry enough to sound enthusiastic when I told the story. "Well, ding-a-ling here decided to break into the Cracker Barrel which was the home of Sissy and Jimmy Redneck - Sissy carrying the fetus of a cannibal rapist and Jimmy being in a wheelchair; and in the process of relieving them of some of their candy, managed to get himself caught."

"It wass awesome. Bryn came in dare and threatened to shoot dat Jimmy guy, and dey let me go. *And* dey let me take da candiess too."

"I appreciate the gesture, Bodo, as I'm sure Bryn does, but really, that kind of risk is only going to get you or one of us killed."

"Yeah. What Peter just said. Times ten," I added.

"Yes, okay. It wass stupid, I admit dat. I won't do it again. I just wanted to do something nice for you guyss, since you're doing so many nice thingks for me."

"Next time, just offer me a foot rub or something instead," I said.

"Really?" he asked.

"No. Not really. Stay away from my feet, weirdo."

"So where are we going … I mean, what's the plan for to-night?" asked Peter.

"Well, since we've gotten an earlier start than I had originally planned, I figured we'd just ride until we can't anymore."

"I don't know if I can make it until eleven again," warned Peter. "That's, like, twelve hours straight of riding."

"Why don't we go for a few hours, stop and have a meal, may-be a little nap, and then go some more?" I suggested.

"Works for me," said Peter, sighing. "I'm going to be really glad when we get to our final destination. I hate riding bikes. I didn't before, but I do now."

"Me too," I agreed.

"How will we know when we're dare?" asked Bodo.

"I haven't figured that part out yet," I admitted. "When we get closer we should look for a tourist shop that has maps and stuff, and pick a spot. I hope we can find a place that has canoes nearby. Then we can take a few of them and go out into the Everglades until we find the right place."

"Da Everglades iss a really big place."

"Yes, I know. But it's made up of lots of different kinds of ter-rain and stuff. We have to find an area that has trees for cover and dry land to build a shelter on."

"And there has to be a lot of game or whatever. Or fish," added Peter.

"I read in da newsspaper, dat dare are snakes so big out dare, dey can eat a deer," said Bodo in his best spooky voice. "Dit you know dat deer are bigger dan people?"

"Shut up, Bodo," I said, quickly losing patience with him. First he scares the crap out of me, making me think he's going to get killed, then he tries to freak me out about man-eating snakes.

"No, he's right. I read that, too," said Peter. "Some people apparently either lost their constrictor snakes or purposely set them free out there, and without any natural predators they've gotten huge. I saw a picture of a giant yellow one. It was freaky. As long as a car ... or longer."

I refused to panic about something I hadn't yet seen with my own eyes. "All that means is a bigger meal for us, as far as I'm concerned."

"We're gonna eat snakes?" asked Bodo, clearly excited about the prospect.

"Why not?" I asked. "It's meat, isn't it?"

"Dat's so cool. Who's gonna catch it?"

"You. That's your job. Snake wrangler."

"Awesome," he said. I think he really meant it, too.

"Smooth," said Peter, quietly, so only I'd hear.

I smiled, pretty proud of myself. "Never doubt my skills, Peter. Never."

"Oh, I won't. Believe me."

"I think we should try to eat gator too. We can use dare hides to make shoess."

"Yeah, you work on that, Bodo. You can be our snake wrangling, alligator wrestling, cobbler."

"I know you're mocking me, Bryn, but I can do it. You'll see."

"Good. I hope you can, because I have no interest whatsoever in doing any of that."

"What *are* you going to do?" asked Bodo. "I have my chob now. What's yours and Peter's going to be?"

"Don't forget to add gardener to your list," I reminded him.

"Of course. I haff promised you tomatoes and you will haff dem. I just haff to find some seedts."

"I have some. In the backpack. My dad bought them for me ... before he died."

"Oh," said Bodo more quietly. "Dat's nice dat he did dat for you. He wass a good guy, huh?"

"Yeah. He was a good guy. A *really* good guy." I think he would have liked my two friends a lot. Peter, because of how strong he ended up being, even with all the adversity he'd suffered, and

Bodo, because of his boundless energy and constant happiness, despite all the reasons he had to be sad.

"My job is going to be getting our food stores set up and contingency plans in place. I also like to cook," said Peter.

"I have no idea what my jobs are going to be, other than teaching you guys how to do some krav maga."

"You are in charch of our defenses. Dat's important. Maybe one of da most important thingks. Without good defenses, we will be da dinner."

I don't know why, but his words made me feel good - like I was important to our group.

We continued on for another two hours in relative silence before Peter spoke up. "Do you guys mind if we stop? I'm tired and really hungry."

"No, I think it's a good idea. How about we stop at a car this time? This part of the highway seems kind of abandoned. I haven't heard any sounds or seen any lights up ahead at all," I said. "Maybe we could sleep on the seats or something ... have a comfortable bed for a change."

"I'm okay to rest for a while," said Bodo.

I pulled up next to a large SUV that was parked on the shoulder. I got off my bike and walked around it, putting my face up to the darkly tinted windows, making sure there weren't any surprises within. I didn't know what I expected to see, but I did it anyway. Nothing seemed out of the ordinary.

Bodo tried all the doors and they were locked.

"Well, that's dumb," said Peter. "Who locks the doors of a car that's out of gas when there's no more gas around?"

"Someone who owned the car, I guess. Old habits die hard."

Bodo went over to the side of the road and came back with a rock, using it to smash the driver's side window so he could reach inside to unlock the doors.

I went over to the passenger side and climbed in, putting Buster down on the floor in the back seat. He immediately sniffed around, investigating all the parts of the car that might have crumbs for small dogs lying around.

Bodo reached over and opened up the glove box. I pulled things out of it, wondering why I'd never thought about doing this before. People usually kept all kinds of good things in their cars. This one had maps and a small flashlight, which I tested and found still worked. I stuck it in the waistband of my pants.

Peter was in the back seat. "Hey! There's gum back here."

He handed a piece up to me and Bodo - they were kind of sad-looking, having suffered the Florida heat for who knows how long. I stuck mine in my pocket for after dinner. "Anything else?"

"Nope. There's a gas can in the back but it's empty. And a blanket."

"We'll take the blanket. We have room on the trailer, I think."

I got out of the car and went over to the trailer, pulling out the things we'd need for our dinner. Bodo came around to help me, and together we set up the small camp stove, the pan and got the noodles and sauce ready.

"Um, guys?" asked Peter from the car.

"Yeah," answered Bodo, busy screwing on the canister of fuel to the stove.

"I think you should come here for a minute."

"What is it?" I asked, busy organizing the few dishes and utensils we had, to try and make a real event of this meal.

"Just come here, please." His voice had taken on a new urgency, so I put the things down I was messing with and walked over.

"What's so dang important that you couldn't just tell me ...?" My voice trailed off as my brain tried to fully appreciate what my eyes were seeing. "Are those ...?"

"I think so," said Peter in a hushed voice. "No wonder the doors were locked."

"What's up, guys?" asked Bodo over my shoulder.

I stepped back so he could take a look.

"Whoa. Dose are tiny bombs!" he said excitedly. "I'll go open da back."

"Grenades, Bodo," corrected Peter, absently, still focused on the SUV's cargo area.

A couple seconds later the back of the SUV opened and Bodo's eager face appeared. He pulled the blanket the rest of the way off of the black, heavy plastic case and slid the whole thing over to the edge of the tailgate, his eyes scanning the contents left and right, up and down. "Dis iss amazing. Dare's, like, sixteen grenades in here."

"I think there's more underneath. It's like two layers of them in foam."

"I wonder why the person didn't take them when they left the car," I said.

"Who knows?" said Peter. "Maybe they got killed. Maybe they're coming back soon. We have no idea when this car was left here - it could have been earlier today."

I backed away from the car and went over to our food. "I vote we eat and get the hell out of here." I pulled a lighter from the side pocket of my backpack and lit the camp stove, adjusting the dial on the fuel tank to make the flame high enough to boil the small amount of water we were using for the noodles. I put the noodles in the water while it was still cold, allowing them to get softer more quickly. They ended up being a little starchier this way but I didn't care. *Maybe it'll help the sauce stick to the pasta better.* I was purposely focusing on the meal instead of freaking out about the real, live grenades that were just five feet away from me.

Bodo came back over to the trailer, carrying the heavy-looking case.

"What are you doing with that thing?" I asked.

"Putting it on da trailer, of course."

"Do you really think we should take it?" I asked, looking from Bodo to Peter.

"If we leave them, they could be used against us some day. I agree with Bodo here. We need to bring them with us, even if we're just going to bury them somewhere."

"Bury dem? No way, don't be crazy like dat. We can use dese in case anyone comes to our new place. You said it yourself. Da canners can go get da military stuff. Now we have some military stuff. It's perfect. Don't worry, it's not a problem, I'll make room. I'm very good with organizing thingks."

I shook my head. *Boys and their war toys.* It reminded me about reading George's journal. I made a mental note to get it out the next time the sun came up and we were stopped, so I could start getting a grasp on what type of situation we might find ourselves in. Maybe some old war veteran would have something to say about using grenades and defending ourselves against a crazed enemy.

CHAPTER
THIRTY-THREE

W E ATE OUR PASTA DINNER and got back on the road, traveling for a full six hours before finally stopping to sleep. We were nearly to our destination, the changing landscape around us becoming more lush and wet. Off in the distance we could see what looked like small bodies of water, and fewer towns, at least on the west side of the highway.

I pulled George's journal out of my backpack while Bodo walked around putting the tarps down and over our things. Peter was busy playing with Buster and laughing at his antics. Bodo and I had an unspoken agreement between us that we did the heavy lifting and manual labor - Peter was still way too skinny for my liking and tired easier than we did. He'd been really cool, trying to keep up, not wanting to slow us down. We did what we could to make our breaks more comfortable for him.

I turned the pages of the journal randomly, noticing George's careful script that never seemed to falter or become sloppy like mine always did when I wrote for longer than five minutes at a time. My fingers had always been much more comfortable on a keyboard.

He hadn't organized the book in any particular order. It seemed as if he'd done the work over a period of time, writing things down as they came to mind. In one section he talked about his friends - who he was serving with in the army; in another he discussed the process they used to dig latrines - bathrooms, I guess.

I read aloud so Bodo and Peter would be able to comment when I was done.

> *"It is important to remember that attack can come from any side. A smart enemy will approach from the place you are least likely to expect; this means, it could even come from your own friendly territory. For this reason, it is important to shore up defenses in every direction, and expect the unexpected."*

"Well, that's encouraging," I said.

"It's goodt advices," said Bodo. "We will need some kindt of lookout that can see in all directions."

"I guess that's why in all those war movies they have those towers at the prisons - so you can see anyone trying to escape no matter where they are. And on pirate ships too."

"Yeah, but in the war movies, the lookout tower is the first thing that's blown up."

"Keep reading. I like what dis guy is saying."

> *"If your manpower is low, due to injury or simply unavailability, you may not have enough bodies to adequately guard your position. Use whatever methods you have at your disposal to act as early warning systems. A popular method used during the most recent wars is land-mines."*

"Too bad we don't have any land-mines," I said sarcastically.

"We haff grenades. They can be attached to a wire that pulls da pin out. I've see dat in several movies."

Peter nodded. "Trip wires. Totally done all the time in jungles."

I shook my head. "We're missing the critical piece - wire."

"We have clear fishing line," corrected Peter. "I don't think it has to be metal."

"I guess you have a point - so long as we don't need the stuff for fishing."

I went back to the book and flipped through some more pages before stopping to read another passage.

> *"One of the biggest problems you will face is boredom. Hours will be spent doing nothing, as you contemplate what the enemy might be doing and when they might strike. Sometimes there is no intel and other times the intel is inaccurate. The important thing is to use your free time wisely. Train, train, train. Practice hand-to-hand combat. Make weapons. Build your stores. Play games with your comrades. But never give in to the boredom and do nothing. Down this path lies insanity."*

Those words sent chills up my spine.

"He's right, you know. There are people going crazy right now, all around us. I don't know if it's boredom doing it or just desperation, but it's definitely happening," said Peter.

"You got that right," I agreed. Canners came to mind, and Sissy and Jimmy too a little bit. I could see how a life spent inside of a Cracker Barrel could lead someone down to crazytown.

I looked through the book some more, noticing that he had sections on making weapons and traps, but deciding to study them later. I was tired and needed a break from thinking about dying, killing, and defending myself against zombie attacks. I thought about the days when my biggest worry was a chemistry exam.

"What are you smiling about?" asked Bodo, looking at me from across the tarp.

I leaned over and shoved the book back into my bag. "Oh, just how my biggest concern used to be a chemistry exam - and now it's whether I'm going to die tomorrow or not."

"Kinda puts things in perspective, doesn't it?" asked Peter.

"I don't know. Call me crazy, but I kindt of prefer dis world to da last one."

"Yeah. No doubt about it," I said, "you're crazy, alright."

"But don't you agree? I mean, here we chust survife with our brains and it doesn't matter who you know or how much money you haff. You just work hard and think about how da world works and you can survife. You can make friends and it doesn't matter what your clothes are or what kindt of car you are driving. Da food is more healthy and da air and da water is better."

"Sure," agreed Peter, "but then you have the whole canner thing. That part's not better. Neither is the fact that we could starve to death or die from a simple cut."

"No, we won't starfe to death. Not in da Everglades. It'ss full of life. Birds and snakes and gators and deer and all kindts of mammals. Dare's so much rain here all da time, we'll never run out of water. And for da injuries, we can make some things like alcohol to kill da germs. I can build dat for sure, it's not a problem."

"You know, Bodo, when you put it like that, it doesn't seem so bad," I said, surprising even myself with what I was saying. "I mean, I know you're creating this little illusion and all, but if I don't think about it too hard, it does seem pretty okay. With you guys in the picture, at least. I don't think I'd want to do all that alone."

"Yes, dats what I mean, too. It's not worth it so much if you are alone. Human beingks were meant to live in groups. You can see dat even when dare were cavemens running around. We survive better in tribes and families." He stopped for a minute and then leaned forward more, looking especially earnest. "And it's not an illusion. It's reality! You have to think positif. Hey, you're Hamerican! Your country was built on the idea dat nothing is impossible! If you can belief it, you can achief it!"

I shook my head at him. He was probably right, but he was so excited about it, he looked just a tad bit deranged. The fact that his hair was sticking out in every direction in clumps wasn't helping.

Peter laughed. "I think you've listened to too many Tony Robbins tapes or something."

"You will see. Bodo is right on dis one." He laid back on the tarp. "Time for sleeping. Goodnight, family."

I watched him close his eyes, and sat there staring at him for a while. He'd wandered in off the highway out of nowhere - a place we really hadn't bothered to ask him about - all alone, with almost nothing to live on in his bag. He was from another country, where they spoke a different language and had a different history. And yet, he was the voice of reason in our lives. He made sense and he made me feel hopeful and happy to be here under a highway overpass in the middle of Florida, headed to a giant swamp filled with lethal creatures.

I looked up at the sky, wondering if my dad were up there, looking down on me and sending people to me who might make my life feel worth living. I sent him a silent message, just in case he could hear me, fingering the ring of his that was hanging at my throat.

Thanks, Dad … for sending Peter and Bodo, and Buster too. I like my new family. I wish you were here too, but even though you aren't, I'm pretty sure I'm going to be okay.

It was the first time I'd felt hopeful about my life in a long time.

CHAPTER
THIRTY-FOUR

BODO WOKE US UP AT four o'clock with a breakfast of Pringles and water, anxious to get going.

"Today is maybe da last day, right?"

I pulled the map book out and studied the mile marker signs as best I could with the tiny flashlight I'd taken from the car with the grenades in it. "Maybe. I'd at least like to hit a tourist shop if nothing else."

"Awesome," said Peter sleepily, shoving the one, still-crunchy potato chip in his mouth.

We packed up our stuff and got on our bikes, pedaling back up to the highway to head south once again.

After three hours of riding we started seeing billboards advertising a huge tourist shop. They promised Maps, Oranges you could ship, Seashells, T-shirts and More! A few also mentioned discount tickets to local attractions. I wondered if any of them were way out of the way and habitable. It was tempting to think of living in a place that was already built for us.

A small town arose from the emptiness in front of us, making me instantly feel nervous. Towns meant people. It was still pretty early for canners, but that didn't make it safe.

"Let's get off at the next exit," I said. "That last billboard said there was a big tourist shop there."

"Should we be aiming for a big one or a small one?" asked Peter.

"Well, either, I guess. What are you thinking?"

"Just that if it's bigger, it's probably already been hit by raiders. Maybe they wouldn't bother with the smaller ones?"

"All of dem are going to be hit - but who'ss gonna take maps into da swamp except for crazy people like us?" He smiled at me, taking any sting out of his words.

"Yeah, you're probably right," Peter conceded.

We got off the exit and coasted to the bottom, following the signs leading us east to the tourist shop. It was located on the edge of the town, near a strip mall - a stand-alone building with the front glass partially smashed in.

Bodo rode his bike up to the front door.

"Watch for glass," warned Peter. "We've made it this far without any flats, let's not get one now."

Bodo backed his bike up a little. "Who's going in?" He looked over his shoulder at us, awaiting an answer.

"You and me. Peter, you wait here with Buster. Shout if anyone comes, and have your gun out and loaded. Shoot anyone who looks at you like you're a steak or invites you to a barbecue."

I winced inside a little at my careless choice of words, but Peter didn't seem to care. He nodded his head, pulling his backpack around and getting the weapon out.

"Come on, Bodo. Let's go see what we can find." I took my gun out and nudged him in the arm with it so he'd take it. He frowned at me but didn't argue, taking the gun and putting it in the back of his waistband.

We stepped through the door frame that remained locked together, using the convenient, giant holes someone had made in their glass fronts to enter. The interior was one big open space. There were rows and rows of shelves that held seashells of every shape, color, and size. Some of them looked native to Florida and others obviously weren't. Someone with a glue gun and way too much time on her hands had made giant shell-covered knick knacks. There were mirrors, lamps, clocks, bowls, vases, jewelry boxes, and a hundred other things. Some of them had their natural shell colors and others had been painted, bedazzled, or shellacked. It was crazy.

Bodo walked over to the gaudiest piece in the entire store and said, "Bryn, imagine dat we livt in da real world, da old one, and dat I am buying dis lovely piece of art for you. As a gift. Happy birthday."

I laughed, walking over to a hula skirt and coconut bra on a hanger, holding it up for him to see. "And imagine that I'm buying this for you, Bodo. Happy birthday."

"Why thank you, Bryn. Dat is very kind of you. I think dat would look very nice on me, especially da bra part. When iss your birthday, anyway?"

"It's next month, actually. When's yours?"

"December twenty-fifth. I am a Christmas baby."

"That sucks."

"Yes. For da presents. But my mom always gafe me extra in June at da half point."

"Your mom sounds cool."

"Yes. She wass very cool, my mom. I miss her sometimes."

I nodded my head. I didn't want to talk about parents anymore right now. I had too many other things to worry about. "Let's go find some maps and brochures about places in the swamps."

We made our way over to a bank of racks holding all kinds of brochures. They advertised water parks, butterfly parks, bird sanctuaries, snake museums, gator wrestling shows, and swamp buggy and airboat rides. Everything and anything a person could do near the humid, hot Everglades was put on display here.

I pulled one of everything off the racks, stacking them in my arms. Bodo helped, going over to the other side and grabbing one of each from there.

"We gonna read these later?"

"Yes. I don't like leaving Peter alone."

"Yeah, me needer."

I put the stack of brochures I had in Bodo's arms. "I'm just going to check behind the register, see if there's anything of any use there.

"Okay. I'll go put dese in da trailer. See you in a minute."

I was rummaging around on the shelves below the cash register when I heard a small noise behind me. I shifted to my left before turning, and I'm pretty sure that's the only thing that saved my life.

A baseball bat came crashing down, glancing off my shoulder to hit the edge of the counter. It snapped off a piece of the formica and left a crack in the underlying particle board.

I dropped to the floor and rolled, coming to the balls of my feet in a not so smooth move on account of the incredible pain shooting through my shoulder. I stood there, slightly off kilter, fighting off the urge to coddle my injured body part. I knew it wouldn't do to let the enemy know where my weakness currently lie.

I found myself facing a girl - a dark-haired angry one. She was spouting all kinds of pissed-off-sounding weird words at me that I didn't recognize, and swinging the bat a little from side to side, as if she were at home plate and getting ready to hit a high fly ball deep into left field.

I held my fists up, ready to let her have it if she came any closer. I almost screamed at the pain that shot up from my injured shoulder. The bone wasn't broken, but man, was it bruised.

"Don't even think about coming near me with that bat again, bitch. I'll friggin' take it away from you and bash your head in with it."

"Oh, so you think you can just come in here to my parents' store and take whatever you want? Steal from me?"

I smiled, for some reason finding the fact that she had stayed to protect her parents' tacky shell emporium hilarious.

"What's so frickin' funny?"

"Is your mom the one with the unhealthy glue gun addiction?"

"What?" she spat, her face the picture of confusion. Slowly, though, realization dawned, and her expression changed to one of incredulity. "Did you just mock my mom's shell crafting?"

"Yeah. I guess I did."

She stood up straighter, the bat falling to her side. "I'll have you know that my mom's shell art was a big seller here."

"Seriously?" I said, truly shocked at the idea. "Who buys that crap?"

She shrugged. "Tourists. People from places where they don't have shells."

"Most of this shit isn't even from Florida," I scoffed.

"So? They don't know that."

I shook my head. "Shell scammers."

She lifted the bat again. "It's not polite to talk ill of the dead."

I held up my hands, wincing at the pain in my shoulder. "You're right. I'm sorry. I'm leaving."

"You planning on going into the Everglades?" She still held the bat up, but I noticed her shoulders relax a little. She wasn't planning on swinging at me now. At least not at this particular moment.

"What's it to you?" I was pissed she'd overheard our conversation. Now there was one more person on this planet who could give our secrets away to the canners.

"I was gonna help you. But maybe I won't now, since you gave me shit about my moms." Her chin came up and she challenged me with a hard stare.

I realized how stupid it was of me to keep fighting with this chick. She lived at this ridiculous shell shop and obviously was from the area.

"I'm sorry about your mom. I do need your help. I want to know where there's a place we can find canoes." I focused on the boats because I was thinking that a tourist place would have canoes where the most scenic parts of the Everglades were - which hopefully meant that it would be in an area with trees, swampy parts, and lots of wildlife. A good place to settle down in anonymity.

The girl backed up out of the area behind the register and walked over to the brochure rack, pulling three fliers off.

"Here," she said, slapping them down on the counter. Then she left the room for a back office area for a second and came back with another one that she placed on top of the others. "This is something you might want to check out too."

I took a tentative step forward, keeping my eye on her bat, occasionally glancing up at her face. I was waiting for any sign that she was about to jump all over me again, but it didn't come. I stopped before I got to the brochures, worried about getting any closer.

"Go ahead and look. I'm not going to hit you."

"Could you back up a few steps? You're making me nervous."

She went two paces back to stand by the entrance to the office.

I pulled the brochures closer to me and looked down at one of them quickly. It was the last one she put down, and I could see immediately that it had something to do with indians.

"What's this place?"

"There are some indian tribes out there. Not all of them live at the casinos, you know."

Her accusatory tone told me more than her words had.

"What tribe are you with?"

"Creek. But there are others. You want to find the Miccosukee. There might be some kids out there who could help you if they feel like it."

"Wow. Thanks." I couldn't believe my luck at almost but not quite being killed by a Creek indian in a shell shop. I reached up and felt the ring at my neck. My dad's spirit had touched me again.

"That your dad's ring?" she asked, a softer tone to her voice now.

"Yeah."

She reached into her shirt and pulled out a smaller version on a silver chain. "This is my mom's."

I got choked up, looking at the expression on her face and watching her hold the small jewelry carefully in one hand, while the bat hung forgotten in the other.

"Can I ask you for a really huge favor?" she said, her eyes going shiny with tears.

"Yeah. Sure." She'd helped me and the guys out more than she could possibly have known. Who was I to say no to something in return?

"Can I have a hug?"

I looked at her like she was crazy. "What?" It was the last thing I had expected her to ask me for.

She leaned the bat up against the wall. "I know it sounds nuts. You probably think I'm going to stab you in the back or something, but I'm not. It's just that … my mom used to hug me all the time … and she's been gone for almost a year. And I miss her terribly." The tears fell down her cheeks. She gritted her teeth together, refusing to sob. I could see her jaw muscles standing out. She looked like a proud indian warrior girl.

I shrugged. "Why not? Just don't stab me, seriously. I'll kill you if you do."

She half choked, half laughed, holding up her hands. "Promise."

We both took two awkward steps toward each other and just stood there for a moment. She was shorter than me, her dark hair hanging in greasy clumps around her face. She had huge brown eyes and wispy eyelashes. I could see why her mom had hugged her a lot. Underneath all her angry bravado, she was just a cute kid, scared about what was going to happen to her.

I grabbed her in a strong hug, feeling her arms come around my waist to settle at my lower back.

She was crying now, her shoulders shaking with the effort.

I just stood there, fighting off my own tears. Life was so friggin' unfair. All these kids, left alone to fend for themselves. Like Bodo said, we weren't meant to be alone.

I rubbed her back a few times and then pulled away. "Listen, we don't have much, but you're welcome to join us."

She shook her head. "No thanks. I'm going to stay here. With my mom's things."

I looked around, seeing the place from her perspective now, my eyes picking out shell-covered objects and seeing them differently. I could picture an older version of this girl, her mom, sitting at a table with her glue gun, taking each small shell and putting it in the exact right position, creating something that someone would buy, making it possible for her to put food on the table for her daughter. And man, did I feel like an asshole for mocking the glue gunning now.

I turned back to face her. "Well, if you change your mind, you know where to find us. Somewhere out there in the swamp."

"It's a big place you know," she said, wiping her nose off with the back of her hand.

"Yeah. I keep hearing that. Well, we'll leave you a sign."

"What kind of sign?"

"I don't know. You'll recognize it when you see it." I was pulling stuff out of my butt now, but whatever. I knew me and my two boys would figure something out.

As I left, she followed me out, pressing a bag of shells in my hand when I got to the door.

"What's this for?"

"A gift. From me and my moms."

I gave her another quick hug and then let her go. "What's your name?"

"Celia."

"Mine's Bryn. Look me up sometime, if you're ever out in the swamps."

She smiled. "I might do that someday. After I sell all this stuff," she said, gesturing around the room.

I laughed. "Good luck with that."

The guys were sitting on their bikes, just watching me with questions in their eyes. I shook my head slightly, telling them silently not to ask until we were gone. I got on my bike and waved goodbye one more time before pedaling away, leading my tribe back to the highway.

We had brochures to study and plans to make, and I didn't want to do it here in a town where lunatics who ate people or lonely girls with bats might be waiting to jump us.

CHAPTER THIRTY-FIVE

WE SAT BEHIND A COPSE of trees near the roadway with the brochures in a pile on the tarp. Buster had decided he liked the feel of shiny paper on his underparts, so did everything he could to spread out on them with his legs poking out behind him, giving him maximum belly exposure to their cool surfaces.

"Ew, Buster, get your wiener off the maps," I said, nudging him to the side.

He just leaned over quickly and licked me in hyperdrive speed every time I tried to touch him.

"He's trying to cool himself off," said Peter, smiling and reaching over to play with Buster's ears. That was one of Buster's favorite things. His eyes went half-closed as he floated off into doggy heaven. In Buster's world, there wasn't anything much better than an ear tickle and a cool belly.

"I think we shouldt check dis place out," said Bodo, looking at the booklet that Celia had brought out from her office.

"What is it? She said it had something to do with indians."

Bodo read from the brochure, "*The Miccosukee indians settled da area generations ago, building villages and structures on da wetlands and Cypress forests of da Everglades."* He turned a couple pages and said, "Dey have houses and stuff dare."

"Well, we don't want houses. At least not a place where there's a bunch of them."

"Why not?" asked Peter. "It'd be a lot less work."

"Yeah. And easy and convenient. Do you *not* remember the whole point of swamp life?"

Peter sighed. "Yes, I remember. We need to go someplace hard to get to and inconvenient to live in."

"Exactly. Keep reading."

"How about this ...," said Peter. *"Canoe and rowboat rental. Discover the forested wilds of the Everglades."*

"Let me see," I said, taking it from him. I looked it over and saw that the pictures were promising. I could see us hiding out in some of the areas depicted there.

"My turn," said Bodo, holding out his hand.

I passed him the brochure.

He looked at the back and then turned to the last page of the other booklet he had, comparing something on the two of them and frowning.

"What?" asked Peter. "What are you looking at?"

"Well ... it looks like on dese maps dat da two places are not very far away from each udder." He put the two maps down side by side next to Buster. "What do you think? Am I crazy?"

Peter and I studied the two illustrations. They probably weren't to scale, but they sure looked almost exactly the same. And the red dots marking the two places weren't very far apart.

"How far are those places from here?" asked Peter.

I pulled the map book from my backpack and found the page that showed where we currently were. "What are the co-ordinates of that map? Can you tell? Is there, like, a landmark of any kind?"

Bodo took the larger book and looked closer. "Oh. Dare are directions here above da map."

As he read them out to me, I followed the track on my map, turning the page over to one that had very little showing on it other than swirls of uninhabited water, wetlands, and green parts that hopefully meant they had trees on them.

"Bingo. Here's the spot where the canoes are. And here's the place where that indian village thing is." I pointed to the two areas on the map for the guys to see, while Buster got up and wiggled around under my arms, using his head to butt up against my hands, insisting on being petted. I sat up straight and dragged him over into my lap, petting his chin absently while we discussed our options.

"That looks like it's about an hour from here," said Peter. "We could do that easy."

"What time is it?" asked Bodo. "We want to get dare at da right time, too."

I checked my watch. "It's about nine or so. Yeah, a bit after, actually. It's getting a little late to travel. Canners will be getting up soon."

"How about if we go to the place with the canoes and see if maybe we can stay there today? Then we can take them out to-morrow morning at four or whatever."

I shook my head. "I really don't want to travel through the swamps at night, in the dark, our first time out. We need to see where we're going not only so we can find a good spot but also so we can find our way back out again."

"I'm agreed with dat," said Bodo. "I think we can risk doing dis today, if we hurry. I doubt dat da canners are going to be out in canoes on da water dis early in da morning. Besides, dare prey is on da land, not in da water."

I looked at Peter and he shrugged, apparently not disagreeing with the plan.

"Fine," I said, looking down and realizing with slight disgust that Buster had taken advantage of my preoccupation and was currently several hundred licks into cleaning my hand. I grabbed his muzzle and closed it, turning his face up to look at me. "You're a punk, you know that, Buster?"

His butt wiggled, carried away again by his tail wagging.

"Stop licking me, you freak." I let him go and he jumped out of my lap, barking once at me, obviously excited about the prospect of being called a punk and a freak. I guess so long as someone was talking to him, he was happy.

It made me think of Celia, all alone in that crazy shell shop. She'd been so starved for affection she'd asked the girl she'd tried to beat to death two minutes earlier for a hug. I looked at Bodo, busy packing up our brochures, and Peter pouring out some water for a happily expectant Buster - and once again thanked my lucky stars I had found them. Or that they had found me.

We were almost to our goal, and knock on wood, we were all still alive - over two hundred and fifty miles later. Now all we had to do was find some water transportation, figure out how to use it, and not get eaten by alligators or deer-eating snakes before we found a place to live. Simple.

CHAPTER
THIRTY-SIX

OUR RIDE OVER TO THE canoe rental place was uneventful. We were no longer on the highway and there were very few abandoned cars on this simple, two-lane side road. We passed an occasional broken down roadside fruit stand, but saw no signs of life aside from ourselves. To our left and right were big waterways, some of them flowing and some of them still, dotted with large sections of treed areas, the edges made up of huge roots that looked like elephant trunks, growing right down into the water.

"Look," said Peter, pointing up ahead. "There's a sign for the canoes."

It promised a turn-off in two-tenths of a mile, and a few minutes later there was a faded red arrow pointing us toward a dirt road that disappeared into a forest of pines and high shrubs. The thick vegetation made it impossible to see more than a few feet in.

A strange harmony, unique to the singing cicada bug, rose up around us, lending a spooky air to the place, as we slowly pedaled our way over the sand and pine-needled pathway. We had to slow down for Peter because his bike tires kept catching in the soft surface, throwing him off balance. Eventually he gave up and walked instead, pushing his bike next to him.

"I luff dat sound," said Bodo, "but I've never seen da bugs dat make it."

"Yeah, me neither, and I've lived my entire life in Florida," I said.

"I have. In a bug museum once, stuck with a pin. They're like a big fly, but longer rather than wide."

"It always reminds me of humidity for some reason," I said quietly.

"They come out in summer, so that's probably why."

Buster's head came up and he sniffed the air. I was a little nervous about his reaction to the area, but when he didn't growl or bark, I figured it wasn't a person he was smelling. Even so, I kept glancing toward him as we moved down the road, ready to take his clues for my early warning sign that something was up.

We came around a bend in the road and a smallish green shack came into view. Next to it was a small picnic area and a pitiful looking playground with a single swing and a faded fiberglass slide. I got off my bike and moved closer to Peter. Bodo dismounted too and moved in front of us, the trailer following smoothly behind.

I stopped for a minute, lifting Buster out of the basket and putting him on the ground. "Go see if anyone's there, Buster."

Peter looked at me and frowned.

"What?" I asked, defensively.

"You're sending the bald poodle in as our front line of attack?"

"Why not? He's little and fast. No one's going to hurt him. And he'll bark if he sees or hears anyone."

Peter shrugged. "I guess."

I pulled my gun out of my backpack, deciding that if someone was hungry enough, they might see Buster as a nice little Happy Meal, and maybe I should be prepared to back him up.

But Buster was totally unconcerned for his safety. He sniffed around gaily, peeing on the edge of the slide, the swing set pole, and then the side of the building before wandering off into the bushes to scare some birds. He only hesitated at the door of the shack and sniffed the air a few seconds before moving on.

Bodo parked his bike near the front door of the shack. It was shut and locked. He rattled the handle a couple times just to be sure.

I put my bike next to his and walked a little farther past where we had stopped. Just beyond the shack was a drop-off that led down to a dock. On a small beach next to the dock was a tall rack with six canoes all stacked on it, three by three, chained together and locked up tight. There were two rowboats and one small outboard motor boat, pulled up on the beach, also chained together.

"We have to get into that shack. All the boats and canoes are locked up. Maybe the key's inside."

Bodo disappeared around the right side of the building and then reappeared a few seconds later on the left.

"Dare's a window here in da front and a small one in da back. Neither one iss broken. I think dat's weird."

"Yeah. It's not like this place is out in the middle of nowhere," said Peter, looking at me fearfully.

I went up to the window and tried to look in, but it was pretty dirty, on the inside and the outside. I turned to the guys. "Should we break it?"

"Do we have a choice?" asked Peter. "We have to get those boats loose. And I'm tired of riding this stupid bike. My butt crack is permanently bruised."

"I hear ya," I said. "Bodo, what do you think? Should we break this window or the one in the back?"

"Dis one. The udder one is too small."

"Fine." I walked up to it and hit it with the butt of my gun. A few seconds later the smell hit me. I threw my hand up to my face and backed up. "Oh, crap. Someone's dead in there."

"That doesn't make any sense," said Peter, his face now hidden by the t-shirt he'd pulled up to cover his nose. "Anyone who died before wouldn't still smell, would they?"

"Well, at least we know it is safe to go in," said Bodo, moving toward the window with a large stick he'd found on the ground. He used it to bust out the rest of the glass.

"Unless, of course, they died of something other than the disease that killed the adults," said Peter.

I shook my head. "Well that's a friggin' sunny thought, isn't it?"

"I'm just saying ... we should be careful. There's got to be a reason this place is pretty untouched."

"Maybe no one bothered to come out here because it's a piece of crap that has nothing but canoes and bait."

Peter's face lit up. "Maybe that's the smell ... rotten bait."

Bodo had cleared all the glass and dragged the trailer over so he could stand on it. He was looking inside when he said, "No, I don't think so. It's definitely people. Two of dem."

"Oh, crap," I said. "Can you tell how long ago it was?"

"Not long. A few days or a week, maybe. I'm not an expert in dead thingks. But dey are not moving, so I'm going in."

He laid the blanket that had been covering the grenades over the windowsill, and lifted himself over the edge, disappearing inside headfirst. His feet were the last things we saw before we heard a crash.

"I'm okay!" came his voice from inside. "I chust knocked over some gas cans. Empty ones."

I went over to the window and climbed up on the trailer to look in. Bodo was getting to his feet when he saw me. "Come andt join me. Dare's food in here!"

I glanced at Peter over my shoulder. "I'm going in too. Are you okay out here with Buster?"

"Sure." He took his backpack off and got his gun out, laying it on his bike seat while keeping a hold of the handle. "I've got it covered."

"Okay. I'm going to find those keys first. Then we'll start loading canoes."

I boosted myself up onto the sill and straddled it. Bodo grabbed my waist from inside and lifted me, setting me down in front of him. I looked up, realizing nervously that we were only inches apart. He was taller than I'd ever noticed before - I had to look up to see his face.

He was smiling and his eyes were practically sparkling he looked so happy. He held out his arms. "Hug for good luck?"

I shoved one of them away, trying not to smile. "Get real. I'm not hugging you with dead bodies behind me."

"Dey can't see you," he said, not at all dissuaded by my rejection, his arms still out and in position.

"Maybe some other time."

"Okay. I'll hold you to dat, you know." He dropped his arms.

"I'm sure you will," I mumbled, as I turned and took a few tentative steps toward the cadavers on the floor.

Both of them had been shot in the head. The small caliber weapon that did the messy work was lying nearby. One of the bodies was much smaller than the other - skinny and sickly looking. I couldn't tell if it was that way from the process of decomposition or from the fact that the living person hadn't been well before the bullet had entered her brain. I could tell she was a girl by the dress she was wearing on the day she died.

"Dare's a note here," said Bodo, picking up a piece of paper from the nearby counter.

"Read it."

"*To whom it may concern … my name is William. My sister's name is Rachel. Dis business used to be ownedt by our parents before dey died. Rachel is really sick. She has leukemia and is dying a very painful death. She asked me to end it for her and I finally agkreed. But I know dat once I do it, I won't want to be here alone, so I'm going to go with her.*" Bodo paused a moment to clear his throat. I could tell it was starting to constrict on him, choking him with the emotions he was trying to hold back. I was suffering the same problem. "*She doesn't know it, and I didn't tell her, because if she knew I planned to shoot myself too, she would change her mind and refuse to let me end her suffering. And I know she really wants to go, so I don't want to stop her. But I wanted someone to know what happened so dey wouldn't think I was just some crazy murderer. I love my sister. She's all I have left. So thanks for reading dis. Take whatever you want. The keys for da boats are in da cash register. Sincerely, William.*"

Halfway through the letter, my throat was hurting with the ache of unshed tears. By the time Bodo was done - his own voice having gone scratchy and heavy with sadness - I had begun to cry.

Bodo came from behind the counter and around the back of the shelves to join me by the window again.

He stood there in front of me for a few seconds before I said, "I've changed my mind about that hug."

He reached out and pulled me to him tightly, dropping his face down to rest his chin on the top of my head.

I put my arms around his back, grabbing his shirt and squeezing it in my fists as I cried. "Why does everything have to suck so much?" I asked through my tears.

"It's not all bad, Bryn. Dey have peace now. Dey're togedder now and with no more pain or suffering. It's better dat way for dem, I think."

"Maybe we should just do it, too. Suicide pact. End all the bullshit."

He squeezed me harder. "No, don't say dat. We stick togedder, we make a new life. It will be good, I promise. I take care of you, you take care of me, and togedder we take care of Peter. Okay?" He pulled away and took my head in his hands, forcing me to look at him.

I reached up quickly to wipe the snot off my face, trying to look down, but he wouldn't let me. He was earnestly staring in my eyes, forcing me to respond.

"Fine," I said sullenly, not ready to agree to a new life with so much hope in it.

"I don't belief you. You're chust trying to make me go away."

I smiled in spite of myself. "Yeah. I am. Go away, would you?"

"No way," he said, pulling me in for another hug. "I finally got you to hug me. Now I'm going to be like a litch."

"What's a litch?" I said into his smelly shirt.

"You know, a litch. Dat thing like a snail dat sucks your blood and doesn't come off. From da water."

"Oh, a leech."

"Dat's what I said. A litch."

I laughed, pushing him away from me. "You smell. Go away."

"To smell me is to luff me."

"I'm pretty sure that's not how the saying goes, Bodo."

He moved to go back around the shelves. "New world, new sayingks."

I kept smiling, avoiding looking over at William and Rachel on the floor. Instead I focused on the piles of canned goods that lined the shelves, grabbing them and throwing them out the window.

"Here you go, Peter!" I said. "Get as many on the trailer as you can."

"Okay!"

I could hear him moving around out there so I put the rest of the cans and other things on the windowsill instead, attempting to avoid clunking him on the head by accident.

His face appeared in the opening as he grabbed two cans of green beans. "Wow, this is cool. We can load an entire canoe just with canned goods."

"Yeah, this stuff can hold us over until we figure out how to kill animals to eat or fish or whatever," I said, not exactly relishing the idea of doing that but knowing it was going to be necessary.

"Maybe we can get Bodo to do that part," whispered Peter conspiratorially.

"I hope so," I said, winking at him.

"So what's the deal with the dead people?" he asked.

"I'll tell you later. It's sad."

Peter studied my face a little closer. "You've been crying."

I turned away to grab some more cans. "Yeah. Like I said. It's sad."

Peter didn't say anything in response - he just grabbed what he could in one armload and left with it to find spots for it in the trailer.

Bodo came over with a ring of keys jingling in his hand. "I got da keys. You want me to go unload da canoes?"

"Yes, please. I'll finish getting stuff out of here. I figure we need to get it all now. We can't expect this place to stay untouched for long, now that its protectors are dead."

"Yeah, you're right. Okay, see you later."

He jumped back up on the sill and fell out head first again.

I shook my head at his antics. I'd never known anyone like him before this life-changing event, and I wondered what I would have thought of him if I had met him a year or two years ago.

I also wondered whether he acted this way back then or if the world having changed had somehow made him different.

I knew it had made an impact on the way I acted. It probably should have made me more distrustful and introverted, but it seemed to be having the opposite effect. I was more open to other people now and had lost some of my preconceived notions about people my age. Where before everyone had appeared so different from me, now they all seemed the same. Maybe they had different wrappers on the outside, but inside we were all just … people - the only exception being the canners. They were nothing like me. Inside they were monsters, hidden on the outside by wrappers that looked normal.

I shook my head, trying to make the visions of the two canners who I'd had the close encounters with leave my mind. I thought of Bodo's eyes instead, how they looked when they stared at me while he reassured me that everything was going to be okay. It brought me a measure of peace, and even made it possible for me to look over at the brother and sister on the floor without feeling sick. I noticed for the first time that they were holding hands.

"Thanks, William and Rachel. We appreciate you sharing your parents' stuff with us. We'll put it to good use, I promise."

"Who are you talking to in there?" asked Peter, his face at the windowsill again.

"No one … myself. Here." I handed him a bag of Doritos.

"Holy crap-on-a-stick, Bryn, it's a bag of nacho cheese Doritos!"

I smiled. "I know. We're going to have a serious party tonight."

CHAPTER
THIRTY-SEVEN

B Y THE TIME I HAD emptied the small shack of anything we could use, Bodo had taken all the canoes down and lined them up on the beach. Each one had two oars inside it, one with a wide paddle-part and one with a narrower one. I'd never used a canoe before so I had no idea what difference the sizes would make. Something told me I was going to find out soon enough.

"Let me help you with that," I said to Peter, as he struggled to maneuver the trailer to the edge of the bank that led down to the canoes.

"Thanks."

Buster kept running down to the canoes and then back up to the trailer, apparently excited about the idea of whatever we were doing. I didn't know about small poodles being much for the water, but he sure seemed to think it was cool.

"We should do an assembly line thing," suggested Peter. "I'll throw stuff down to you one at a time and you can pass it to Bodo to put in the canoe."

"Works for me," I said, looking over to Bodo for his approval.

"Sure. Go aheadt. I'm ready."

Peter began with the canned goods. I managed to only drop about one out of every ten cans, but I blamed it on Peter and his not so amazing tossing skills.

"I'm over here, Peter, not over there."

"Sor-ry. I'm trying to get them right to you but they're different sizes. It's hard to estimate the force exactly right."

"Excuses, excuses," I teased.

"I'm not going to throw the chips. I don't want to break the seals on the bags."

"Good thinking."

Once we'd moved the lighter items, the last things remaining were the grenades, backpacks, and the bikes and trailer themselves. One canoe was almost completely full of the other stuff. Bodo came up to join Peter and me at the top of the bank.

"What are we going to do with da bikes?" he asked.

"I don't know. It's not like we can ride them in the water or use them in the small bits of floating forests there are out there."

"Yeah," said Peter, "but we're going to want to have them to go look for things when we need to later ... back in that town. I mean, we're not going to be out in the swamps forever and ever without ever leaving for anything, right?"

I shook my head. "Probably not."

"So we need to keep dem. But do we need to take dem with us is da question."

"I don't think we should leave them here. Someone will eventually find them and take them."

"Okay, den. So we bring dem with us. We need to disconnect da trailer."

"I'll get on that. You guys get the other two bikes down there and the sensitive cargo that's left in the trailer."

Thirty minutes later we had everything to our names piled up in three canoes. We tried to stack all the bikes in one, but it made it too top-heavy and it looked like it could tip over too easy. We sat on the dock, drinking water from our bottles and eating a bag of the chips we had found in the shack. I handed a few to Buster who crunched away at them and then licked up every single crumb that dropped.

He drank water out of my cupped hand for a few seconds and then gave up, running down to the water's edge to drink from there.

"So do we go in one canoe together and pull the other ones somehow? Or are we going to each take one alone?" asked Peter.

"I will tell you what I think," said Bodo. "You guyss go in two empty canoes, with Peter in da front. We can attach da three canoes with our stuff to you, Bryn, and each udder. Den, I can follow in a canoe with all da udder boats behindt me."

"Like a big convoy," said Peter, smiling.

"It's not ideal, but I guess it's the only way we can make sure that we don't leave behind a boat for someone to follow us with."

"Is the current strong?" asked Peter.

"I have no idea. I guess we're going to find out."

"We can handle it. It's not a problem." Bodo beamed at us, rubbing his hands together in excitement. "We are almost home, guyss! I can feel it! And I haff extra energy right now, so we should use it before I get tiredt again."

"You're right," I said, standing up and brushing myself off. I wasn't really sure why I bothered, since my jeans were beyond ever being clean again. Maybe because old habits die hard. "Might as well do this now. I don't want to be fighting currents or alligators when the canners might be out and about, listening."

"Alligators?" asked Peter meekly. "Are you serious?"

"Kind of. I mean, they do live here, you know."

"Yeah, but they're shy right?"

I shrugged. "Let's hope so."

Peter stood up. "Bryn, sometimes I don't know if your lack of concern is bravery or … something else."

"Tell me you weren't going to say stupidity."

"I didn't say it," said Peter, trying to look innocent.

"Go ahead, call me stupid. But I got us this far."

"Yes, you did," soothed Bodo. "You're not stupid, you're brave. Maybe a little more creatif dan udder people, but dat's a good thing to me."

"Thank you, Bodo," I said, just before sticking my tongue out at Peter.

"I'm sorry, he's right. Without you I would have been sitting in my aunt's house still, looking at my last batch of tomato sauce and wondering where I was going to find my next meal."

I smiled hugely. "And here you are, getting ready to float away with a bunch of boats filled with baked beans and nacho cheese Doritos instead! How can you possibly doubt my awesomeness?"

"It's gonna be gassy in this swamp," he said, giggling.

"You'd better not, Peter. You'll get kicked off the island. I'm not kidding."

He just shrugged, stepping off the dock and going over to an empty canoe. "What are we connecting these things together with?"

"Da chain," said Bodo, picking up one end of it and passing it through a metal loop on the front of an empty canoe. He dragged it down the length of the boat, clanking and banging it along its side until he got to the next one. He only had three of them strung together when he ran out of links. "We think needt a rope."

"I saw one in the shack," I said.

"I'll go get it," offered Peter, scrambling up the bank.

"It's behind the counter!" I yelled. "Grab the blanket off the windowsill on your way back!"

"Okay!"

"I probably should have already taken that rope. I didn't think we'd need it but that was stupid."

"Don't worry about it. We can come back and get da last few thingks later. Nobody expects you to be perfect all da time."

"I do," I said, thinking about how hard my dad had worked to be precise and careful with his decisions and actions. I kept thinking that if I just did what I could now to live up to his standards, it would somehow keep him from floating away out of my memory or something. I was afraid to think that at some point, I was going to start forgetting what his face looked like.

I pulled the picture of him and me out of my pocket and stared at it while I waited for Peter to come back.

Bodo came over and stood next to me. "Is dat your dad?"

"Yeah. We were somewhere here in the Everglades."

"Dat's cool. Dat means his spirit is already here."

I smiled. "Yeah, I guess so. I never thought of it that way."

Peter came back with the rope still coiled and the blanket, much more subdued than he was before. "There are some slivers of glass in this thing. I don't know what you want to do about that."

"Just fold it over to cover them. We'll worry about getting them out later. I think we can still use it."

Peter balled up the blanket and shoved it in the canoe with our backpacks. "Are we ready?" he asked, standing in the sand and looking down at the ground.

"What's wrong with you?" I asked. His sudden change of mood was strange.

"I saw the two kids in there."

"Oh. Yeah. I'll tell you about them later."

"I read the note."

I walked over and gave his shoulders a quick squeeze. "Sorry. It sucks, I know."

"I know it's better that she's not suffering anymore. Maybe they're the smart ones."

"No, they're not. Come on, let's get out of here. It's too depressing. Let's go find our new hang out."

Peter picked up Buster and walked over to the canoe in front and sat inside at the back of it, putting Buster down by his feet. "I'm ready whenever you guys are."

Bodo and I exchanged glances, saying nothing.

CHAPTER
THIRTY-EIGHT

BODO WENT INTO THE WATER and pulled the first canoe out with Peter on board, pointing it toward the center of the waterway.

"Go aheadt. Get in," he said, gesturing to me and the canoe behind Peter that was now in a few feet of water.

"No, I'm going to help you get the rest of these in, first."

"Yeah, okay. Maybe dat's better," he said, looking worriedly at the group of boats that still needed to go out.

Together we wrestled the heavy ones into the water and got them floating behind Peter.

Peter's boat kept trying to go diagonal on him, and he was having a heck of a time trying to keep it straight.

"Try the other paddle," I suggested.

"What difference does it make?" he said, clearly frustrated.

"One has a bigger paddle part. Maybe it won't make any difference, I don't know."

He threw the one he was using behind him in the boat and dragged the other one forward, looking at the end with a critical eye. "I don't see any difference." He put it in the water and moved it around. "Oh, wait. There is a difference. Cancel my last complaint."

I smiled, noticing his boat was already more under control.

"I think when you haff two people in da boat, da one riding in da back gets the bigger paddle," said Bodo, watching Peter stroke it through the water. Even just a small movement made the boat adjust quickly.

"Yeah, I think you're right," agreed Peter, sounding a lot more confident now. Buster let out a sharp, happy bark, looking at us with his tongue hanging out.

There was just one last boat, the one with the tiny engine on it, left to push out.

"Go get in your canoe, Bryn. I got dis one."

I waded out into the water, trying not to stress out over the fact that it was getting pretty deep and that any alligator that wanted a snack could be under there and I'd never see it until it was too late.

I gave up on walking all the way to the boat, since the water was too deep, and used the rope to pull it closer to me instead. Once it was in front of my chest, I put my hands on the edge to jump in; but as soon as I pushed down on it, the whole thing tipped sideways. I tried three times before I smacked the water in frustration.

"How the heck am I supposed to get in this friggin' thing?"

Buster was dancing around and whining, dipping the front of his body down toward me. He looked like he was thinking of jumping in to help me. I was relieved to see Peter put his hand on the dog's back, settling him down. Buster abandoned the idea of saving me in favor of lick-attacking Peter's hand.

"Wait a minute. I'm coming."

Bodo swam over and got on the opposite side of the canoe. "I'll hold dis side down. Now you use the edge to pull yourself in."

This time when I grabbed it, the leverage Bodo gave me on the other side kept the canoe from tipping. The water added another forty pounds or so to my body weight, at least that's what it felt like, but I was finally able to pull myself in and flop over into the boat. The seat shelf that was moulded to the inside of the canoe jammed into my back, and I knew I was going to be feeling that for a few days after.

"Thanks, Bodo. Pull yours up next to me so I can help you."

I nearly flipped my own canoe trying to provide him the counterbalance for his entry, but eventually we were all in our own boats and no longer tethered to dry land. It was a weird sensation, floating freely while also being connected to everything and everyone that meant something to me.

"I wonder if this is what Christopher Columbus felt like," said Peter, paddling. He was already looking like a semi-pro the way he was maneuvering his canoe.

I followed behind, trying the different paddles so I could get a feel for them. I wasn't nearly as coordinated as Peter was, no matter which one I used.

"Hey! You're pulling my rear end off balance," he accused, struggling to paddle backward with his oar and readjust his position.

"I'm not even touching your rear end, you big baby."

"You're connected to it, though. Steer straighter."

"I'm trying. It's not that easy." My canoe seemed to have a mind of its own, the nose of it first going left and then right.

"Less muscle, more finesse," suggested Peter.

"Fine," I grumbled. I didn't like not being good at things. Usually when I tried something and put a lot of effort into it, I was successful. Canoes, so far, were one of my few failures, but I wasn't going to give up so easily.

"Looks good from back here," said Bodo. "I think we're gonna be okay."

"Not a problem!" shouted Peter.

"Yeah, it's not a problem, Bodo," I said, smiling with the happiness of our team-level success and the joy of mocking my friend.

"You guyss are making fun of me again, I know dat. But da joke iss on you, because now you are using my words. Dat means I am a leader and you are my followerss!"

"All hail King Bodo!" I said in a thundering voice.

"We are not worthy," joined in Peter. He turned to shoot me a huge grin, making me thrilled to see him so happy. It was the first time in a couple days that the shroud of sorrow had truly lifted from his face for just a few seconds.

We continued down the easy-flowing waterway for what seemed like miles. It twisted and turned, making its way farther and farther into a more heavily-treed area. There were huge cypress hammocks surrounding us now, with long tresses of Spanish moss hanging down. The roots of the trees had grown into strange shapes, some of them stretching out to join the limbs and roots of nearby trees, causing them to look almost like people holding hands ... or in some cases, strangling each other. The filtered light and the little bugs flying lazily around lent a very spooky feeling to the place. It was almost as if we were in another world entirely.

The current picked up, making controlling our canoes more difficult. The more heavily-laden boats got pulled this way and that, making the control of our three manned boats almost impossible. Peter's canoe ran into an outcropping of a bank for the fifth time in as many minutes.

"Dammit!" he yelled. "I can't get this thing to go straight anymore." He was paddling backward madly when he suddenly stopped and sat up straighter. "Oh my god," he said, sounding like a happy child. "They are so cool!"

Buster ran to the front of the canoe, barking like crazy. He paused only to run over to Peter and then back to the front one before going nuts again. Something was seriously exciting to the fuzzy pink guy.

"What's so cool?" I said absently, trying to keep from dragging the rear end of Peter's boat around again, since it was making him so cranky. It was taking most of my concentration and back muscles.

"There's like five ... no seven ... well, more like twenty pretty salamander gecko things here. They're crawling all over this tree root mess."

I looked up to see what he was talking about. We had plenty of those kinds of creatures in Florida. A person couldn't walk across a sidewalk without twenty lizards scrambling to get out of the way. I swear, they stood on the edges of walkways and dared each other to cross whenever a giant human came by.

I couldn't see the salamanders because they were too far away and hidden. The place where Peter was gesturing toward was behind a big root that blocked my view. Buster sure seemed pretty excited about them, though.

"I can't see dem," said Bodo. "What are dey doing?"

"They're crawling all over. And swimming too! I've never seen geckos swim before."

Neither had I.

"What do they look like?" I asked.

"They're black with yellow stripes on them. Long tails."

Something was clicking in my brain, nagging me that these gecko salamanders were something I remembered seeing before.

"How many of them are there?" I asked again.

"A ton. More than ten. Maybe more than twenty. They're everywhere. It's like a nest of them or something."

The word 'nest' set off the alarm bells. Then Bodo's next words sent my pulse into overdrive.

"Um, guyss? I think dare's a gator coming dis way."

I turned around as fast as I could to look at him, ready to scream at him if he was joking around; but he was pointing just off to my right, and when I looked in the direction he was pointing, I saw that sure enough, a huge log-looking thing was making a beeline for Peter's boat, its eyes and snout visible above the water as it cut a V through the current. It was moving fast - a hell of a lot faster than we were.

"Peter, those aren't geckos! They're baby gators! Get the hell out of there!"

Peter screamed like a girl and back-paddled as fast as his skinny arms could take him.

I did the same, feeling the burn in the muscles of my arms and back as I strained them to the maximum, trying to pull not only my boat, but Peter's away from the nest.

Buster changed his focus from the nest to the gator. He ran to the side of the canoe and barked like a dog possessed. He wanted to get out of that boat and tear that gator to shreds, from the sound of it.

"Ohmygod, ohmygod, ohmygod," cried Peter, his boat now moving back only a few inches from the nest. "Buster! Shut up!"

The gator was about fifteen feet away.

"Bodo, help!" I yelled.

I felt a jerking motion coming from behind me. Bodo had taken the rope tying us all together and was hauling back on it. It moved us toward him a little, but it moved him toward us too.

"Wait!" I yelled, dropping my oar. "You paddle back. I'll pull Peter!"

Bodo grabbed his big oar and got up to kneel in the bottom of the boat. I spared him just a glance before I grabbed the chain that held Peter's boat to mine. As soon as I felt my boat moving backward, I pulled on Peter's.

The gator was now only five feet away. Peter's boat was less than two feet from the nest.

"Keep going!" he screeched. "She's coming!"

As soon as the end of Peter's boat bumped into mine, I dropped the chain and scooted on my butt up to the front, leaning over to take the edge of his boat in hand. I jerked back on it hard, using the leverage of Bodo's backward pull to keep my boat from moving forward.

Peter's body leaned forward involuntarily as I pulled his canoe up alongside mine, putting a good six feet between us and the baby gators. He snatched at Buster and pulled him into his arms, putting his hand over the dog's mouth to try and muzzle him.

Bodo continued to pull us back a few more feet, while Peter and I watched silently. The momma gator swam up to her babies and opened her mouth. Several jumped in, and for a second, I thought she was going to eat them. But then I noticed several more getting on top of her head. She closed her mouth partway and then climbed up out of the water, into the roots of the tree that had sheltered her babies.

"Holy crap. Did you just see that?" said Peter in hushed tones. Buster continued to struggle and whine in his arms, but Peter kept a hold on him.

"Yes. And I never *ever* want to see it again."

"Paddles, guyss, paddles. Bodo iss getting tiredt."

"Oh, yeah ... sorry," I mumbled, scrambling to my spot at the back of the boat and picking up my paddle on the way. I used the end of it to shove Peter's boat away from me.

"Peter, if you don't mind, I'd prefer it if you could avoid running into gator nests for the rest of this trip."

"Shut up," he said, putting Buster back down and stroking his oar into the water, moving to lead our convoy again. "It wasn't me. It was the paddle."

CHAPTER
THIRTY-NINE

I DECIDED THAT GIVING PETER a hard time about his paddling was a bad idea. My lack of canoeing skills was a slow form of torture for all of us.

"Here I go again," sighed Peter. "Pushed into the bank because someone can't seem to stop dragging my ass end over into the Netherlands. Good thing there's no gator nest on this one."

I laughed. "The Netherlands?"

"It's the best I could come up with," he said, slapping the water with his paddle. "Can we stop for a while, please. I'm too tired to go any farther. I give up." He rested the paddle across his thighs, looking back at us.

"I think dat's a good idea," said Bodo from behind me.

"Okay, I'm outvoted. First good pull-over spot you see, park your canoe, Peter. We'll figure out the rest."

Peter paddled with renewed energy, and five minutes later pointed out his choice. "There! That's where I'm aiming."

We were in a darker part of the cypress bog now, trees completely covering the space above our heads, leaving a canopy that started about fifteen feet up. Peter had taken a fork in the river to the left about a mile back. I would have gone right, following the small and unobtrusive signs the canoe rental people had attached to nearby trees, but I was letting him lead the way.

The spot Peter was planning to have our picnic was spooky - definitely not the spot I would have chosen - but I knew he was at his wit's end, so kept my mouth shut about it.

His canoe ran into a system of tangled roots that belonged to a huge tree with branches hanging over the water to reach the other side. Peter scrambled not very gracefully out of his boat and balanced on a long narrow root, his sneakers bending in half over it, making him look like a giant scraggly bird gripping the thing with its talons. He was doing what he could to hold the canoe in place, so we could join him. "Ready for you, guys," he said, grunting a little with the effort of holding his canoe.

Buster was the first to follow his orders. He jumped out easily, sniffing around ambitiously.

I decided to forget trying to paddle into any sort of organized parking spot next to him since my capabilities were so limited. I eyed the water, looking all around me for clues that a gator was waiting to eat me, slapping at the mosquitos that had come out in the shade to suck my tired blood.

Deciding that there were no hungry-looking gators in evidence, I got out of the boat and into the water, grumbling to myself the whole way. "Stupid swamp … Stupid mosquitoes … Stupid gators."

"Stupid canoes!" added Bodo.

I looked up at him from the water and smiled, knowing that at least for me, the old adage was true: misery loves company.

Peter held his hand out and helped me schlep out of the water. I hated the squishy feeling in my shoes, but tried to ignore it. We were going to be living in a swamp; chances are, squishy shoes were going to be a regular part of my life. Buster came up and started licking them.

I shooed him away so I could use the chain and then the rope to secure the boats to our landing site without squashing him.

Bodo was the last to arrive, getting out in the water like I had to come join us. "Well," he said, a huge grin on his face, "dat was exciting, wasn't it?"

Peter looked at him, just shaking his head. "Are all Germans as crazy as you, Bodo?"

"Maybe. If you think being happy about life is crazy, den yes."

"Bodo, how is it that you were wandering around the highway all by yourself that day that we saw you?" It was a huge puzzle to me that a guy like him, funny and so positive, had been alone. It seemed like he'd be the type of guy that would have a flock of people around him.

"Well, maybe I will tell you dat story anudder time. Right now, I want to eat. All dat gator evasion hass made me hungry." He was massaging his biceps for effect, looking over to the boats that held our food.

I studied his face in profile, trying to figure out if he was purposely avoiding my question or if he was just being a guy - more concerned with his stomach than anything else. I decided to give him the benefit of the doubt. Eventually we'd learn his story. I didn't ever feel threatened around him, so I wasn't worried that he was going to spring a I'm-a-reformed-canner-story on us.

"What do you guys want to eat?" I asked.

"Nothing that has to be heated. Too much trouble," said Peter.

"Beans and chips iss good," suggested Bodo.

"Beans and chips it is."

We dragged the boats over and busied ourselves with handing out food and water for everyone. Gathering the water bottles to hand them out, I noticed that we were low.

"As soon as we find our final spot, we need to set up a water catcher. Or just later today, if we haven't found something by then. This is the last of the good stuff," I said, holding up my bottle that was half empty.

Peter stood. "I'm going to go take care of business," he frowned at me, "and don't say what I know you're thinking about saying, Bryn. Just because we're swamp dwellers now, doesn't mean we have to act déclassé."

"Oooh, gettin' all fancy on us now, are we? What is that? French?"

"Shut up," he said, disappearing into the trees with Buster happily bouncing off behind him, leaving Bodo and me alone.

"What does dat word mean dat he said … déclassé?"

"It means common. Don't act rude, basically. He doesn't like it when I ask him if he's going to doodle."

"What is doodle? Dat's when you draw on a paper, right?"

I smiled. "Yeah. That's what it means."

"I don't understand why he gets mad about drawing. It's not rude to draw. I am good with doodling myself, actually."

I tried to hide the smile on my face behind my water bottle. "Oh, you are, huh?"

"Oh yes. You would be surprised, I think. I doodle all over da place when I'm in da mood."

"Like, where?" I laughed out.

Bodo looked at me confused, but continued. "I doodle in da house, of course, and also at school."

"Doesn't everyone, though?" I asked, all innocence.

"Yes, but does everyone doodle in the bathroom? I don't think so. Dat's where I do it sometimes."

"Oh, I do it there all the time. Or I used to anyway. Now I just do it outside."

"Yes, well, when we find a new place, I'm gonna doodle dare."

"No, you're not." I said with a straight face.

"Yes, I am," he assured me. "You will see. I'm gonna doodle right on our house, to make it look nicer."

Peter came walking up. "What are you guys talking about?"

I smiled. "Well, Bodo was just telling me here that he likes to doodle. He doodles all over the place. In fact, he's planning to doodle right on our house, to make it prettier."

Peter looked at Bodo aghast. "What is your problem? That's just sick! I'm not going to let you guys turn into savages just because we're living in this wild place."

Bodo's face was the picture of cluelessness. "I don't understand. What is so wrong with drawing pictures on our house? Dey will be very nice, I promise."

Peter rolled his eyes and sighed loudly at Bodo, and then glared at me. "Bryn. That is so, so wrong. On *so* many levels."

I was laughing, unable to stop. When Bodo asked Peter, "What is dis? Why is she laughing?" And Peter answered, "Doodle is another word for poop. As in shit? Get it?" I lost it completely. Bodo giving me the evil eye, and then swearing he was going to get me back, only made it worse.

"Bodo," said Peter, taking on his hoity-toity tone, "I'm going to address this next question to the grown-ups in the room. Do you want to go see the awesomely amazing thing that I saw when I was … away just a minute ago?"

"Doodling!" I gasped out before collapsing in giggles again. I had no idea why bodily functions were so entertaining to me right now, but I decided not to fight it. I was getting totally high from the brain chemicals and I wanted more.

"Come on," said Peter, leading Bodo away.

Bodo cast a few bemused glances back my way, making me think that I'd probably shown him one of the uglier sides of my American personality, but I totally didn't care. If he couldn't like me for me, he could go join Celia at her shell shop.

My laughter faded out, tempered a little by the idea of Bodo leaving to be with another girl somewhere else. My stomach felt a little funny, and not in a good way. *Is that jealously I'm feeling? Weird.* I'd never really had that feeling in relation to a guy before - probably because I'd never really had a boyfriend or wanted one so badly that I let thoughts of competition bother me. The only thing I could remember being jealous of in the past was someone's krav maga level. *Interesting.*

I wasn't sure if I was pleased or distressed by my growing feelings for Bodo. It made me uncomfortable that they seemed to have a life of their own, completely out of my conscious control; but they also made me happy in a way. I pictured what it would be like to kiss him and felt my face going pink. I quickly brushed the thought out of my mind. The last thing I needed to be doing was mooning over some guy who was probably only playing around when he asked for hugs. Unrequited crushes sucked. I'd had them before, so I knew.

A few minutes later, after I'd cleaned up our lunch mess, Peter and Bodo returned with Buster at their heels, the expressions on their faces telling me something big was up.

"Bryn, you have to come see dis," said Bodo, holding out his hand to help me up. "Come on. We'll show you."

I took it and stood. "What is it?"

Peter walked back the way he had come. "Just come on. You'll see."

I followed behind the guys, trying to keep up in my slippery shoes. I could hear gross squishing sounds as my weight pushed water out of all of their crevices, making me wonder what would happen to the skin of my feet if they stayed wet all the time. *Are they going to be permanently pruned? Start to rot off?*

Before I could contemplate the full magnitude of that awfulness, a structure appeared. Rising up out of the swamp was a shack. Actually, it was more than a shack. It was like a full-fledged hut, with a palm-thatched roof and poles holding it up above the water and everything. The only thing it was missing was walls, which probably didn't matter much because it was so damn hot and humid in here, they would have just blocked the breeze anyway.

"What the heck?" I said, walking up to stand next to Bodo and holding onto his arm to keep from slipping down into the roots that were woven beneath my feet and keeping us suspended over the water.

Peter whispered, "See the paintings on that post over there? I think this is indian land."

"Yeah," whispered Bodo loudly. "Dose are da kind of doodles I wass talking about." He gave me a quick frown before looking back at the structure.

I stifled a laugh. "Is it empty?" I prayed it was, because we had stupidly left all of our weapons back at the canoes. I had no sooner gotten that prayer completed when I heard a voice behind me that made my hair stand on end.

CHAPTER
FORTY

W HO ARE YOU?" BUSTER WAS barking his head off, running over to get in between me and the newcomer.

I turned slowly to face him, my eyes nearly bugging out of my head at the sight that greeted me. I felt like I'd been transported into the pages of my high school history book. I reached my foot out and hooked it around Buster's chest, dragging him back to me and then shoving him farther over so Peter could pick him up and try to quiet him down.

"Wow," said Bodo, taking in the guy's shaved head and the tribal tattoos that covered his chest and arms, obscured only by a small vest made out of some kind of cloth that had bright designs woven into it. "Now dat's what I call some warrior doodles."

Peter cleared his throat while he held the dog's mouth shut. "We're not a threat to you. We just came here looking for a place to live. Away from the crazy people." Buster struggled a little bit, some muffled barks making their way out.

God, how I prayed this guy wasn't one of those kooks … because he had an arrow pointed at my heart and his fingers looked like they were itching to let it fly.

"This is Miccosukee land. You're trespassing. We don't want you here."

I don't know what possessed me to speak, but once the words were out it was too late and useless to regret them. "Not anymore it's not."

He sneered at me. "We claim all of the Kahayatle for our own. You think you can take it away from us?"

I raised an eyebrow. "Kaha-*what*? Who's *us*? I don't know what the hell you just said, but all I see standing here is you."

"Then you see like all the other white men who came before you. *Not very well.*"

My hackles rose and my eyes darted around, looking for others. I couldn't see anyone but the guy in front of me, so I figured he was bluffing. I took one step forward, working to adjust my footing so I was better-balanced and in a position to immobilize him, should he decide to get frisky. He didn't move, so we were just two feet away from each other now.

He lifted his bow a little bit higher and pulled the arrow back farther. "Don't move or I *will* kill you." He was aiming for a face shot now.

"Not today, you won't," I said softly. A split second later I slashed my arm out toward him, knocking his bow to the side, while simultaneously leaning over to protect myself from any flying arrows. His now un-notched weapon, loosened by my fist's impact, fell to the ground and wedged its lethal end in the roots at our feet.

I heard the slick, deadly soft sound of a knife leaving its sheath and quickly brought my other forearm across in a flattened arch, connecting with his wrist with enough force to send the weapon flying from his hand. I caught a quick flash of it out of the corner of my eye, noticing that its blade was a nasty one, meant for skinning animals and sawing through tendon and bone. A spasm of relief that I hadn't been gutted by that thing skittered across my brain as I continued to exercise the well-practiced motions I had often used to bring a man who out-weighed me by fifty pounds down to my level on the practice mat.

I swept my foot low and backward, taking him out by the ankles, ending the move by slamming myself down on top of him with one foot at his throat. I leaned back, grabbing his leg and pulling it up to keep him from hooking me with it. I could feel his body tense up beneath me, as he got ready to try and throw me off.

"I wouldn't do that if I were you!" I warned. I pushed my foot up into his chin harder, making it painfully clear that my intentions were serious and that my final move would be even worse for him than my earlier ones had already been.

"Fine!" he grunted out through gritted teeth. "I give."

Buster got loose from Peter's arms and ran over to start licking the guy's face, taking a few precious seconds in between licks to bark at all of us in excitement.

I ignored the rest of the dog's performance and looked up briefly at Bodo who was standing there and staring at us on the ground, as if in a trance.

"Check him for weapons, Bodo." I waited for him to obey, not moving my foot an inch.

Bodo came over and bent down, touching the guy's body all over and pulling out another small knife from a strap around his ankle, hidden under his pants.

"I can't check da back of him. You haff to get off."

I grabbed onto Bodo's forearm and pulled myself up, hopping on one foot a couple times until I could get my other one under me. I reached down and grabbed the indian kid by his vest, hauling him roughly to his feet and spinning him around once he was upright. He lifted his arm up and I tensed, ready to take him down again, until I realized he was just wiping the dog slobber off his face.

"Check him now," I said, angrily, pissed that this guy had made me do this to him. It just felt wrong to take out an indian on his own land like that. I hadn't really meant it earlier when I'd said it wasn't his. *Who the hell am I to decide whose land is whose?*

"He's got nothing."

I turned him around and released him, stepping back to give him some space. I saw him look on the ground toward his fallen bow.

"Don't even *think* about it, Mikko."

His head jerked back up. "What'd you call me?"

"Mikko. Miccosukee, right?"

His eyes narrowed at me.

I raised an eyebrow at him in challenge.

"My name isn't Mikko. It's Yokci."

"What does it mean?" asked Peter, stepping up to stand beside me.

"None of your business," he said, now a proud, stubborn look on his face.

"I think it means loner," I said.

"No, it doesn't."

"Bald guy?"

"No." The tiniest flicker of amusement appeared at the corner of his mouth, and then was quickly replaced with a scowl.

"Swamp thing."

He sighed, looking wistfully at his bow again. "Close."

"Your name means *Swamp Thing?*" I asked, not believing I had actually guessed it.

"No. If you must know, it means *turtle.*"

I tried not to laugh but it was really, really hard. No one said anything. It was totally quiet for a few seconds until I lost it and snorted, no longer able to hold in my mirth. I held up my hand, saying, "I'm sorry. That's *so* bad of me to laugh, I know."

"She has a problem," said Peter. "We're working on it with her."

"He wass pretty slow, dough, wasn't he? Just like a turtle," said Bodo, "Bryn took him down in less dan ten seconds. It wass pretty cool, actually."

The guy frowned. "That depends on your perspective."

"Says the turtle," I quipped.

He glared at me.

I decided to appease him by sharing some of my more positive thoughts. "Love the tattoos."

He glanced down at his arms without expression. "Thanks."

"Do they mean anything?" asked Peter, staring a little too hard at Yokci's chest which was plainly visible through the opening in his undone vest. The body art was pretty cool and the body they were on wasn't bad either. Peter looked like he was going to start salivating any second.

"Yes." He didn't volunteer anything else and still remained totally passive, making me wonder if they taught that whole in-dian-brave-of-few-words-thing in the cradle.

"So what are we going to do now?" asked Bodo, once he real-ized that Yokci wasn't going to elaborate.

"Yokci, we're from up north of here ... Orlando area. We're looking for a new place to live, out of the way of ... other people," I said. "This place looks pretty cool." I gestured toward the hut. "Is is free?" It didn't look like it was being used, but that was probably the beauty of it. Maybe the area behind it was full of painted warriors with arrows pointed at us. I liked the idea of being able to surprise unsuspecting canners who stupidly came looking for their next meal in the Kaha-*whatever-whatever* that Yokci had called this place.

"That is a ceremonial lodge that we use ... or used to use some-times. It's empty now, but you can't have it."

"Why not?" asked Peter, putting his hands on his hips. Even he was starting to sound feisty now.

"Because, we plan to use it for rituals. Once we have our ... situation figured out."

"What situation?" asked Bodo.

"Tribe business."

I rolled my eyes. "Whatever. If we want the place, we'll take it; it's as simple as that. Give me a better reason why I shouldn't want it, Yokci. Otherwise, I'm gonna go stick my flag in it or whatever." When I said it, I was picturing Neil Armstrong on the moon. I didn't even have a flag, nor did I know what my flag would look like, if I were to design a new one. *Maybe a giant 'Canner' with a circle around it and a line drawn through the middle?* I didn't think Bodo's bright orange bicycle flag would make the statement I was going for.

"You don't want this place for lots of reasons. Mainly, though, because there are better ones elsewhere." He ran his hands across his bald head, rubbing it back and forth a few times. There was still a tuft of hair on the back part, which was tied in several places like a ponytail, kind of. It hung down to a spot just above his shoulder blades. I had to admit - it totally went with the badass indian warrior thing he had going on. Too bad his fighting skills sucked so bad.

"Where?" asked Peter. I could practically read his mind - he was hoping he didn't have to do too much more paddling with me behind him jerking his canoe all over the place.

Yokci turned and gestured toward where our canoes were sitting. "Continue on that waterway where you were going, take the next two splits to the left, and you'll find it."

"Why shouldt we belief you?" asked Bodo.

"Because he's going to go with us and show us personally, aren't you, Turtle?"

"No," he said, all offended now.

"Yeah. You are. And I'm going to have your pretty knife at your back the whole time too, while you paddle my canoe." I bent over and pulled it out of the roots where it had landed, wiping it off on my pants and slapping the flat of its blade in my hand. The thing was seriously heavy.

Peter looked at me and nodded his head. "Nicely done, Bryn ... getting the escort to do all the work."

I shrugged. "Just want to be sure he's not going to lead us into a trap, is all."

"It's not a trap. And if you try to take me with you, you'll be captured and either killed or sent out of the Kahayatle with nothing."

"He means Everglades," said Peter.

"I know what he means," I said, a challenge now in my voice. "I think he's full of crap. He's the only one here and he's just trying to intimidate us."

He shrugged nonchalantly. "Think what you want, but consider yourself warned."

"Why haven't dey come to rescue you? Where are all dese friendts of yourss when Bryn wass taking you down?"

"Good question," said Yokci, before letting out an earsplitting whistle that almost sounded like a bird.

Several answering calls came from out in the swamp. At least four of them that I could make out.

"Shit, he wasn't kidding, Bryn," whined Peter, tiptoeing over to stand right next to me. He grabbed onto my arm, but I shook him off. I couldn't have him hanging on me if I was going to have to make some moves on this guy again, otherwise, both of us would end up getting hurt.

Bodo spun around and looked out into the trees. "I don't see anything."

"I do," I said, looking out behind Yokci. Coming out from the far side of a big tree was another indian kid. This one was bigger and also tattooed all over his bare arms and chest with a bald head and a topknot ponytail thing. He even had a tattoo on his cheek. It was one black stripe, going from below his eye to his jawbone. He moved over the lumpy tangle of roots without looking down and without faltering. He looked graceful and dangerous.

"Nice of you to show up," said Yokci sarcastically to the tribesman coming up to stand beside him.

The guy held his hand out as if to shake mine. His bow and arrows stayed on his back, but I just stood there and stared at his hand. He looked down at it and up at me, raising an eyebrow, as if daring me to take it.

I slapped my hand into it, squeezing it hard, making sure he knew I was not to be messed with. He stared me dead in the eye the whole time, and I was pretty sure he knew that letting me touch him like this was a risky proposition for him.

"Kowi," he said.

"What does that mean? Hello?"

"No. Hello is 'chehuntamo'. Kowi is my name."

I let go of his hand. "What's it mean?"

"Panther."

I nodded. It suited him. "Did you always have that name or did you take it … recently?"

"The name given to me by my mother was Michael. I took my new name when the disease took our parents and elders and we were forced to adopt some of our older and almost forgotten customs."

"Is that when you added the tattoos too?" asked Peter.

He nodded, still only looking at me. "Why are you here?"

I decided the best way to deal with this panther guy was to be dead honest. Obviously, there were more indians around us right now, how many I had no idea, and I wasn't exactly sure what had kept us alive to this point, but maybe it was curiosity or even kindness. I prayed it wasn't the meat on our bones.

"We came from Orlando. Kids are going nuts out there and eating other kids. We just want to find a place where we can live in peace."

"You do not seem to be a peaceful person to me. You've been trained to fight."

"I've been trained to protect myself and my family." I looked briefly at Bodo and Peter who was now standing beside me, holding Buster in his arms. For the first time in his furry life with me, he wasn't spazzing out when he had all the right to be. "I don't go looking for trouble, but when it points an arrow at me or pulls a knife on me, then yes, I'll fight."

Kowi looked at Yokci and said, "Nokosi."

Peter leaned in and whispered, "I think that means butt kicker."

Kowi smiled. "It means bear. Gentle unless its family is threatened. Not afraid of its own power. Deadly when annoyed."

I smiled. "Yeah. That about sums me up, I guess." I didn't mind being compared to a bear. At least not until turtle-boy spoke up.

"Smell bad, too."

Peter giggled.

"Hey, watch it, turtle-boy. I haven't had access to a shower in months. It's not my fault the friggin' world came to an end."

"So what'd da deal, guys?" asked Bodo. "Are you going to kill us and eat us or what?

Both of the newcomers frowned. "The Miccosukee do not eat human flesh," said Kowi.

"Yeah, that's just disgusting," added Yokci. "Besides, we don't need to. Kahayatle provides everything we need."

"That's why we're here," said Peter enthusiastically. "We don't want to eat anyone or do anything to hurt people, either. We just want to … eat snakes or whatever and leave you alone. Just help us find a place to stay and you'll never hear from us again, we promise."

I smiled watching him. He looked so earnest, his eyes all shiny as he bounced on his toes. He was like our little diplomat.

"We'll help you," said Kowi.

Yokci folded his arms, not looking all that thrilled with the idea.

"But not for nothing," Kowi continued.

"We have nothing to give," I said angrily. "We have barely enough food to last a week for the three of us."

"You have more than that."

Another indian came walking up, this one a girl, small and wiry. She didn't have any tattoos and was fully clothed, her long black hair handing in a braid down her back. "They have military-grade grenades," she said. "And bikes with a trailer. They took whatever was in the Colemans' shack."

"They were dead," said Peter. "We didn't steal anything, and we didn't kill them either."

"You better not take any of dat stuff," warned Bodo. "We made a lot of work to get dat here."

Kowi looked at us impassively. "We're not interested in your things, although the grenades … we may take those. But no, you have something more valuable to us than these things. If you agree to share it, we will agree to let you live on our land."

"What's that?" I asked, ready for anything.

"Fighting skills. We need you to teach us."

CHAPTER
FORTY-ONE

I EYED HIM WARILY. "YOU'RE going to give us a place to live, on your land, in exchange for krav maga training?"

"Yes. We have weapons that can be used at a distance, but as you can see, when it comes to hand-to-hand combat, our skills are lacking." He frowned at Yokci who stared at the ground in shame.

I looked at Peter and Bodo. "What do you guys think?"

"I say, hell yes," agreed Bodo without hesitation. "Dey are a tribe, we are a tribe. Let's make an accord."

"You sound like we're in the model U.N. at school," I said.

"Yeah, it's kind of like dat, actually. We are two nations, only very small oness. We each have something to share dat the udder one needs. Togedder we are stronger." Bodo's accent was getting heavier with his enthusiasm.

"Well, I feel kind of bad that Bryn's the only one who could contribute to this ... peace accord," said Peter.

"There will be other things I'm sure you can help with," said Kowi. "We may be separate people, but we don't believe in living in isolation. That was the case when the first settlers came to the United States and it's the case now. Times have changed a lot of things, but not our basic nature."

"So does that mean you still scalp people who piss you off?" I said.

"I suggest you not try to find out," said Kowi without missing a beat.

I smiled. I was talking to a fellow badass and it was amazing to think my boys and I might have what was left of the Miccosukee nation watching our backs. It made the prospect of meeting up with canners almost something to look forward to. I held out my hand.

"You've got yourself a deal … on one more condition."

He paused before taking my hand. "What?"

"We keep the grenades, with our promise that we won't use them on you."

"You keep half, we get half," he countered.

I looked at the guys and they both nodded.

"Fine."

We shook hands, and as soon as they went up and down together one time, a group of crazy birdcalls rang out around us. Bodies were coming out of everywhere, formerly hidden behind trees and clumps of rotted trunks and moss. When everyone was finally gathered in our small space near the hut, there were three of us and twelve of them - eight Miccosukee guys and four girls.

"Wow. I'm glad you made that deal," said Peter, quietly so only I'd hear him.

I was thinking the exact same thing. *Talk about outnumbered.*

CHAPTER
FORTY-TWO

W E WENT BACK TO OUR canoes, and the entire group of
Miccosukee came with us. They all piled into the different
boats, making the paddling and rowing a complete breeze. These
people knew what they were doing. Kowi rode with me and two
other guys who were all heavily tattooed and shaved. Turtle boy
was in the boat with Peter and two of the girls. The rest of them
were spaced out with Bodo and the formerly empty boats.

"How come you left these canoes and boats with Rachel and
her brother?" I asked. It didn't seem very smart for them to have
provided the vehicles that brought us this far toward their home.
We could just as easily have been canners.

"They belonged to the Coleman family and were always kept
locked up. The last time any of us saw them they were still alive.
Rachel was very sick, though."

"Yeah, well, she asked her brother to stop the pain with a bullet and then he decided to join her," I said, softly. It didn't seem
right to speak so casually about their pact, especially since if it
hadn't been for their boats, it was hard to imagine what we'd be
doing right now - probably still trying to outrun and hide from
the canners. We owed them big time.

"I'm not surprised," said Kowi. "They were close. She took care of him until she couldn't anymore. Then he took over."

I thought about Peter and his sister, guessing that it had been the same with them. Lily, I knew, was younger; but Peter was the type that seemed to need taking care of. I could see the back of Peter's head and his slumped shoulders, telling me he was listening to us.

We took the left turns that Yokci had mentioned earlier and pulled into a small cove of root outcroppings. It didn't look like anything special to me - it appeared to be pretty much the same as the other place, and there were no huts in site. I tried not to feel suspicious, since the indian kids seemed to be acting normally and none of them were shooting each other any funny looks, but living in this messed up world had made that impossible; now everything and everyone was suspect until proven otherwise. Since I couldn't get rid of my sense of unease, I worked instead at hiding it behind a smile at the dog.

Buster jumped enthusiastically onto the bank and then ran back and forth, waiting for the rest of us to disembark. He was on happy-dog hyper drive, lifting his head up over and over as if to say, "Come on, guys! This is fun! Let's go!"

"Leave the boats and things here for now. You can look first and decide if you want to stay," said Kowi.

Yokci led the way, moving quickly through the heavily wooded area, ducking under moss and low hanging branches, and finally at one point, climbing through a crazy growth of trees whose branches had melded together over the years to create a widely spaced web of wood and leaves. Once I got through to the other side, I realized it was acting as a screen, blocking the view from the boat area of the two small huts we were standing in front of now.

Kowi came up and stood beside me. "These are two chickee huts that you can have, if you want them, in exchange for the training help and the grenades. They have sides you can put up when the rain comes or during the few weeks out of the year it gets cold."

"*Half* of da grenades," said Bodo, pushing past us to go get a closer look. Buster went running after him, looking every bit the klutz as he fell through the roots several times and scrambled like mad to get back on track.

Kowi said nothing more. He just stood in place, waiting for our reaction.

Peter and I followed behind Bodo. I didn't see as how we had much choice other than to accept Kowi's offer, really. It's not like we could walk away and say, *Thanks, but no thanks*. Even if we wanted to, and I was pretty sure I didn't, this was almost exactly what we had come looking for; it would have been stupid to turn away when it seemed so right. I'd actually been prepared for something more primitive when we'd set out to live in the swamp.

I stepped up into the closest chickee hut and felt like I'd practically just been offered a canner-free, four-star hotel room. I followed Bodo into the second one and Peter came in behind me. These huts were partially over root systems and partially over water, lifted up above all of it by several feet, on thick poles that almost looked like the ones used for holding telephone wires up in towns. We all stood in the center together, looking around and then back out at the group of fierce-looking indians on the bank.

"So, what do you think?" I asked quietly, trying to have a private meeting with my mini-tribe.

"I think we got very lucky," said Peter softly.

"I like it," said Bodo. "But I'm a little bit worried dat dey just accepted us so easily. Dare's something going on with dem."

"You know, me too; something bugs me about this whole thing a little. But I don't see as how we have any other options right now. Do you really think they'd let us say no thanks and row right out of here?"

"Probably not," said Peter, looking scared now. "So are we staying or testing that theory?"

I looked at their two faces, not wanting to be the one to make the decision for all of us and take responsibility for their lives like that. But they were waiting for me to do it, and I couldn't imagine chickening out now. My dad had raised me to fight when I was being attacked - to be strong when adversity came my way. Now was not the time to go all wimpy on my friends.

"Let's stay, but keep our eyes and ears open. Anytime one of us sees anything at all that looks wrong, we talk about it, no matter what. Deal?"

They both nodded.

Buster came over and licked my exposed ankle, looking up at me with his happy doggy eyes. One bark was all it took for me to know that he was on board with our plan too.

CHAPTER
FORTY-THREE

TWELVE SETS OF HANDS ADDED to our three made quick work of our boat unloading chore. Within thirty minutes we had everything inside the chickee hut nearest the landing place of our boats.

"You keep the grenades for now," said Kowi. "We will come for our share when we have something to keep them in."

"Where can we put our boats?" asked Bodo. "We don't want to lose dem."

"We'll secure them where they are for now. Once you're ready, we'll show you a good place to keep them out of sight and where you can come and go - it's not the same way you came in."

"Thanks, Kowi," I said. "We really appreciate you doing this for us and not shooting us full of arrows."

He smiled. "I'm glad we sent Yokci in to greet you first."

"Why? Because he sucks at fighting?"

"Let's just say, he's a little slower to anger than some of the others."

"Or you can chust say he's slower and dat's all," said Bodo.

I tried not to laugh at his stark honesty, but I probably shouldn't have bothered since Kowi chuckled.

"I like you ... Bodo is it? You're from Germany, right?"

"Yes. How didt you know?"

"Just a lucky guess," he said, winking at me.

One of the girls from his tribe came up and stood next to him. She stopped close enough to him and stared me down hard enough that I got the picture immediately. I half-expected her to pee on the guy's leg, she was being so obviously territorial. "Everything is done," she said.

Kowi glanced at her and said, "This is my girlfriend, Coli."

"Hi," I said, warily. I didn't have a lot of patience for jealous girlfriends, especially when there was no need for it. Kowi was not my type.

"Hi," she said, putting her hand on Kowi's arm.

I rolled my eyes, turning away so she wouldn't see it. "Okay, then. So, when do you want to start training?" I asked, going over to stand at the entrance to the hut with Bodo and Peter, who were going through our things. Peter had already started organizing the food on a small set of shelves that were built in to the far side of the hut.

"Tomorrow. And if you want, you can come have dinner with us tonight."

"She needs to take a shower, first," said Coli.

I took a deep breath so I wouldn't be tempted to walk over there and slap her across the face. Her tone couldn't have been more rude.

Peter was giggling behind me.

"I'd love a shower, actually. Unfortunately, the world came to an end and all of the water that I was used to having come out of my faucet dried up. So forgive me if I'm a little bit pungent right now, but it's not my friggin' *fault.*"

Kowi was trying like heck to keep a straight face. "You can use ours. Eventually you can find a place to hook up your own if you want."

I looked at him incredulously. "You guys have showers? *Here?*"

"In a manner of speaking," he answered mysteriously. "I'm sure Coli will be happy to show you where they are, since she so generously proposed that you take one."

She opened her mouth to protest but one look from her tattooed boyfriend shut her up in a flash.

I smiled at her smugly. She might smell better than me, but I didn't have to jump when some half-naked guy told me to, like she apparently did. At least I had that going for me.

I looked back at Peter and Bodo. "Do you guys mind if I go get cleaned up?"

"No!" they both yelled in unison, causing Coli to smile bitchily back at me.

"Jerks," I said under my breath. I stormed over to get the freshest clothes I could find out of my bag, picking out a tank top, shorts, and a fresh pair of socks that I'd taken from the army-navy store. My shoes were soaked, but I didn't have anything else for my feet.

"Come on," she said, walking off quickly, not looking back to see if I was following.

I trailed behind her for five minutes, picking my way along as best I could over the lumpy surface. It eventually got less rooty and more like regular ground, even though it still felt pretty springy underfoot. We reached a small clearing that the sun was able to penetrate and burn into brightly.

"Over there, behind that curtain, is the shower. The water is heated from the sun. Don't run it continuously. Just run it to get wet and rinse off. Soap and shampoo is there too."

She turned to leave me.

"You guys have soap?" I asked. I was in shock. I hadn't touched soap in months. It was one of those things my dad had kind of forgotten when he was trying to set me up with supplies before he died. I had all kinds of camping gear and bleach, but no soap. I'd used up the last bit I had a month after he died, and had depended on my pool water to keep me as clean as possible for the next couple - but the algae had soon taken over and made the whole cleanliness thing a dream I left in the past.

"We make our own."

"That's friggin' nuts," was all I could say.

She shrugged. "Our tribe has always been self-sustaining. We might have integrated into the white man's world once, but that didn't mean we let the old ways disappear."

"Well, thank God for that," I said, impressed as hell.

A hint of a smile crossed her face before it was replaced again with her scowl. "I assume you can find your way back."

I laughed somewhat bitterly. "You assume wrong, actually."

She stopped her exit and turned around. "Seriously? You expect me to stay here while you shower?"

"It's not like it's going to take me forever," I said, slightly offended that she found my company so distasteful.

"The way you smell? Uh, yeah. It is."

I threw my arms up and stalked off. "Whatever. Leave then, jerk. See if I care." I was pretty damn sick and tired of everyone making comments about my stink.

"I was only kidding," she said, not sounding at all contrite.

I looked over my shoulder and she was still standing there. She looked fragile and unhappy, but I ignored her and whatever her issues were as I continued to the shower.

The curtain that I'd been able to see from far away was actually a small enclosure, set up using nearby tree branches as support for the animal hides that hung down. I wasn't exactly sure what kind of animal they were, but thought maybe deer.

I quickly shucked off my clothes and stepped over to the black hose that was hanging down at the far end. I could see that it was coming from a large black rubber bladder thing above my head, the entire side of which was in the full sun, getting heated by the rays attracted to its dark color. There was another bladder next to it, but this one was gray and hidden in the shade, not directly exposed to the sun. Both of their hoses were tied together with twine, and a giant clip thingy kept the water from coming out with the force of gravity. I walked up and squeezed the end of the clip gently, allowing a little of the water to escape. It was a mix of very hot stuff from the black tank and cool stuff from the gray one, combining to make a perfect temperature for a shower.

I hurriedly pulled the rubber band out of the bottom of my braid, sliding it onto my wrist so I wouldn't lose it, and tried to finger comb all of my hair. I brushed it every day, regardless of the fact that it was disgustingly dirty, so there weren't any tangles to speak of.

I looked on the ground and noticed some plastic water bottles filled with a cloudy white liquid. I unscrewed the cap of one and then the other, deciding which one was the shampoo by the way they smelled. One had the light scent of flowers, and the other smelled more like the harsh kind of cleanser they had at my school in the art room - the stuff we used to wash the paint off our hands.

I went back over to the hoses, squeezing the clip so enough water would come out to soak my hair and body. Then I lathered the heck out of both, using generous amounts of the soaps. I hated to be selfish and use more than my share, but like everyone was so fond of saying recently, I stank to high heaven; and it was going to take some industrial-strength stuff and lots of it to get me back to normal again.

Coli's voice came to me from a lot closer than it had been before. "There's a bucket of sand there. You can take handfuls and use it to scrub your skin clean with the soap added to it."

I looked over and saw the dry sand, grabbing some eagerly and using it to slough off the dried, stained skin on my elbows and hands. I ended up using it everywhere but my most sensitive parts, scrubbing until my skin turned pink. It almost hurt, but it felt so damn good to be clean again, I didn't care. I even used it on my face and neck, totally thrilled with the feeling of non-oily skin. My face hadn't felt this soft and smooth in forever. I wanted to sing with joy.

I shampooed my hair three times, letting the soap sit in it for several minutes, hoping the harsh cleaning product was cutting through and dissolving the smelly hair grease that had plagued me for months. When I finally rinsed it out, I could feel that my hair was almost completely dried out, which made me so happy I couldn't stop smiling. That's how my hair had felt when my dad was alive. I'd used gallons of conditioner over the years to try and get rid of that feeling, but now I just wanted to let it explode all over my head. Maybe, possibly, if we could get along with these Miccosukee indians, I'd never have to have oily hair again. *A girl can dream.*

Once I was finished removing an entire layer or two of skin from my body with the scratchy sand and soap, I rinsed off. I stood out in the sun for a little while with my arms up in the air, letting its warm rays and the slight puffs of breeze that made their way into the enclosure dry me off. When I was almost totally dry again, I got dressed. The shorts were too big since I'd lost some weight, so I rolled the waistband down. I didn't bother with a bra since I didn't have a clean one anyway. My chest wasn't that big, so it didn't make a noticeable difference that I could tell. I slipped the tank top over my head and pulled it down to cover the top of the shorts.

I stepped out from behind the curtain expecting to be alone, but Coli was still there, standing back again at the entrance to the glade. I walked over to meet her, combing my hair out with my fingers as best I could before putting it up in a quick ponytail. It was getting too long, so I planned to cut it when I got back; just a few inches and I'd be all set. Now I just had to find some dry shoes.

"You didn't put your shoes on," said Coli, looking at my feet.

"My shoes are wet and they reek like dead monkeys."

"We have moccasins you can have. But it's dangerous to walk around here in bare feet in the meantime."

"Why?" I asked as we set off to go back to the hut.

"Cuts lead to infections. And there are spiders and any number of other creatures on the ground that don't like humans walking on them."

I stopped immediately and slid my bare feet into my smelly shoes. I didn't need to hear the word *spiders* more than once.

Coli waited for me to finish before continuing again.

"So how long have you and Kowi been dating?"

"Six months."

"Oh." That meant the love affair had begun after the apocalypse. Interesting. I asked what I thought was a stupid question next, just to keep the conversation flowing. "So, you're Miccosukee?"

"No."

I stopped walking for a second, trying to decide if she was messing with me. "Well, if you're not Miccosukee, what are you?"

"Creek."

"Like Celia," I said before I thought too hard about it.

Coli stopped walking and spun around, coming back to stand way too close to me. "What do you know about a Creek indian named Celia?" she demanded.

I took a step back to restore my personal space. "I met her earlier today. At the shell shop."

"So you're saying she's still alive." She said it like she didn't believe me - a statement not a question.

"Yyyeeah ... " I was trying to figure this girl out. *Is she happy or mad about Celia still being alive?*

Coli turned back around to walk again.

"So, what's the deal, then? Are you guys, like, friends or something?"

"No."

"Sisters?"

"Hell no."

"Enemies?"

Coli sighed loudly. "We're cousins."

"Cousins who don't get along." I was fishing for info.

"Cousins who don't agree on what they should be doing with their lives."

I waited a few more seconds to see if she had anything to add, but she was done. "You know, Coli, I'm just wondering something..."

"What?"

"If you could be any more mysterious."

I was trying to get a laugh out of her, but I shouldn't have bothered.

"I don't share my business with outsiders."

I was going to say something sharp back at her, but then I decided that it wouldn't be fair.

When I stayed silent, she looked back over her shoulder. "What? You've got nothing to say to that?"

"No, not really. I don't blame you for it. I'd feel the same way."

She stopped, waiting for me to draw up next to her.

"I worry about my family," she said, staring straight ahead, her face set in a stern mask.

"Me too. I'll do whatever it takes to keep them safe."

I looked at her and she turned to meet my gaze.

"So will I."

I smiled. "Good. Then we have an understanding. You keep your hands off my boys, and I'll keep my hands off yours."

She smiled back briefly. "Deal." Her mask of unhappiness slid back in place, making me wonder if I'd even seen the smile at all or if I had just imagined it.

CHAPTER
FORTY-FOUR

I GOT BACK TO THE chickee hut and Coli disappeared. I turned to thank her for her help and she wasn't there.

"Damn, she's good," I said, walking into the hut.

I started talking to Peter and Bodo without paying any attention to what they were doing. "That shower is amazing, guys. Now that I'm all clean, I can smell your reekage, so you'd better get over there soon. No stink masters in the hut allowed." I threw my dirty things in a corner. "We need to figure out how they wash clothes around here. If I can't scrub the holy hell out of these things I'm going to have to burn them." I was digging through my pack, unable to find what I was looking for. Buster came over to investigate, sniffing in the open pockets. "Have you guys seen my underwear anywhere? I'm totally commando now. I hate going commando."

No one was answering, so I looked up. Peter and Bodo were just staring at me.

"What?"

They said nothing, making me nervous, so I abandoned my search for panties and stood up. *"What?!"*

Peter blinked a few times before finally answering. "You look … much better."

"Thanks." I narrowed my eyes at Bodo. "What's your problem?"

"I hat no idea dare was dis woman under all dat dirt."

I picked up my smelly t-shirt and threw it at him. "Shut up, you idiot."

Bodo dodged out of the way, looking back at the t-shirt in horror. "You just threw a grenade at me?" He tried to look horrified but couldn't pull it off, his facial expression way too exaggerated to be real.

Peter laughed hysterically.

I stormed over and retrieved my shirt, holding it up and shaking it at him. "Yeah, buddy. A stink grenade. Better watch your back. You have to sleep eventually, you know."

Bodo lifted up his fingers and pinched his nose. "I will learn how to sleep like dis, den."

I went to run after him, but he took off, getting far ahead of me in seconds. The guy had some seriously long legs. Buster went barking after him, probably thinking Bodo was doing it just to play a game with him. I gave up the chase quickly and came back to the hut, throwing my stuff down on the ground again.

Peter eyed me warily, trying hard to erase the smile from his face.

"I'm glad you think my being without a shower and suffering the natural consequences of it is so funny. You don't smell so hot yourself, you know."

"I know. I'm just playing with you, Bryn. It's funny to watch you get all mad for some reason."

"Nice," I said sarcastically, now totally giving up on finding any underwear. I was just getting ready to pick it up to zip it, when I saw something move out of the corner of my eye. I looked up quickly, expecting to see one of the indians out in the trees, but there was no one there.

I walked over and nudged Peter on the arm, gesturing casually with my hand as I zipped up my backpack. "Do you see anything over there?" I asked quietly.

Peter looked over to where I had pointed. "No. Where?"

"Between those trees - the ones that look like they have faces on them."

Peter shook his head. "I don't see anything but tree trunks, branches, and leaves."

"Huh," I said, wondering if I'd been imagining things or if someone was spying on us. I wouldn't put it past them; we were strangers after all. And they'd done a great job of hiding eleven people from my not very observant eyes earlier, so it was entirely possible there was a whole contingent of Miccosukee watching us, and we'd never know. It crossed my mind that I should have traded some of my training for lessons in how to hide and sneak around, Miccosukee-style.

"Okay, Bryn," said Peter, ignoring my paranoia and walking over to the shelves that were now covered in our food. "I have organized our pantry. There are canned goods down here, chips here, water here, and miscellaneous here." He smiled proudly. "Home sweet home."

I walked over and pulled a can of beans off the shelf and put them up with the chips. "What happens if I do this?"

Peter frowned at me. "Then I do this," he said sassily, moving the beans back to their original shelf, turning the label so it faced out, perfectly straight.

"And what happens if I do this?" I asked, quickly grabbing two cans of beans, putting one with the chips and one with the water. I finished by tipping one of the bottles over on its side.

Peter crossed his arms. "Do you really want to go there with me? Seriously?"

I smiled. "Sometimes, yeah, I do. You're fun to rile up."

"So are you, Smellykins, so you'd better not start a war you might lose."

"What did you just call me?" I asked in mock outrage.

"You heard me ... *Smellykins!*"

I rushed over and started tickling him, pleased to find that he was amazingly sensitive, especially around the ribcage. He was shrieking with laughter that sounded so much like a five-year-old girl I couldn't help but laugh myself. Eventually I had to quit attacking him because I was too weak from my own hysteria to continue.

Bodo came back to find us sitting on the floor, holding our stomachs.

I looked up when I saw him approach, a huge smile left over from our tickle fest on my face; but it slowly melted off as my eyes feasted on the glorious Bodo before me.

He'd found the shower and used it well. No more dirt, no more matted hair, and no more shirt. Bodo had been hiding a six-pack and a seriously nice set of pecs under all of it, and I was having a hard time breathing just looking at him. I prayed Coli and none of her tribeswomen were around, because a big part of me right now didn't want anyone but me seeing this vision of utter hotness.

Peter tried to say something, but it came out as something sounding like, "Gah!" and then he started choking. I whacked him on the back a few times, my eyes never leaving Bodo's chest.

"Holy hell, Bodo," I said before I could stop myself.

"What?" he asked innocently. I looked up at his face and saw that he was totally aware of what he was doing to poor Peter. And probably to me, too.

"You know exactly what. Put a damn shirt on, before Peter has a stroke."

"Sorry, Peter," he said, bending down to pull a shirt out of my bag.

"Sure, help yourself to one of mine," I said sarcastically.

"I don't haff anymore. You don't want me to put da smelly one on, do you?

Actually, I'd prefer you stayed shirtless. "No. Go ahead, I'm just messing with you."

Bodo came over and sat down next to me. He pulled the shirt on over his head and down to his waist before leaning over and whispering in my ear. "Did you like what you saw?"

I laughed, pushing him away. "Get out of here." I had to fight to keep the smile from my face.

"Seriously," he said quietly. "I'm ready for dat hug anytime."

I could feel my face burning red again. "I'll keep that in mind, Hulk."

"Ah. You called me da Hulk. Dat means you likedt it." He smiled hugely, obviously beyond pleased that he'd figured me out.

"Yes, but I didn't call you Ironman now, did I?" I got up to kick all of our dirty things into a big pile, sneaking a look over at Bodo.

His brow was furrowed and he was pouting his lips in thought, before he said, "Iss dat a problem?"

I laughed. "No. It's not a problem, Bodo. You're hot. You've got a kickass set of abs. Go ahead and strut your stuff around here. Peter and I will just admire you from afar."

Bodo smiled again. "Dat's good den. I will do dat if it makes you happy."

I decided to let it drop since poor Peter was going to start suffering soon. Bodo was obviously a hell of a male specimen, but he wasn't batting for Peter's team. Odds were, there were guys out there for Peter, but so far, we hadn't seen any. What would I do if I lived in a world full of just girls? I'd be fine with it for a while, but eventually, I'd want a straight guy's company. Peter was right; everyone needed a cuddle every now and then. I looked over at Bodo as casually as I could. It was nice to know he was offering when and if that time came.

"Did you see the organizing Peter did, Bodo?"

"Yes, I dit. It's very nice. It pleases my Cherman heart to see everything so neat."

I smiled, knowing now that I had the power to mess with two of my housemates at the same time with a simple switching of pantry items. I would use this power sparingly and with great care - a zen master of teasing awesomeness. I couldn't wait for my first opportunity.

"Thank you," said Peter, trying to act all modest. "I have other things in mind for this place, but I need to get those wall parts."

"Yeah, what was that all about?" I asked. "This thing has movable walls?"

"More like removable. See those hooks up there? I think they have these hides that connect and hang down to keep out the rain and stuff."

"Cool." I'd never been in the Everglades during a rain, but I knew it could come down pretty damn hard in central Florida - there was no reason to think it'd be any different here.

"Well, I don't know about you guys, but I'm pretty damn tired. Anyone else up for a nap?"

"Yes. Me," said Bodo.

"I have to shower first. Can you show me where it is?" Peter asked both of us.

"Better have Bodo do it. I was following Coli the whole time."

"Come on. I'll bring you. Bryn, you can get our bed ready." He winked at me.

"Try beds. Plural," I said.

Bodo pouted for a second before reverting back to his default Bodo look. "Come on, Peter. I will show you. Bring your clean clothes."

They disappeared a minute later, and I got to work making a bed of sorts. I took the blanket that had glass pieces in it and worked on picking them out, putting the shards in a small pile on the top shelf of the pantry. It was relatively easy work since they were all in a neat line and big enough to see.

Once the blanket was cleaned up, I opened it and laid it down on the floor of the second hut. I figured one hut should be for living in and one for sleeping in. I went to my backpack to get my mosquito spray out. I still had almost an entire bottle of it, using it only in emergencies. Right now felt like one of those times, since I had so much skin showing. The cool spray was a relief on my hot, itchy skin. At least five bites had appeared in the last fifteen minutes, and it was the middle of the day. The evening was going to be awful. I wondered if the indians had a homemade brew of some sort that kept them away, because at this rate, my bottle would be empty in a few weeks at the most.

Bodo came back alone a few minutes later.

"Peter all set?" I asked.

"Yeah. He's taking a shower. I wanted to give him some privacy."

"Good thinking."

"Is dat our bed?" he asked, gesturing to the blanket on the floor.

"It's part of it." I pulled my sleeping bag from my backpack. "Here's the other part of mine."

"Oh. I don't haff one of dose."

"Maybe Peter will share," I said, unrolling mine and putting it down on the blanket.

"I'd radder not," he said, coming over and lying on the edge of the blanket, next to my sleeping bag. "You sleep in the middle. Udderwise, I'm going to get too hot."

"Fine." I tended to get cold in the middle of the night, so I didn't mind having a warm body on either side of me.

Bodo folded his arms behind his head. "So, what do you think of these people here ... dese indians?"

I came over and laid down on top of my sleeping bag, bringing my mosquito repellant with me and pulling one of his arms out to spray it for him. He allowed me to manhandle him, putting each arm back when I was done. "I guess they're okay. That girl Coli told me that she's not Miccosukee. She's Creek, like the girl at the shell shop. They're cousins."

"I'll bet all of da indians around here are related in some way."

"Probably. I wonder if it's normal for Creek indians and Miccosukee indians to get together like that."

"Dats what the Seminoles are," said Bodo.

I put my spray off to the side and laid down on my side, turning to look at him. He was staring up at the ceiling. "What do you mean? Seminoles are Seminoles."

"I did a study of Native Americans when I was doing my semester abroad here. I lived near da casino, so it was interesting to me. In Chermany, indians and cowboys are a big deal ... very mysterious and exciting. I chose dis subject because I always wondered about it when I was a little boy."

"So what's the deal with the Seminoles then?"

"Dey are a tribe made up of other tribes. All of dem came together with an alliance. It made dem stronger and more powerful."

"What tribes?"

"I don't remember all of dem, but I do remember Miccosukee and Creek were includedt."

"Coli hinted around, and so did Kowi, of some sort of issue going on with their tribes. Do you think this Seminole business is a problem for them right now?"

Bodo's voice was sounding sleepy. "I don't know. Maybe. Dey might have different ideass about who owns da Everglades now."

"Yeah," I said, my voice drifting off to my own ears. "That makes sense." I rolled onto my back, my eyes closing of their own accord.

The sound of Bodo's light snoring put me to sleep. To my exhausted brain and newly washed and relaxed body, it almost seemed liked I was falling asleep by the beach, resting in the shade of a palm and listening to the sound of the waves. In and out they were going, a light breeze keeping the humidity and heat at bay, a soft bed of sand beneath me.

CHAPTER
FORTY-FIVE

I WOKE SOMETIME LATER, SITTING up and wondering why there was so little light showing between the trees. I looked at my watch and was shocked to see that I had slept for several hours. Bodo was still snoring next to me.

I nudged him with my hand. "Get up."

He turned in his sleep and reached his arm out, putting it across my lap.

I looked down at it for a second, liking the feel of its weight there and the warmth that quickly spread from it. I looked to see what Peter was up to, and for the first time, realized he wasn't there. A quick scan of the hut we were in and the one next to us told me he wasn't anywhere around.

I lifted Bodo's arm off me and let it drop at his side awkwardly. "Bodo, get up. Peter's not here."

Bodo mumbled something in his sleep and turned on his back again. His mouth was hanging open, a snore coming out.

"Bodo!" I said more sharply, pushing on him with two hands. "Get up! Peter is missing."

Bodo's eyes opened three times in quick succession. He was blinking them over and over; I could tell he was trying to figure out where he was and who this person was that was pushing on him and telling him to leave his peaceful sleep.

"It's me, Bryn. I know you're tired, but I need you to help me find our roommate."

Bodo sat up, scrubbing his face. "Oh, yeah. Sure. What's da problem?"

I sighed. "Peter is missing. We've been sleeping for three hours and I don't think he's been back yet from his shower." I stood up and could see there were no signs of his clothes on the floor, and I knew Peter well enough by now to know that he would never have showered and put dirty stuff back on.

Bodo got up and did a few jumping jacks.

"What are you doing?"

"I neet to get da blood flowing better. I'm too tired to think right now."

I nodded. "Whatever works." I went into the other hut and kicked the dirty clothes around. There was nothing there of Peter's.

"Let's go to the shower and see if he's maybe lost over there."

"Follow me," said Bodo, taking the lead.

We arrived at the shower and I was not happy with what I saw there. Peter's dirty clothes were sitting in a pile, soaked from the shower, left there as if discarded.

"Peter would never leave his clothes like this," I said, picking up his cammo shirt and then letting it drop.

"I agree. Something is wrong here."

I looked at the surrounding trees. "Do you think he wandered off? Maybe he's going to the bathroom somewhere."

"We can sit and wait for a while. But I still don't think he wouldt just leave his clothes like dat on the ground. It's not like him to be making a mess."

I felt sick to my stomach. Someone had taken him, I just knew it. "Who did this?" I asked, not expecting an answer, really.

"Let's go findt those indians and ask dem."

"Do you think they did it?"

"No, do you?"

"No. It seems weird that they'd offer us a place to live and then kidnap one of us."

"Exactly. So it's someone else, but probably someone dey know. Dey sneak aroundt in dese trees and dis swamp all da time. Dey must know everyone who iss here."

I nodded. "You're right. Let's go back to the hut and see if we can figure out how to get in touch with them." I was kicking myself that I hadn't thought to ask them where they actually lived.

We went back and roamed around the area immediately surrounding our huts. I gave up finding clues of their whereabouts and just yelled instead. Bodo looked at me but didn't tell me to stop.

"Hey! Kowi! Coli! Someone! Where are you?!"

After a few long and stressful minutes of no response, Bodo lifted his fingers up to his mouth. "You might want to cover your earss," he said, just before taking in a big breath.

I covered them just in time, but it still wasn't enough to totally block out the sound waves.

When he was done I pulled my hands away. "Holy crap, Bodo. Are you full of some serious hot air or what?"

He smiled. "I'm good at da football games, belief me."

Yokci came walking up from behind some trees. "You called?"

"Yeah, sorry about that. We didn't know where to find you."

"What's so urgent you have to let every person within three miles know that you're here?"

I ignored his scolding tone. "Peter's missing. We need your help finding him."

Yokci frowned. "What do you mean, he's missing?"

"I mean, he's not here. He went to take a shower and disappeared ... never came back."

"Are you sure he isn't just taking a break?"

"For three hours?"

Yokci shrugged. "I don't know him. It's possible."

"Not Peter. And he left his clothes in a pile at the shower. He'd never do that."

"How do you know?"

I gestured angrily toward our pantry. "Hello? He's totally anal about organizing things. Look!"

Yokci scanned the canned goods and other items, all neatly lined up and evenly spaced on the shelves. The labels all pointed in the exact same direction and it looked as if he'd used some sort of spacer to make sure that each can was separated from the one next to it by the exact same distance.

"Wow. It's even alphabetized."

"See? So are you going to help us find him or what?"

"Yeah. We'd better. It's getting late."

He stepped outside the hut and let out his bird whistle call. I tried to figure out how he was doing it, but all he was using was his tongue and teeth. I seriously had to figure out how to do that.

I heard a soft whistling sound and turned in time to catch Bodo trying to imitate it. He stopped when he saw me watching and smiled self-consciously.

A few more bodies came out of the trees, Kowi and Coli among them.

"What's up?" asked Kowi, striding toward us.

"Their friend is missing," said Yokci. "I'm thinking Creek."

Coli's bottom jaw stuck out in anger. "You always think that, Yokci."

"Shut up, Coli," he said, not even looking at her.

"Both of you, shut up," said Kowi, turning to face me. "When was the last time you saw him?"

"Three hours ago, when he went to take a shower." The look on all their faces and their body language was screaming out to the world. There was some messed up shit going on around here. "What the hell is this all about, Kowi? Did some Creek indians take him?"

Kowi sighed heavily. "It's possible."

Yokci snorted. "More like probable."

Coli leaped forward and shoved him. He fell back a couple paces and moved quickly to regain his footing, acting like he was going to go after her. Coli stood there, her hands in fists at her side, her jaw thrust out. "Go ahead, Yokci!"

I almost expected her to say make my day next, but Kowi got in the middle of them and stopped it from going any further.

"Enough!" he shouted. "This is not the time or the place. Coli, go get the others. Yokci, go start tracking him from the shower area."

They both shot each other a death glare and then moved on to obey his orders.

I crossed my arms over my chest. "You have some explaining to do, Kowi. I feel like we've been lied to."

Kowi's face was a mask of no expression. He closed his eyes for a few seconds before opening them again to stare at me and then Bodo.

"We haven't lied to you. But we haven't exactly told you everything, either. Let's sit down and I'll tell you what I can."

CHAPTER
FORTY-SIX

ISAT ON THE FLOOR of the hut near enough to Bodo that I could feel his body heat. It was comforting, since I knew he was the only person in this place who I could trust right now.

Kowi explained, "We're having a little bit of trouble with a neighboring tribe, the Creeks."

"That's what Coli is," I said.

"Yes. Our … relationship is supposed to help the tribes get along. So far it's only having limited success."

"You might have tried to find a happier bride."

He tilted his head, his face still giving nothing away. "One does not always get to choose who he ends up with."

I raised an eyebrow at that, not even really sure what he meant, but I was pretty sure Coli wouldn't have liked hearing it. Was he saying she had been chosen only for tribal purposes? Or that he'd fallen in love with a woman who'd never be happy? It was impossible to tell with his emotionless delivery.

"So what's happening, den? Seemss like da Creeks must not be very happy if dey're kidnapping your friends."

"They've been causing general trouble with us for months … stealing supplies, food, occasionally trying to take our women. But we've never had them take one of our men before."

"Probably because they're more difficult targets."

"Except for dat Yokci guy," added Bodo, totally straight-faced
I couldn't help but smile at that, wishing Yokci had heard it.

"Yes, our men - all of them - are difficult targets." He glared at
Bodo, now letting some of his anger slip through.

I brushed off their macho pissing contest. "Why would they
take Peter, though? I mean, no offense to my friend, but he's totally useless as a warrior or whatever."

"They know he's valuable to us, or we wouldn't have let him
stay here. They don't have to know what his value is, just that he
is important."

"So what ... he's like a bargaining chip now?"

"Maybe. Either that or they'll just plan on integrating him into
their tribe somehow. Or ... "

Bodo leaned in toward me and said, "He iss good at organizing and cleaning thingks."

I shoved him with my elbow. Now was no time to joke about
Peter's obsessive compulsive disorder.

"Or what?"

"Or they'll deliver him out of Kahayatle and send him on his
way. He's an outsider - a trespasser. He has no right to be here."

I instantly felt sick, imagining Peter wandering around out there
without supplies or a way to defend himself. He'd be lunch before
dinner. "I want him back. They can't have him and I won't allow anyone to kick him out of here." I seared Kowi with a look, letting him
know there would be hell to pay if anything happened to my friend.

"I know that, Nokosi. We're going to find him and bring him
back to you."

"You'd better," I said, getting up to storm out of the hut. I paced
back and forth in front of it, frustrated that there was nothing I
could do.

Bodo came up and joined me, standing off to the side, talking
quietly.

"Don't worry, Bryn, dey're going to bring him back to us."

"They'd better, or I'm gonna go American white girl all over
their asses. I'm serious, Bodo."

"I know you are. I'm not exactly sure what dat means, what you just said about asses, but it sounds scary. I'm sure dey won't sendt him out of da swamp."

"Oh really?!" I said, looking at him and letting my anger get the most of me. "And how do you know that, Bodo? Did your book report delve into the psychological mindset of the Creek indians?"

"No," he said, without emotion.

"Oh, well, maybe you're using your German mind-reading skills then."

"No, I don't have any of dose."

I threw my hands up. He was impossible to make angry which only made me more frustrated.

He put up his fists in his pitiful imitation of a mock martial arts stance. "Do you want to fight me? Causs I'm pretty sure I could take you down."

I shook my head. "Don't be stupid, Bodo. I'll break your friggin' arms off."

He gestured with his head, egging me on. "Come on, little girl. Little Smellykinder. Give me your best shot. I can take it."

My arms were twitching, I wanted to take him up on his offer so badly. "I'm warning you, Bodo ..."

He stepped right up to me and play-slapped me on the cheek. "Dare you go. I got you now."

I shook my head, bewildered by the fact that he was begging for a butt whooping so insistently.

"You're scared. Dat's the problem. I don't blame you really. Now you'f seen my muscles and you're scared of what I can do to you. Dat's okay. You'd better just take a pass, den."

He lowered his arms and I couldn't stop myself. I ran at him full force, taking him down like a football dummy.

He tried to grab me around the waist, but I slammed him into a tree, instantly breaking his grip. He pushed himself up to meet me again, stepping forward aggressively.

"Bodo! Cut it out! I'm not messing around, you're going to get hurt." I tried to back up away from him.

"Not me!" he said, grinning evilly.

I shook my head. "Fine, idiot. But don't blame me when you're in pain later." I took four quick swipes at him, landing some bruising blows and keeping him busy blocking me, all the while making him move backward to avoid the worst of it. He couldn't see where he was going, but I could.

"Next time," I grunted, giving him a jab to the abdomen with my left, "...think harder ..." my right came next, following up after the left "... about who you pick..." I used both fists this time in the middle of his solar plexus "...a fight with." My last move was a kick to his lower abdomen, folding him nearly in half and sending him flying backward into the shallow body of water behind him.

His arms and legs went flailing, but nothing could stop his backward motion. He landed on his back in the water with a big splash.

I heard clapping off to the side and saw three guys standing there, Kowi and two others I didn't recognize, admiring my performance.

Bodo jumped up out of the water, whipping his shirt off and standing there half naked, dripping wet, yelling, "Oh, I see your plan! You just wanted to see me with my shirt off again! Very tricky, Bryn, very tricky. I didn't see dat coming at all."

I shook my head and walked away, but only after getting an eyeful of that gorgeous chest of his again. *Man, do I have it bad.*

I tried to stay mad, but his little devious plan had worked. My mind had been taken off our problem with Peter and the frustration was temporarily out of my system. I wondered if Bodo was going to be my self-designated punching bag now that he'd so accurately guessed the most efficient way I knew of to calm my runaway emotions - fight therapy.

CHAPTER
FORTY-SEVEN

IT WAS GETTING DARK. OCCASIONALLY guys would come back to our hut to let Kowi know what was going on. It was clear that he was the official or unofficial chief of this tribe now. Everyone reported to him and followed his orders. I guess that made Coli the indian princess or whatever.

Her disposition hadn't changed. She at least wasn't outwardly aggressive toward me, but it was probably only temporary, merely done out of respect for the fact that I was worried about Peter. She wasn't here now, having left with the last group of people who went out tracking him.

Two guys came running into the clearing by the huts about an hour later and went immediately to Kowi. I got the sense that they had important news, so I rushed over to listen in on their conversation. I didn't catch any of it since it was over before I got there, but I did hear Kowi's response.

"Tell them that's unacceptable."

"Tell who *what* is unacceptable?" I asked.

Bodo came and stood beside me, casting nervous glances between Kowi and me.

Kowi looked at his cohorts and sighed before answering. "The Creek have Peter. They said that they're going to send him out of the Kahayatle unless we agree to their demands."

"What demands?"

"It doesn't matter. We won't agree to them."

"You have to agree to them!" I yelled. "You can't let them send him out of here! He'll get killed inside of ten minutes!"

Kowi shook his head very slowly. "Don't forget your place here, Nokosi. You are not Miccosukee. You stay at our pleasure. You are in no position to tell me what I can and cannot do."

I stepped closer to him - close enough that I knew he could feel the angry heat coming off my body. "Listen here, cougar. I came here and brought you gifts in the form of bombs. I agreed to train your people. Without me you'll always be the Creeks' little bitches. Is that what you want?"

His upper lip curled an instant before he tried to push me away, but I was ready for it, easily blocking his arms and throwing them out to the side, making him look like a goofy pinwheel.

Buster was barking like a maniac and I heard Bodo trying to calm him down in the background.

Kowi wasn't expecting to be thrown off so easily, so his ego-bruised man instincts took over, causing him to make his second mistake. He reached an arm back to punch me and I watched it travel through space from his shoulder to my face, easily dodging it by leaning to the side and then around him. I let the force of his own move throw him forward, helping to increase the momentum by driving my elbow into his back hard.

He stumbled forward, but tried to recover and take me down by spinning around and grabbing my leg.

Unfortunately for him, krav maga taught me that any move was legal, so long as it resulted in me getting free of my attacker. I adjusted my footing and centered myself, using the knee he'd brought toward him to connect with his nuts. I knew I caught at least one of them when all the air burst out of him and he crumpled to the floor.

His two friends jumped me, each one grabbing one of my arms. Sure that they had me in hand, the didn't bother doing anything else but hold on. I judged the one on my right to be the one with the strongest grip, so I used his force on my arm as leverage to lift my legs high enough off the ground to deliver a heavy-duty side kick to his friend, sending the guy flying off the edge of the hut. His hip caught the railing and the upper half of his body kept going, flipping him over the top and into the water.

Now I had one guy, a big one, holding me by the arm. He stood there almost frozen in shock. I stopped for a second and looked down at the meaty hands holding me. Then I looked up at him, raising one of my eyebrows for effect. "You sure you wanna do that?"

"Say, no, buddy," urged Bodo from off on the sidelines. "She's gonna kick your nuts too. You don't want dat. You know dat feeling you get in your stomach that takes forever to stop hurting?"

"Just walk away," I said softly.

He looked down at his chief and at his friend getting up out of the water. I knew the moment he made his decision. These indians thought they were all cool with their stone cold lack of facial expression, but their bodies spoke volumes.

I grabbed the fingers of his hand and bent two of them back until I heard a crunch. He screamed out in pain and roared at the same time, his other hand coming up to grab my hair.

I was pissed I hadn't cut it yet. If I had, he probably wouldn't have been able to get me so easily. And he was pulling on it like it was his lifeline or something - if I didn't do something quick, I was going to be scalped by having my hair ripped out at the roots.

I punched him hard in the thigh, bringing on what I hoped was one hell of a charlie horse. His knee buckled with the pain, but he held on tight to my hair. I reached up and slammed my arm down on the inside of his elbow which hurt my head like hell, but brought me closer to him.

I swung my hand in an upper-cut arch, coming from way back to clamp down on his balls hard. The fist holding my hair went slack, making it possible for me to flip my head up so I could watch his face turned white.

"Oooof, oh, man ... I tried to warn you," said Bodo, a pained expression on his face.

The guy bent over in pain and I finished him off with a hammer strike to the back of the head. He fell to the ground onto his face and didn't move.

"Oh, my *godt!*" said Bodo, half laughing, clapping his hands together slowly, "dat was ... oh man, dat was unreal! Dat was *not* real! Whoot!"

Kowi stood up slowly, keeping his hand on his upper thigh, which I knew was his way of trying to manage the pain still radiating up from his groin.

I put my fists up in a defensive position, ready on the balls of my feet if he decided to get stupid, but he held his hand up in surrender.

"No. No more fighting. You've made your point."

"I want Peter back. *Here,*" I said from behind my fists.

"Yeah. I got that." He looked over and motioned to the guy who'd finally gotten out of the swampy water and was now dripping just outside the entrance to the hut.

"Go tell the Creeks we will agree to their terms."

"But...!" he argued.

"Just go!" he yelled, looking down at his friend on the ground.

I could tell from the look on the wet indian's face that something huge was being sacrificed here.

"Bryn," said Bodo, and I could almost read his mind.

"Wait," I said to the guy who was getting ready to leave to deliver the message, putting my arms down and relaxing. "Before you go run off all half-cocked, why not tell us exactly what's going on here? Maybe we can help you resolve this without your sacrifice and without mine."

"It's tribe business," said Kowi.

"Don't be like that, Kowi. I want to help. We all do." I looked over at Bodo and he was nodding his head enthusiastically.

Kowi looked like he was weighing his options, so I continued my plea. "The world is a different place. It's never been like this, even when your ancestors were here greeting the friggin' settlers. Back then the settlers just wanted to survive at first, figure out how to grow food and live. The people who are out there now

... want to *eat* you guys. I mean seriously ... we're all fighting the same enemy here."

"Yeah," said Bodo, "da zombies."

"Let us help you. We've already shown you we have skills and we're determined."

"We made it all da way down here from over two hundredt and fifty miles away. Through zombieland," said Bodo.

"I can't just bring you into our tribe business without talking to the others."

"Just do it, Kowi," said the wet guy.

I looked over at him, surprised his ego would allow those words to come out of his mouth.

He shrugged. "We need the help. Obviously." He walked over and kicked his fallen comrade. "Get up, asshole."

The guy on the ground moaned. He slowly rolled over and we got a look at his face. He'd broken his nose in his fall.

"Oops, sorry about that," I said. I looked over at Kowi. "Do you want me to fix that before he's fully awake?"

"You can do that?" he asked, looking a little shocked.

"I've seen my dad do it enough times." I went over and straddled him, sitting on his chest. "Bodo, get on his legs, would you?"

"Dat's not a problem," he said coming over and lying across them.

"Grab his arms, Kowi."

Kowi limped over and kneeled down, taking the guy's arms and holding them on the ground above his head.

"Here goes nothing," I said, as I put my hands on either side of his smooshed nose, yanking it back to the front.

A loud crunch and a fresh gush of blood told me that I'd at least gotten it back in the general direction; the loud screaming and bucking from the kid told me that it had hurt. He passed out in a few seconds, finally going still. I got up and rolled him over on his side so he wouldn't choke on his own blood.

I walked down to the swamp to rinse my hands off in the water. "He might not look pretty, but at least his nose won't be sideways." I scrubbed my palms together and watching the blood dissolve away.

I didn't get a response, so I turned around to look at them. They were all staring at me. I self-consciously reached up and wiped my nose with the back of my hand. I was hoping I hadn't ruined the whole effect of my fighting skills by having a boog hanging out or something.

"What?" I said, tired of the silent treatment. "Why are you guys staring at me? Cut it out."

Bodo spoke first. "I don't know why dey are staring at you, but I'm doing it because I'm admiring your muscles. You really know how to make a guy feel like a wimp."

I looked down at my arms, noticing for the first time that they were a little pumped from their recent workout. I had almost zero body fat left, so they did look pretty ripped. I glanced back up at him, "I hope that's not a problem for any of you." It would be just my luck that I'd ruin any chance of ever having a boyfriend by scaring them all away.

"It's not a problem for me," said Bodo, shaking his head slowly side to side. "Not a problem ..."

I smiled, ignoring the responses from the other guys. The more I got to know Bodo, the more I thought I might have a chance at finding a guy my dad would have loved.

CHAPTER
FORTY-EIGHT

W E SAT IN OUR HUT, surrounded by a big group of Miccosukee. I didn't bother counting all of them. Kowi and Coli
sat at the center, and everyone was listening closely to what Kowi
was saying.

"As you all know, the Creek of Kahayatle have taken the friend
of Bryn and Bodo, named Peter, and they are demanding that we
turn over the grenades to them in exchange for Peter."

I gasped. *How could they possibly know we brought grenades?*

"My first answer was to say no. Then Bryn was kind enough to
show me the error of my ways."

"She kicked our asses," said the wet indian, who I now knew
as Paci. A few of the group laughed, including Kowi. Kowi's girlfriend just glowered at me.

"Yeah, so after we had our … discussion with Bryn, we decided to go ahead and agree to their terms. But she convinced us to
reconsider and share with her and Bodo the details of the Creeks'
demands, which we have now done. We've asked all of you to come
here tonight so that we can discuss this situation before we make
our decision about what to do. Those of us who are on the council
have agreed to include Bryn and Bodo in our conversation."

I looked around and could see that all but a few of the members were okay with it. Paci looked like he was on Team Bryn, and he seemed like the gregarious type. I had a feeling he'd been campaigning for us. He smiled and lifted his chin at me, acknowledging my presence.

I looked over at Bodo in time to see him narrow his eyes a little bit at Paci. *Jealousy maybe?* I tried not to be too excited over the idea. Jealousy was usually bad news, even if in the beginning it was a little flattering. I'd seen enough girls leaving the mini krav maga self-defense workshops talking about stalker ex-boyfriends who'd always started out being the jealous type; the same ones they were now trying to learn how to fight off. I didn't need to be fighting my own people over stupid stuff like that.

Kowi began talking again. "Bryn wanted the chance to speak, so I gave her my permission. Does anyone have a problem with that?"

I could see Coli itching to say something, but she kept her mouth shut.

Kowi looked at me. "Go ahead. Say what you wanted to say."

I stood up, wiping my hands nervously on my shorts. "I just wanted to say a few things, maybe share some ideas."

I looked at Bodo and he nodded, urging me forward with his quiet confidence in me.

"The Creek have my friend Peter. He's not a violent person in any way and he's pretty much helpless. If they set him loose outside of the Everglades, he'll never survive. He'll get eaten."

I saw from a few faces around that the idea didn't seem all that likely to them.

"I don't know how much you guys have gotten out of the swamps lately, but in case you're living in a fantasy world that doesn't include zombies, let me enlighten you - there are cannibals out there. Kids are eating kids." I waited a few seconds to let that sink in.

Someone in the back spoke up. "That's isolated stuff. It's not all over."

"Don't be so sure," said Bodo, standing up next to me. "I came from West Palm Beach. She and Peter came from Orlando. Dare

are zombies in both placess and in between. Dat's like almost two hundredt miles."

"Right," I said. "So it's not just one group or one isolated situation. It's all over and probably spreading as the resources dry up. This whole fighting thing you're doing with the Creeks is a bad idea. You need to get together and make one big tribe instead of a bunch of small ones disagreeing and fighting over grenades."

"It takes both sides agreeing," said Coli, "and that's not going to happen."

I looked at her with disapproval. "Well I guess you only have yourself to blame for that, don't you?"

She stood up suddenly, taking a step toward me.

Kowi held out his arm, bracing it across her legs. "Trust me, Coli. You don't want to go there."

She looked down at him in disgust. "You guys might have bowed down to her little games, but I'm not going to."

Kowi pulled his hand away and used it instead to gesture in my direction. "Well, then, by all means. Have at it. But don't come crying to me later when she hands you your ass."

Coli seemed to be considering the idea of being publicly humiliated in front of her tribe and decided to stay by her man's side. But that didn't change her opinion about me one bit.

I sighed. "Seriously, Coli. You're Creek for god's sake. Why can't you go talk to them?"

She folded her arms. "I'm not going to get in the middle like that."

"Why the heck not?" I demanded. "You're the girlfriend of the chief over here. You're second in command. It's your job to make peace with neighboring nations, isn't it?"

She stuck her chin out in defiance but didn't seem to have anything to say back.

"Are you guys all crazy out here, or what? Can't you see what's happening right under your noses?" I stared Coli down. "How did they know about the grenades, anyway? Did you tell them? Maybe you're a mole."

She gasped at me, clearly outraged that I'd even suggested it. Or at least, she was acting outraged. She took a step forward and

Kowi stood, taking her by the shoulders and pulling her back. "No. You're not going to fight her. I like your face the way it is."

He looked at me. "I think the Creek were tracking you before you got here. That's how they knew about the grenades."

"Dat's not likely," said Bodo. "Dey were covered all da time. You probably got a spy in here. I bet it's her," he said, pointing to Coli.

She struggled to get out of Kowi's arms. If she were guilty, she was doing a good job of hiding it.

"Whatever. It doesn't matter," I said. "Actually, it just underlines the fact that this thing, this conflict you have with the Creek, is dangerous. You can't trust each other. You're all working against your common interests." I took a deep breath and continued. "Let me go talk to them. Maybe I can help negotiate some kind of truce." I stared at Coli. "I'll bring her with me. She can prove to everyone she's not a spy."

She jerked her arms out of Kowi's grasp and practically spat at me. "I don't have to prove to you or anyone else that I'm not a spy."

"Yes, you do," said Paci. He stepped forward from the group. "You were gone and no one could find you. You disappear like that all the time. And someone had to tell them about those grenades. I think it was you."

I saw the murderous look on Kowi's face and knew these words were not being spoken or taken lightly. Coli looked stricken.

"Okay, so whatever," I said hurriedly, not wanting to lose the momentum we had. "I'll take Bodo and Coli and we'll go talk to the Creek. If we can get them to agree to a truce, then will you guys be in favor? Will you honor it?"

"I'm going too," said Paci. "You can trust me to bring back accurate information, brother." He was addressing Kowi, and now I could see a strong resemblance between the two. He didn't mean just tribe brothers in this case - they had the same parents for sure.

Kowi nodded. "Fine. You go represent our tribe with the negotiators." He looked at his girlfriend. "Coli, you go too. Talk to your family and help them to see the sense in this."

"But you're my family now, Kowi." Her eyes were pleading with him along with her voice. It was kind of sad, really. I was starting to get the feeling that their relationship was somewhat one-sided.

"We'll see," was all he said.

Her face dropped and she looked down at the ground. There had to be tears in her eyes; even someone made of stone would have cried at a rejection that cold and that public.

"Come on," I said. "We're burning daylight. How far away are they?"

"Twenty minutes, if we move fast. Come on," said Paci, separating himself from the group and heading for the trees.

I looked at Coli. "Coming?"

She just stared at me for a second and then moved away to follow Paci, saying nothing.

I rolled my eyes. I thought teen drama had been left behind in the old world. Today, the Miccosukee has taught me otherwise. Bodo came up to walk beside me.

"Dat was some smooth talking back dare."

I smiled. "You think so?"

"Yes. Remindt me never to argue with you about anything. I guess it wouldt be a waste of time for me."

"I'm glad you've figured that out so early in our relationship, Bodo." The import of my words didn't really hit me until he responded.

"Dat's what we have, issn't it? A relationship."

"I guess," I said, noncommittally.

"Maybe some day you'll let me call you my girlfriendt."

I laughed. "Yeah. Some day when we're not running away from cannibals and indian warriors."

"Okay. I'm gonna hold you to dat."

I smiled but said nothing. The idea of a world without fear and Bodo calling me his girlfriend didn't sound half bad.

CHAPTER
FORTY-NINE

W E CLIMBED INTO A CANOE that was docked near our
hut, leaving Buster behind with one of the Miccosukee
girls who promised to take good care of him and feed him. Buster
seemed perfectly happy with the arrangement, especially when
she pulled a nugget of something edible out of her pocket and
gave it to him. I sighed, watching him scamper away, jumping up
so much on her that he looked like he wanted to climb right up
her leg. *Loyalty - taken by a simple scrap of food.*

Paci rode in the back and Coli in front, both of them doing
all the paddling while Bodo and I just rode. It was pretty nice,
actually, if I didn't think about the purpose for the trip. No one
said anything, so the only sounds to be heard were those of the
wildlife around us. There were squawks, croaks, and ribbets and
an errant caw now and again, floating out above the sounds of
rustling bushes and leaves. The banks of the river seemed like
they were full of animals, rushing to hide whenever we came by.

Eventually we stopped and Coli got out, pulling out the line
they kept attached to the front of the canoe and wrapping it
around a nearby tree. We disembarked when she was done, following her into the trees. A light was visible up ahead, and as

we approached, I could see that it was a circle of torches stuck in the ground, all centered around a fire.

Coli stopped well outside the circle of lights and made a sound like a birdcall. Less than a minute later, we were joined by three indians in more tribal-looking dress than I saw the Miccosukee wearing, making them look more intimidating.

"Coli," said one of them. "Tired of those Meeks? Ready to come back home?"

"Shut up, Jeremy. I need to see Trip."

"Trip's busy. Who are these people?"

Coli sighed. "You're not high enough on the food chain to know that information. Just go get him."

"You know, Coli, one of these days that mouth of yours is going to get you into trouble."

"Yeah, well, maybe you'll be lucky enough to be around to see it."

"Maybe I will," he said, before storming off.

"Nice guy," I said, when he was gone.

"He's my brother."

I had nothing to say to that. The guy was obviously a jerk but I couldn't very well say that to his sister.

A couple minutes later another guy appeared. "Trip says you can come in the circle."

"Wow. How big of him," said Coli sarcastically.

I grabbed her arm to hold her back, letting Paci take the lead. "Do you think maybe you could just try to get along here?"

She jerked herself free. "You have no idea what you're talking about."

"Yeah, actually, I do. I'm talking about getting my friend Peter back without anyone getting hurt; and I'm talking about possibly saving your whole damn tribe. I'd think that would be a little more important to you than whatever little personal issues you have going on."

She walked away from me without saying a word.

"Don't bother," said Bodo softly. "She's a lost person. She can't hear anything you're saying."

"That's too bad," I said.

"Yeah."

We were soon at the edge of the lighted circle, looking at a group of faces, all of them painted red and black. Even Peter's. He was sitting off to the side, his shirt off, looking very dejected. He was the sorriest excuse for an indian warrior I'd ever seen in my life.

"Wow. Look at Peter," said Bodo. "He's got paint on his face."

"And his chest."

"Dat's his chest? Wow. He's so white he almost glows in da dark. I thought it wass a t-shirt."

A big guy separated himself from the group in the circle of fire and came over to greet us. He had long black hair, hanging loose around his shoulders. It had some beads and pieces of string wrapped around chunks of it. He'd painted his face and his chest with lines, dots, and primitive-looking birds. I was pretty sure they were the washable kind of tattoos, but regardless, they looked freaky. I almost felt afraid.

"Coli," he said, briefly looking at her and then swiveling his head slowly to stare at me.

"Why are you on my land, Paci? You know you aren't welcome here." He didn't even bother to look at the guy when he was speaking to him; I was no expert on indian customs, but it sure felt like an insult to me.

Paci apparently didn't care. "Yo, Trip, what's up, man? How's it hangin'?"

"Coli, why did you bring this mongrel to our place? You know better than that."

"He's here to represent his brother. You know … the chief? My boyfriend?"

Trip leaned over and spit on the ground.

"Who's this?" he said, gesturing at me with his chin, still not breaking eye contact with me.

I kept my gaze steady. I'd seen guys like him before. He was a class-A ego maniac, totally convinced of his own superiority. Every one of those guys had a serious weakness and it started with that ego giving them false bravado and an over-inflated sense of their own fighting skill-level.

"That … is a white girl."

"I can see that. What's her name and why is she here?"

I sighed. "Okay, guys, really … I appreciate the whole ceremonial stuff and everything, but we don't have a lot of time. It's getting late, I haven't eaten all day, and my friend Peter over there is not looking well. I'd like to get this wrapped up so we can head out of here in the next half hour, tops."

"So you think you're going to just walk on my land and claim your Peter and walk away?"

I tried not to laugh at his choice of words but it was impossible. I put my hand over my mouth to try to hide it, but then gave up and said, "Did you just say I came to claim *my peter?*"

I heard Coli snicker next to me, and then Paci joined in. Finally, Bodo got in on the game.

"Oh, dat's funny. I just got dat." Bodo leaned over and asked me in a loud whisper, "Do you think he knows what dat word means?"

"Yes, I know what that word means," said an angry Trip. "Stop laughing, you idiots. It wasn't that funny."

"Yeah. It kinda was," admitted Coli. "You were totally pulling off that badass indian chief thing and then you started talking about peters."

Peter's head came up. "Bryn? Is that you?"

"Yeah, it's me. I'll be right there." I turned my attention to Trip. "Sorry for laughing. I'm really tired and hungry, like I said. I'm here to talk to you about a ceasefire or a truce or whatever."

"A truce over what?"

"Between you and the Miccosukee."

He laughed. "What? You speak for the high and mighty Kowi now?"

"Don't talk about him like that, Trip," warned Coli.

"Whatever. I just think it's pretty funny that he's got some white girl coming over here for him to try and tell me what to do."

"She ain't just a regular white girl, Trip. Trust me," said Paci.

"Trust you? Yeah, right."

"Fine. Don't say I didn't warn you later if you decide to tangle with her."

Trip raised an eyebrow at me. "So what does this white girl who's got all the Meeks all scared got to say to me?"

"What I have to say is, first of all, you're not getting any of the grenades I brought with me, and also that I'm taking Peter with me tonight back to my hut where he lives. And finally, maybe most importantly, you and the Meeks, as you call them, need to kiss and make up, before it's too late."

He laughed overly loud and took his time about it. Then he stopped all of a sudden and got instantly serious, giving the distinct impression that he was a little mentally off balance.

"You've got to be kidding me," he said, all traces of laughter gone.

"No. I'm not. Let's go sit down and talk."

He nodded his head slowly. "Talk. Okay, we can do that. Just you, though. The rest of them can stay here." He gestured to his group behind him and said, "Watch them. No one leaves." He took me by the arm and led me past the fire pit, toward a chickee hut that had the walls up.

As I passed by Peter I leaned behind Trip and said, "Be right back!"

I ignored Peter's stark look of fear.

Trip and I entered the empty hut and he gestured to the floor. "Have a seat."

"I prefer to stand." I knew that my chances of defeating him in any physical match were better if we weren't on the ground; there he had the advantage of size and weight. Standing I had the element of surprise and my quick strike ability. I hoped I wouldn't need to use it, but if my dad had taught me nothing else, he'd taught me to expect the unexpected and that the worst case was always a possible scenario.

Trip moved to the center of the hut and then turned to look at me, his thumbs casually hooked in the band that went around his waist, the one that was holding up a cloth that hung down in front of his man-parts, covered in decorations. I couldn't tell if they were painted on or woven in - it was too dark to see details with only a little bit of the torchlight reaching in between cracks of the wall hangings. I didn't want to spend too much time studying it for obvious reasons. He wore leather breeches on his legs and moccasins, no shirt. His muscled chest was painted like his face in reds and blacks. He didn't have the permanent tattoos that Kowi and his tribesmen had, I could see that now. He was slightly slouched over and it almost looked as if he were flexing his chest and abs a little. I smiled, thinking to myself that this guy was almost as bad as a peacock.

"Let's start with you telling me who you are," he said.

"My name's Bryn Mathis. I'm from the Orlando area. Maitland."

"What about the other ones?"

"Bodo's from Germany, stuck here after a year abroad program, and Peter's from Sanford."

"Why are you in my swamp?"

I decided not to debate the ownership of the Everglades at this juncture. "We came here to escape the canners - the cannibals that are out there."

He scoffed at that. "Cannibals. Yeah, right."

"Yeah, cannibals. It's the truth."

"Why should I believe you?"

"Because I have no reason to lie?"

"Sure you do."

"Oh yeah? Enlighten me."

"So you could come here and steal from me."

"Steal what? I've got news for you, Trip ... there are at least fifty creatures probably within twenty feet of me that could kill me right now. Does that sound like something a girl like me purposely goes to live with if she has any other choice?"

"Not really."

"Exactly. And I don't go hanging around mosquito infested swamps so I can steal some soap."

He unhooked his thumbs and came a little closer. "Maybe you're here for something else."

I raised an eyebrow. "Please don't be suggesting what I think you're suggesting."

"What's that?" he asked, giving me a slightly devious smile.

"Trip, you're a good looking guy, we both can see that. But in case you didn't notice, I brought one of those with me. So, no, I did not come here to be graced with your awesomeness. I came here to survive. To live."

He gave me one courtesy chuckle. "Well, that's too bad, isn't it?"

"Why?"

"Because these are *my* swamps and I say who stays and who goes. And I say you go." His smile left his face, leaving behind stone cold anger.

"I'll fight you for 'em," I said, my tone low and controlled.

He smirked at me. "What a joke."

"Do I look like I'm joking?"

"You look like a hundred pound chick who doesn't know when to stop talking. You're no match for me." He clenched his fists and flexed his pecs - I'm not even totally sure it was intentional.

"Then why say no if you're not scared?"

"There's nothing to be scared of," he said, coming even closer. I could smell the musky maleness of him now.

Man oh man is he putting off the testosterone or what?

He continued in a softer but more dangerous-sounding tone. "I think you're the one who should be scared. You're in this place, all alone with me. Your friends aren't going to be able to come and save you. What are you going to do if I get too close?" He was practically touching me now, his hands remaining at his sides. He loomed over me, taller by at least six inches.

I didn't move. I got the impression from his body language and the look in his eyes that he was playing a game, calling my bluff. I wouldn't have a lot of room to maneuver, if at any point in the game he decided to change his mind about his intentions, but I'd figure out a way to deal with that if it happened. The important thing right now was to not show any fear.

I looked up at him, refusing to break eye contact. "If you get too close, and I have to warn you, you're almost to that point, I'm going to have to take you down. And I can promise you ... it's gonna hurt."

He smiled, this time without malice. "I like you. Why is that?"

"I have no idea."

"Doesn't matter. Because it doesn't change the fact that you're not staying here, and your friend Peter will be delivered into the nearest town at daybreak."

"No."

He laughed. "No?"

"That's what I said. I don't recognize your authority over these swamps. Since you won't fight me for that right, they're up for grabs."

"According to who?"

"According to the laws of nature, stupid. The strongest survive. That's obviously me."

He grabbed my wrist and squeezed it. "You are either really brave or really stupid."

"Yeah. I've heard that before." I jerked my arm away. "Fight me for it. Fight me for the swamp if you're not afraid of losing it to a hundred pound white girl."

"Fine. You want to get humiliated in front of two tribes and your friends? Be my guest. Let's go." He pushed past me, knocking me to the side, storming out of the hut. I let him get away with that part of the intimidation game so he'd continue to think I was easy prey. I had the advantage as long as I was being underestimated.

I followed him out of the hut, silently praying to my dad, in case he was up there listening, to send me the strength and control that I was going to need to earn the right to stay and live in the Kahayatle with my family.

CHAPTER
FIFTY

A SPACE WAS CLEARED NEAR the fire, giving us room to hold our fight. The Creek indians were laughing and elbowing each other in the ribs, their gazes alternating between me and their fearless leader. He was pacing around in the circle, occasionally hitting himself in the chest like an ape, getting his anger stoked up and his brain chemicals firing. I'm not sure if he was aware of the actual physical changes he was bringing about for himself, but it didn't matter. For the next few minutes he'd have more strength and power than usual and it would help him enhance whatever fighting skills he already had. I couldn't assume he had none.

I allowed the reality of my situation to naturally increase the levels of adrenaline in my system. This guy was almost twice my size, outweighed me by a good seventy pounds - maybe more - and he had something to prove to the entire Creek tribe. On top of all that, he had a giant ego that would only let him lose if he was down to taking his last, dying breath.

Maybe the Creek tribe was only made up of the twenty odd people here, or maybe it was a hundred of them - but it didn't matter. A guy like this with his ego on the line would go to just about any lengths to protect it, and that was enough to let my brain know that I needed whatever performance enhancing chemicals it had on hand, and I needed them now.

"Bryn, I wish you wouldn't do this," said Peter. He sounded exhausted.

"Oh, you'd rather get thrown out on your butt back in town?"

"Heck no. But do you really need to go this far to keep that from happening?"

"There's more at stake here than just that. These guys need to kiss and make up with the Miccosukee."

He rolled his eyes. "Tell me about it. They spent half the night talking about them. You're going to have a problem with them getting together. Too many roosters, if you know what I mean."

"Must have been fun for you," I said wiggling my eyebrows and giving him a look. "All these sweaty, half-naked man-bodies."

"A small consolation for my otherwise hellish experience as a kidnap victim."

"Yeah. There is that whole kidnapping thing, you're right. You'll have to give me the details later. Right now, I have to go all American white girl on this guy's ass."

Peter chuckled. "You go do that. I'm too tired to worry about you. Just don't get killed, okay?" His nonchalance about my up-coming battle translated in my mind into confidence in my skills, which made me feel a little better.

Bodo sat, just listening to our conversation. As I stood to walk away, he got up too, taking my hand and pulling me over to him before I could go out into the circle with Trip.

"Before you go out dare and kick dat guy in da balls, I just wanted to say good luck."

I looked into his eyes and saw they were full of concern. "My dad always said luck is where opportunity meets preparation."

"He's right. As soon as his balls are giving you da opportunity for a good kick, take it." Bodo leaned down before I realized what he was planning to do, and kissed me quickly on the lips. "Kiss for good luck. Try not to let him hurt you. I'm not a very goodt doctor."

I was stunned into silence for a few seconds, my brain process-ing what my lips had felt. I broke eye contact with him and looked out at the angry indian in the fighting ring. Then I looked at Peter watching me, and Bodo, holding my hand. I didn't want that kiss to make me soft, vulnerable for the benefit of Trip. I hardened my heart to the emotions that wanted to dance and sing right now. It was a confusing situation to analyze later. Right now I had to defend my family and our right to live in this safe haven.

I squeezed Bodo's hand once and pulled mine from his grasp. "Just stay out of my way, that's all I ask."

"Dat's not a problem," said Bodo, stepping back to sit with Peter.

"Bryn!" whispered Peter loudly.

I turned my head sideways and whispered back, "What?"

"Trip has a knife near his ankle somewhere. I saw it earlier."

I nodded. Trip probably had one on each ankle if he were smart. I'd bet he wasn't the kind of guy to tell a girl that before a fight, either. I moved slowly into the area designated for our challenge, watching him move, looking to see where he might have a tell - the thing that would show me his favorite move or his biggest weakness. So far, all I saw was a guy dancing around on the balls of his feet with excellent balance. The shape of his upper body muscles told me that he liked to use a punching bag when he worked out, which meant I was going to have to take as few punches from him as possible if I wanted to stay conscious. Quick and mean strikes in critical zones had to be my methods here. He was too big to use simple power plays on, and too in shape to outlast.

"Just so everyone's clear," I said loudly as I walked around the ring, keeping him on the opposite side of it, "we're fighting for control of the swamp ... of the Everglades. I win, I decide who stays and who goes; Trip wins, he decides."

Trip laughed. "Understood! Now come on over here and get your ass kickin', girl."

"You're gonna whoop a girl?" yelled out one of his tribesmen, half laughing, half sounding as if he didn't believe it.

"She asked for it!" said Trip. "Practically *begged* me, even."

"Somebody wants a piece of the chief!" yelled another one,

making everyone laugh in lecherous tones. A few of them hooted in excitement.

Oh, gag. Leave it to a group of guys to turn a power challenge match into a naked mud wrestling event. I let their disrespect sink in and fuel my determination.

Trip made the first move like I knew he would - bold and simple, a straight up face to face attack that he obviously hoped would be the first and last move he had to make tonight.

I waited for him to come, balanced on the balls of my feet, ready to make the maneuver I would need to stop the aggression before it got the better of me.

He came at me like a bull, arms slightly cocked, hands hovering near his chest, just below his pecs. He was going to shove me. Hard. A tiny part of me was relieved to see he was taking the least brutal approach to his assault at the beginning - it suggested he might respect girls enough to not punch them in the face ... at least not right away.

I knew he was going to make contact; I couldn't stop that. But I could change the trajectory of my body once it got hit and remove some of the power from it. I also planned to slow him down for at least a short period of time.

The sounds of the crowd dulled and then disappeared altogether. My brain was focused on only one thing - the man in front of me with the evil intention of taking me down.

At the moment just before he reached out to hit me with over a hundred pounds of force, I shot my hand out in a choking position and jammed the space between my thumb and forefinger into his larynx, twisting a little to the side so I'd be able to reach beyond his arm length and so that only one of his hands would actually hit me.

I felt the hard cartilage of his throat flex a little and the immediate response of his body to begin choking and gasping for air. Meanwhile, his right hand hit me hard in the chest, sending me spinning off to the side. I almost went down.

I continued the movement of my body on purpose, catching myself after a full rotation to end up behind him, knowing I had to take advantage of his temporary inability to breathe. I took one step and stomped the bottom of my foot into the back of his left knee, causing it to bend and bring him down closer to the ground. I ran over to bring my fists down at the back of his neck in a double hammer that was meant to drop him, using the force of my hips and shoulders to drive it toward the ground as powerfully as I could. But he was tougher than I anticipated, and all they did was bounce off.

I did the only thing that was left to me at that point and delivered a punishing kick to his face. I hated to mar the beauty there, but this was my only chance to save my friends.

His body flew back with the force of the blow, but only enough to give him the leverage he needed to stand back up. He used his arm behind him on the ground to get his legs under him and then he straightened. And boy, was he pissed.

Blood was coming from a cut by his eye that I'd just put there with my kick. A bruise was starting to form already around his throat. I knew he'd be sore there for days. His voice told me he was already feeling the worst of it.

"You're gonna fucking die," he croaked out.

Wow, he really means that.

I watched as he reached down and pulled a knife out from under his pant leg near his shoe, never breaking eye contact with me. I let my eyes widen and fear enter them, hoping that he'd take that as a sign of weakness to exploit.

He moved sideways, looking for an opening he could take so he could give me a new orifice.

Grumbling from the sidelines filtered into my consciousness, making me think that not everyone was okay with the whole knife and death threat thing he had going on. But I assumed that no one would be bold enough to actually say so, since that would probably mean they'd be on the other end of his anger instead of me. It was one thing to disapprove - a whole other to volunteer to take my place. I was totally okay with that, though. This guy was a special case. I doubted anyone here had what was needed to take him out. I knew I did, but every fight was different. Sometimes things happened that pushed the odds in the weaker fighter's favor and the stronger man went down. I was hoping that wouldn't happen here - I was the one with the better skills. I knew that with every fiber of my being.

I knew he was going to come for me at any second. His hand and shoulder positioning told me he was going to slash at me, stomach-height, from his left to his right. He was holding the knife in his right hand and it had already started swinging ever so slightly, showing me the plans he was making in his mind. I doubted he even knew he was making them consciously.

He came at me in a mad rush, leaving me little time to prepare my response. I did what came naturally to me, after years and years of practice with guys much bigger than me or him. I waited until the last second - when he thought he had me and started his arc - to jump back and curl my body into a u-shape, allowing the blade to slice the air where my belly had just been.

The momentum of his strong stroke meeting nothing of resistance caused his arm to continue its sideways motion, leaving his abdomen open and unprotected. His legs were spread for balance, and I took advantage, kicking high and hard, intending to check him in the balls.

He swiveled at the last second, causing my kick to go into his thigh instead. It didn't destroy him like I wanted it to, but I knew he felt it. He struck me once hard in the face with his open palm and then danced back, putting some distance between me and his precious parts.

"You bitch. You're gonna pay for that."

"Not if I can help it," I said, breathing heavy not with the exertion, but with the amped up reaction to his threats and the chemicals in my veins. My face stung where he'd gotten a piece of me. I took some deep breaths, calming myself for the battle that was to come. I could feel blood dripping down my face from my cheek.

This was the hardest part, when the opponent realizes he's underestimated your skills. He's more careful now, more studied in his decisions. There would be less weaknesses for me to exploit. And I hadn't managed to relieve Trip of that knife, or the other one I was sure he had in his other pant leg. Now was when I had to be exacting in my work. No mercy could be shown and no quarter given. It was do or die right now, and I chose do.

I'd been on the defensive for the whole time so far. Now it was time to attack. I approached him, praying that he'd take the opportunity to try and use that knife against me and that he'd try a lower stroke this time since he knew the higher aim hadn't worked out so well.

He didn't disappoint me. He pulled the knife back and then leaned over, bringing it forward to slice up under my arms.

I bent over in half again, making sure that knife couldn't make contact with my body and crossed my arms in front of me, throwing them out, connecting at their juncture with his knife arm, about four inches up from his wrist. As soon as the forward motion of the knife swing was stopped, I slid my right arm out of its crossed position, up to his elbow, pulling it toward me while simultaneously using my other hand to twist his wrist around and bend his arm up around his back.

Now the knife was in his hand and pointed at his own back. One shove from me on the bottom of the handle and I could take out his kidney, making it game over.

Instead, I just pushed a little. One pop from my fist, enough to sink the blade in a half-inch, before I grabbed it out of his semi-limp hand and tossed it out of our circle. I pushed his bent-over form away from me and backed up.

I heard gasps around the circle as I danced back and forth on my toes. He had blood running down his back, smearing his paint, making his injury look way more gruesome than it really was. He was going to be pissed, but I had to try and end this without someone getting more hurt.

"I didn't push the knife all the way in, but I could have. Fight's over. I won."

He stumbled one step before standing up most of the way, a murderous look in his eye.

"Bullshit!" he yelled, before he charged me, hands out, ready to choke the life out of me.

I let him come.

As soon as his hands locked on my throat, I reached up, my hands facing down in a cupped and hooked position, coming up and over his arms to meet in the center in front of my throat. I used the couple inches of space between my hands and the inside of his wrists to power his hands away from each other, releasing them from my throat, and more importantly, my windpipe.

I held his hands tight, knowing if he got them back I'd be starting all over. My leg came up and delivered a punishing blow to his balls. I'd finally made contact, but only because he'd thought he had me with the brutal force of his very strong hands, and left them dangling out in the open on a silver platter.

I used the muscles in my back to bring my right elbow forward. I pushed his hands down, ones he was still holding tense in an effort to use his strength against me, causing them to lower his face into the perfect position. I slammed his left cheek with the pointy bone in my elbow, and then pushed his head to the other side with the forearm that was following through, still holding his right arm up against my shoulder.

As he bent in half with the pressure of my arm and the pain in his midsection, I drove my knee upwards into his chest, one, two, three times, knocking the rest of the wind out of him.

My last move was to stomp his right knee that was bent and pointed out to the side. I eased up a little at the end, sparing him from a break that could mean his death without proper medical care. Instead, I bashed it hard enough that he'd feel it for a couple weeks. And maybe every time it rained, he'd get a reminder of the little white girl who'd gone American all over his ass.

He fell to the ground, gasping like a fish out of water, one hand holding his nuts and the other stretching toward his knee.

I reached down and pulled out the other knife he had, from the sheath at his ankle, swinging it over to put the tip to his neck. Out of the corner of my eye, I saw a guy move like he was going to come after me; but Paci and one of the Creek grabbed him by the arms, shaking their heads at him. He stopped and stepped back, for the moment agreeing to wait and see what I would do.

I pushed the tip of the knife until it drew a little blood, before stopping. I announced in a loud voice, "This challenge is over. I won. Call me the winner, Trip, or I'm going to gut you right here."

He didn't say anything at first. Then he spit and said in a hoarse voice, "You win."

I stood up, pulling the knife away from his neck. I was just about to start talking to the crowd when I felt a hand grab my ankle. I didn't stop to think, I just reacted. I twisted around and dropped my whole body down, slamming my elbow into Trip's temple, knocking him unconscious. His grip on my ankle went slack.

I adjusted my body so I was no longer lying on my back across his. Instead, I moved so I was sitting on him, my legs bent up in front of me, my feet on the ground. I rested my forearms on my knees, letting the knife stay solidly in my hand, assassin-grip-style. For all intents and purposes, I looked like I was sitting on a fresh kill. I smiled with the knowledge of the visual impact it was having on Trip's faithful.

They might not have liked the situation one bit, but I had wiped the ground of the Kahayatle with his butt fair and square, and they had to respect that. A lot of the rules in our world had changed, but not the most basic one of all: our chances of survival were entirely dependent on our ability and willingness to dominate others. I'd shown I was not only willing but able to do that - to their leader. The Kahayatle was my world now, at least temporarily, and we were going to be making some changes.

CHAPTER
FIFTY-ONE

PACI CAME WALKING OVER ACROSS the open space and offered me his hand. I took it and stood.

"Well done, Nokosi."

"Thanks, Paci. He's going to be fine, you know. I didn't kill him."

He laughed. "Yeah, I know. Too bad. Trip will live another day to make an ass of himself."

Bodo and Peter came over, Peter with a wet cloth someone had given him. He reached up to wipe the blood off my cheek, causing me to wince when it made contact with the wound.

"That looks like it might need stitches."

"Oh, well. No chance of that out here."

"I can stitch it," said Coli, walking up and only glancing casually at the still form of Trip.

"Uh, no thanks," I said, almost laughing at the idea of letting this cranky girl put a needle in my face.

"Our father was a doctor. He taught her how to do it," said Jeremy, coming over to join our little group. "So what now? You won the right to make some decisions. I'm not sure how much right you actually won, but at least I agree you can take your friend back."

"As far as I'm concerned, I've won whatever the hell I want." I held up my hands to appease the people with feathers starting to ruffle. "But ... I don't want a lot, so hopefully this will be pretty painless. At least more painless than it was for Trip."

I got a good laugh out of that one, and it helped people feel more at ease. I could tell by the frowns disappearing and the folded arms dropping. The only one who still looked pissed was Coli and I was starting to get used to that.

"Here's what I want: First, Peter's coming with me. Second, he, Bodo and I will be living here full time until we decide we don't want to anymore - and I expect everyone here to not only respect that but also to make sure others respect it. Last, I want all of you to get together with the Miccosukee and find a way to live together and cooperate. Put together a new tribe or an alliance or whatever you want to call it. Just get it done ... like soon. Tomorrow."

"Why are you so fixated on this alliance?" asked Jeremy, loud enough that everyone could hear.

"Because we've been outside the swamp, as far north as Sanford, and there are groups of cannibals forming out there - gangs - who are moving around and terrorizing all the towns that we saw on our way down here. They're going after and eating other kids. And let me tell you, those cannibals are fat, okay? They're not just doing it to survive. They're enjoying it. Enough freaks are moving into leadership roles out there and they're brainwashing everyone with them to think it's okay to eat people."

"So, what does that mean to us if a bunch of white people are eating each other? Let 'em," said Jeremy.

"Right. And how long do you think it'll take them to realize you've got some prime beef right here in the swamp?" I reached out and pushed on Trip's body with my foot. "You guys are easy pickins if you keep your tribes separate. They have guns. They're going to find more ammo and they're going to eventually find the rocket launchers and bazookas and everything else. You need to get your shit together and grow your community. We need more people to fight against them when they come. And they will come, I guarantee it."

Several of the onlookers began talking in low tones to one another. I couldn't hear what anyone was saying. Jeremy took the bull by the horns and said the words I wanted to hear.

"What you're saying makes sense. We have some history with the Meeks. Our parents were once friends … at least some of them were." He gave a pointed look to his sister. "We heard rumors, from Celia, that there's some weird stuff going on out there." He looked at his tribesmen. "What do you guys think? Trip's out of commission but I'm his second. I'm willing to take a vote and suffer the consequences from Trip's temper later. Who's in favor of discussing an alliance?"

Most of the hands went up.

Jeremy shrugged. "Looks like the majority says we do that."

"Good. I'm going back to my hut now. Why don't you guys come tomorrow afternoon to the hut used for rituals, and we'll have a meeting there. We can figure out the details with the whole group together."

"We'll eat together," said Coli, standing up straight. "Like our people used to do when there were tribal gatherings."

"Good idea," I said. "It's potluck. Bring your covered dishes and we'll see you in …," I looked down at my watch, "… fifteen hours, give or take."

Bodo put his hands on my shoulders from behind, giving me a strong, quick massage as we walked back toward the canoe. "Dat wass amazsing. I can't wait to learn dat stuff."

I smiled tiredly. Now that I'd kicked butt and taken names, I was exhausted. I hadn't eaten enough calories to do what I'd done today - I was going to have to find a belt to hold up my shorts or pretty soon I'd have to run around in one of those breechcloths too.

"You're giving lessons?" asked Jeremy.

"Yeah. That's what I agreed to do in exchange for a place to live."

"I'd like to get in on that."

"Sign up with the Miccosukee and you can."

He didn't say anything in response, but I knew it was helping our cause that free krav maga lessons had just been thrown into the pot.

We reached the canoe and Bodo helped both Peter and me climb into it. I was really glad I wasn't being called on to paddle because my arms felt like they were made of rubber - the super flimsy kind.

"I guess we'll see you tomorrow, Nokosi," said Jeremy.

Now he was going to use the nickname too, I guess. I lifted my hand in a weak wave. "See ya."

"Wouldn't wanna be ya," said Peter, in a voice so quiet only those in the canoe could hear him.

We all giggled as we pulled away, letting the current and a lazy paddle dipping in the water spin our boat around and point us back home.

CHAPTER FIFTY-TWO

I NEARLY CRIED WHEN I got back to our hut and found three small mattresses lying on the floor and Buster's fuzzy butt parked right in the center of the middle one. He came running over with a bark to greet me, making me feel like a million bucks. I bent over to give him the attention he craved and to accept his five hundred licks of welcome.

"Holy mackerel, mother of little baby fishes, is that a bed?" whispered Peter. His hands came together up at his chest, making a bunch of rapid little claps, his face glowing with deranged delight, which only served to get Buster even more excited. He left me to go lick-attack Peter's ankles.

I put my hand on Peter's painted shoulder, patting him with my fingers. "Ease up there, Mary."

He swatted me away and clapped some more. "Shut up. You're spoiling my prayers."

"Who are you praying to? Holy mackerel?"

"No, to the swamp gods."

"Swamp gods."

"Yes. Shush." He closed his eyes and moved his lips in silent prayer.

I rolled my eyes. "I think you're more apt to find a swamp monster out here than a god, but whatever floats your boat." I dragged my tired butt over to the mattress, the middle one of the three, and sat down with my legs crossed, making room in my lap for Mr. Wiggly Fuzzy Buns himself; I giggled with sleepy-silliness, thinking about how my dad used to call this sitting 'indian-style'.

"Someone left some food here for us," said Bodo, his mouth already full. "I think it's deer meat. Delicious."

I held up my hand above my head and behind my back. "Hand me some. I'm too tired to move."

Peter came over shortly with a wooden platter, covered in meat and some grilled vegetables I didn't recognize. I did care what they were - I inhaled them all, and then licked the plate clean, only giving Buster a few little pieces - I was quite certain he'd already been fed if his round belly were any indication. My stomach groaned loudly with the sudden influx of food - more than it'd had in there in a long time. I chugged the fresh water from the bottle Bodo gave me when he came to sit down on the mattress to my left. When I was finished, I put both the empty bottle and the platter on the ground near the head of my mattress and laid down on my back. Buster settled between my legs and rested his head on my thigh.

"So, you are da queen of da swamp. How does dat make you feel?"

I sighed. "It makes me feel loaded down with responsibility."

Bodo laid back and turned his head to look at me, folding his arms behind his head. "Don't worry. You haff me and Peter to help you."

"That's good to know … no great to know," I said, as I lost the battle to stay awake and drifted off to sleep.

CHAPTER FIFTY-THREE

W E SLEPT THROUGH THE NIGHT and into half of the next day. Nobody bothered to wake us up, but when I stood up to go pee, I found another pile of food on the shelves that looked as if it had recently been brought in. I walked over and tore off a hunk of heavy bread filled with whole grains, seeds and nuts. I sniffed it first, finding it smelled just like the yeasty breads I was used to from back in the old days, when my dad would shop at the local organic market.

I took a bite and breathed out a sigh of pleasure. *Damn, that tastes good.*

I popped the rest of it in my mouth and moved off to find some privacy. Buster followed along beside me, sniffing as he went.

By the time we got back, the guys were sitting up and we had company - Kowi and Coli, standing just outside the hut.

"Hey," he said, his eyes going to the cut on my cheek.

"Hey. What's up?"

"Well, I hear we have a meal to put on tonight."

"Yeah. Sorry about the short notice."

He smiled. "Not a problem. We started preparing last night as soon as you guys got back. Sounds like you made quite an impression over there."

I noticed Coli didn't look quite as cranky as usual today for some reason. I wondered if it had anything to do with our activities of last night or whether it was Kowi's reaction to it. She was almost pretty when she wasn't scowling. It was probably best not to comment on it, though, or it would probably disappear like a puff of smoke.

"Yeah, I guess you could say that. I'm not so sure Trip appreciated it when he woke up."

"Trip will be fine," said Coli, a slight smile on her face. "He needed to be taken down a peg or two, anyway."

"I doubt he'll agree with that," I said.

"Don't worry about him. He's a good sport, deep down," said Kowi.

"Very deep," clarified Coli.

"Good," I said, "because I'm not interested in fighting him again. Once was enough for me."

"Yeah, he's tough. He's gotten the best of every single one of us at one time or another. That's part of the problem we've had, which is what I came to talk to you about," said Kowi.

"Okaaaay ... why don't we all have a seat?" I gestured to the living room part of our quarters rather than the area with the mattresses.

Bodo and Peter came out of the other room and grabbed their food off the shelves, joining us to sit in a circle on the floor.

I reached over and snagged my share of food, pulling it into pieces with my fingers and putting it in my mouth while Kowi talked. Buster begged for his share and Peter made sure he got it.

"When our parents, grandparents, and little sisters and brothers died, we were all living together - us, the Creek and the few Hitchitis and Oconees that are still around. The whole Seminole Nation just kind of crumbled into its original pieces, but we were still kind of together. After a few months, though, we had some disagreements about who was going to be in charge and how we were going to do things - plus who was going to have access to certain hunting grounds. So eventually we split into two groups:

the Miccosukee who absorbed most of the Hitchitis, and the Creek who took the Oconees. Trip took the role of chief over there, since he's the strongest and has the most aggressive personality. I took the role here."

"Kowi was voted on by us. He didn't take the role by force like Trip did," said Coli.

Kowi continued as if she hadn't spoken. "Trip and I were friends in high school. We hung out and played sports together. He's changed since then, yeah ... we all have. But deep down he's a good guy. He always played fair on the field, and I think he'll play fair with us now."

"He fought kindt of dirty last night," said Bodo.

"No, I don't consider what he did dirty," I said. "It was an anything-goes fight. We both knew that."

"Yeah, but you didn't bring any weapons. He did," said Peter.

Coli blew a snort of air out. "She is a weapon."

I nodded at the unexpected words of respect coming from the person I had considered the least likely to ever give any.

She sniffed and looked away.

"It doesn't matter now," said Kowi. "It's over, and everyone knows you won. You hold all the cards here, so I just wanted to let you know what I think and what I'd like to see happen."

I held up my hand, shaking my head. "Save it. We'll all talk about it at the meeting."

"But don't you want to hear what he has to say now?" asked Peter.

"Yes. But I don't want what he thinks to taint my opinions over in his favor. I want this to be fair for everyone, not just the Miccosukee. If the Creek think I'm playing favorites, they're going to get bitter. And you guys can't afford to have bitter comrades watching your backs."

Kowi nodded once and stood. "Fair enough. We'll see you at the ceremonial hut around four, then."

Coli followed him out, looking back once at me and hesitating as if she were going to say something, but then leaving quietly a second later.

"I'd like to go take a shower," said Peter, "but no way in heck am I going alone this time."

"I'll go with you," I said. "I have to wash the fight club grime off me anyway."

"You do know we're not showering together, right?" asked Peter, eyeing me suspiciously.

"Are you *trying* to make me vomit my lunch?"

Peter shrugged, getting up to find his clothes. "I just wanted to be sure. No need to be so prickly about it."

Bodo kept me company while Peter showered on the other side of the curtain, and then escorted Peter back to the hut while I took mine.

I was almost ready to walk back when I heard a rustling in the bushes next to the enclosure. I froze in place, not sure if it was an animal or human, but it was definitely not the wind.

"Who's there?" I called out.

"It's me. Trip." His voice was hoarse.

I stepped out from behind the screen to greet him. He was standing at the edge of the trees. He looked like crap.

"Wow. Sorry about your face."

He had a bruise on the corner of his eye, a swollen cheek just under it, and a big purple bruise on his neck. He gave me a lop-sided grin. "Yeah. I guess I kind of deserved it."

"I won't hold it against you."

"Good. Listen ... I'm sorry to interrupt your shower, but I just wanted to talk to you for a second about the meeting tonight."

"If you're here to plead your case, I'll tell you the same thing I told Kowi."

"Oh, yeah? What's that?"

"Save it. I'm not playing favorites. We'll all get it out in the open tonight with everyone around."

Trip just stared at me and nodded for a couple seconds before he said, "You're smart. I misjudged you. On many levels."

"Thanks. I think."

"I guess I'll see you later."

"See ya."

He stepped back and soon disappeared into the trees.

I made my way back to the huts, deep in thought about to-night's festivities. I was going to need Peter's and Bodo's help to pull this off. They'd seen as much or more than I had out there. We had one shot to convince these guys that their tribes were in danger. Someone had to paint a picture of their possible future that would burn itself into their skulls.

CHAPTER
FIFTY-FOUR

PEOPLE FILTERED INTO THE AREA near the ceremonial lodge a half hour before the actual meeting. We'd gone with Buster since we had nothing else to do, Peter having organized and re-organized our living space three times already.

"I feel better when my life has order and structure," he'd said.

As we walked up to the meeting place, I saw the truth of his words - at least the truth they held for him. He actually looked happy and not scared for the first time … maybe even hopeful. It made me feel like we were definitely doing the right thing. Buster took off in search of lizards or something more interesting than a bunch of feet that could step on him.

Coli came walking up to me and handed me something folded up, soft, and dark blue in color.

"What's this?"

"It's a shirt."

"Why are you giving it to me?"

She shrugged. "I thought you might like to wear something other than that awful t-shirt you have on."

I laughed. "Wow. Okay … so who should I thank for this?"

"Whoever you want," she said, starting to walk away.

I reached out to stop her. "Who made it?"

"I did," she said, before returning to the trees.

"She's got issues," said Bodo. "But I think she likes you anyway."

I unfolded the shirt, which wasn't the shape of a regular shirt, and saw that it was made of some kind of cotton cloth that had designs woven into it, mostly patterns of small diamonds together in rows. There were several colors in these small shapes, but the dominant color was the bright but deep blue.

"It matchess your eyess," said Bodo.

The shirt was more like a cape that fit over my shoulders and hung down to my waist. I was going to keep my regular shirt on underneath. I looked at other girls coming into the area and noticed that they were all dressed up in clothing that had the same general look as this one. Most of them were wearing full skirts that matched too.

"Oh well. Might as well join the party," I said, putting it on over my head. I felt like a caped crusader.

"It's cute," said Peter. "Bright colors suit you, I think."

"Thanks," I said, smiling as I watched two other girls come up with shirts in their hands. One was for Peter and one for Bodo. "Let's see 'em, guys. You can play dress-up with us now, too."

Bodo put his on without even looking at it. It was a vest with the same colors and patterns as mine. Peter's was bright red, yellow, and green. It reminded me of a parrot.

Peter stroked the front of it and flattened it against his chest, smiling. "I like it."

I couldn't help but giggle. "It's loud and proud, that's for sure … shows off your inner Peter."

"That sounds so wrong," he said shaking his head while looking down, still admiring his new duds. I could see him trying not to smile.

We stood off to the side in our new clothes and watched people filter in. Trip showed up with several boat loads of Creek, all of them decked out in finery too. I couldn't help but be impressed with Trip's outfit. He had colors, feathers, beads and all kinds of other things hanging off him that I couldn't identify. I think there were even some animal quills or tails or something in a headdress he wore.

"Daaaamn," said Peter, his mouth hanging open.

"Wow, dat's some kinda hat he's wearing. He looks like he has a mohawk."

The fur or quills that made up his head piece did stand straight up and go down in a row, flowing down past his neck. I had to admit - it was pretty badass.

Kowi and Paci were the last to come in, with Coli walking just in front of her boyfriend. The couple looked like an indian king and queen - or chief and princess, I wasn't sure what the right terms were. They were an explosion of colors, feathers, fur, and beads. Their arms were still bare though, which was probably to make sure they didn't suffocate in this heat. They had to be hot - I knew I was with my simple cape. Apparently even Native Americans have to get uncomfortably dressed up once in a while.

Kowi raised his hands up to get everyone's attention. After a few seconds of jostling around and nudging, the crowd went quiet. It was divided in two groups - Creeks on one side, Miccosukees on the other.

"Thanks for coming, everyone; it's been a long time. I suggest we eat before we begin our business." He turned and gestured to some girls standing behind him holding trays of food. "In the interest of our mutual distrust of each other, we will begin the feast with one person from each tribe eating a sample of their own food, chosen at random by the other."

Trip spoke up. "We agree to this."

I looked at Bodo and Peter, a big question mark on my face. I leaned over toward Peter and whispered, "What the heck is he talking about?"

"I have no clue."

We watched as a Miccosukee and a Creek walked up to one another, each carrying some food. The Miccosukee indian took a fork and speared a piece of the Creek food and gave it to the Creek indian to eat it. Then the Creek indian reached over and speared a piece of the Miccosukee dish and the Miccosukee indian ate it.

They continued with this ritual until every dish of food - over thirty in all - had been tested by someone of the opposite tribe.

"What the hell?" I said quietly.

"Dey're checking for poison," said Bodo.

"Whaaaat?!" I whisper-yelled.

"I guess dey had a problem before with da food or something."

"Wow," said Peter. "That's what I call distrust."

"This is hopeless," I said to no one in particular. I had no idea these people would be so vicious as to poison one another when inviting them over for dinner.

Paci came wandering over, the taste test done. "You like that? Kinda weird, huh?"

"You could say that," I answered, trying to be neutral but my facial expression wasn't very convincing.

"Yeah, it is. We know it. But better to be safe than sorry, you know? We can be pretty creative with our revenge."

"I guess."

Everyone was walking over to get wooden plates and forks. We joined the line and then helped ourselves to a small sample of food from every dish. It all looked simply-prepared but delicious to me. There were lots of vegetables, some fruit, and plenty of meat. I grabbed a hunk of heavy bread to add to my meal before finding a spot on the ground just inside the hut where I could eat it.

"So, we have to talk," said Kowi, once everyone had food and was sitting down. "Bryn's here to tell us about this problem we supposedly have."

"Say what you have to say, Bryn," said Trip, shoving a huge hunk of meat in his mouth.

I put my plate on the ground in front of me and stood up, adjusting my cape self-consciously. "What I have to say is that your plan to stay as separate tribes is a mistake." I looked around at the faces staring up at me and I saw mostly open-minded expressions. A couple of the bigger guys looked doubtful, but I expected that - big guys often think themselves invincible.

"We've come from north of here. All the way down from there to here we saw canners ... cannibals. We got into altercations with two different groups of them, one in my house and one in an orange grove about a day's ride north of here."

"They came into your house?" asked a girl.

"Yes. They're doing that all over."

"We thought there was an unspoken rule that houses were off limits."

"It used to be that way, but not anymore. All the empty houses have been raided until there's nothing left to eat. All the grocery stores are empty and so are the warehouses. Most of the kids, at least in this state, don't know how to grow or raise their own food. So they're going after the easiest prey."

"Other kids," said Peter, standing up next to me.

I held his hand for support because he was shaking like a leaf on a tree, and I knew what he was going to tell them.

"I'm from Sanford. I lived there up until about three weeks ago with my little sister, Lily." He paused a moment to let that fact sink in.

Naturally, everyone was wondering where Lily was.

"One day we were outside our house, and a gang of kids was walking down the street. They came after us and we tried to escape, but Lily fell down and hurt herself. She couldn't run anymore."

The faces around us showed fear. Some of them probably either thought they knew what was coming next in the story or they suspected it was pretty bad.

Peter's voice was quaking now. "They caught us and took her away. They left me behind and wouldn't let me go with them."

"Where is she now?" asked someone.

Peter's voice cracked and became almost a screech. "She's *dead!*" He dropped his face into his hands and sobbed.

I put my arm across his back and continued the story. "I wasn't there, but Peter told me the whole thing. I'm going to tell you … not to shock you, but to make you see that this is serious. More serious than you can imagine." I looked around to make sure I had everyone's attention. No one was even eating anymore.

"After they caught his sister, he followed them at a distance so they wouldn't see him. He saw them take her to someone's house, so he ran back home to get his gun; but by the time he got back, it was too late. They had killed her … and they were dismembering her and cooking her body parts to eat her." My stomach rolled queasily. I saw three girls and one guy get up from their seats and run into the woods. The sounds of their retching echoed across the silent space.

Then the only sound to be heard in the swamp was Peter's sobbing. Bodo came up and put his arms around him, patting him on the back, his own eyes wet with tears. "I'm so, so sorry for you, Peter. Dat's a terrible thing … terrible." He cleared his throat a couple times and looked up at the ceiling of the hut, trying to manage his emotions.

"So you see," I continued, "we have a really big problem out there and we need to do whatever we can to plan for these … monsters who will eventually be coming this way."

"But you said they're up north of here," said one girl, weakly. "Sorry, I don't mean any disrespect, Peter."

He shook his head but said nothing, still hiding his face.

"They're spreading out. Kids I used to know were ganging together, abandoning their houses. You know that once these few maniacs who are leading these groups start letting people think cannibalism is okay, the idea that it's not will start to fade for the weak. And there are plenty of weak-minded people out there."

"She's talking sense, people," said Paci. "Our own history shows the same kind of thing happening to our ancestors."

"No one ate our ancestors, idiot," said Jeremy sarcastically.

"No. But they murdered them didn't they? In cold blood. People do strange things, bad things, when they're fighting for resources like land and food. You may have been all busy with your football and your nice shiny SUV and off-res parties, Jeremy, but you have to remember the basics we all learned when we were little kids in school."

"Even we learned those stories," I said.

Jeremy had nothing to say in response.

Trip stood up and said, "Maybe we all agree that together we're better off - stronger - as a nation rather than individual tribes. But that doesn't solve our biggest problem. Who's gonna be chief?"

Everyone looked from Kowi to Trip, the tension growing with every second.

I watched the two of them. They were both big, proud, teens - almost men. And maybe this virus that killed our parents was dead now and wouldn't kill us when we turned twenty, so they would grow to lead these people as they got married and had families. It didn't make sense to sacrifice all of that for silly things like pride and egos.

"I think you should both be chief."

"There can't be two chiefs," said Trip.

"Why not?"

"Because someone has to make the final decision; someone has to have the final say," said Kowi.

"Fine. Have a council, and majority rules."

"They'll just do what they did before we split," said Coli. "They'll each have their people side with them and it'll just be a split decision all the time."

"Have a fifth member," I suggested, at the end of my list of brilliant ideas. "That way there will always be one tie-breaker."

"Who's it going to be?" asked Jeremy. If it's Creek, they'll vote Creek. If it's Miccosukee, they'll vote Miccosukee.

I threw up my hands. "I don't know! Geez, can't you guys just come up with a solution?"

"I have one," said Coli, standing now, her brightly-colored dress blazing with its designs. "Why don't we let one of the white kids be the tie breaker if we need one?"

You could have knocked me over with a feather when those words came out of her mouth. I waited for the arguments and yelling, but they never came.

"Fine with me," said Trip. "She already proved to me she's capable of fighting."

"Fine with me, too," said Kowi. "We need her skills. If we tie her to us more permanently, she'll have no choice but to help."

"Hello ... I'm standing right here." I shook my head. "And I already told you I'd train you. You don't need to appoint me as a tie breaker." I wasn't even sure I wanted that kind of responsibility or permanent connection to these people. I was happy just being a three-person tribe.

Voices rose as everyone discussed the pros and cons of having a white girl, namely *me*, involved in their day-to-day decision-making. I couldn't blame the people who had negative opinions on the matter - our American history classes had made it abundantly clear that the white man had been viciously unfair to the Native Americans in years past. They probably figured the apple didn't fall far from the tree.

I wasn't sure which way the decision was going at that point, but I knew exactly when it changed in favor of bringing me and my friends on board.

A sound broke through the many voices buzzing with discussion, and began to filter into our collective consciousness. First it registered in my mind as a moaning or a crying. I thought it was the wind and then maybe an animal. But then the weeping took on a very human tone, and Buster's barking made it obvious that whatever it was, it was nearby and he didn't like it. He took off, racing toward the water, howling his butt off.

Several people followed, using the sounds of Buster's hysteria as their guide. I stood back with Peter and Bodo, waiting to get news from those by the water of what was happening.

We heard screams a few seconds later, not just from one person but several. Some were crying hysterically. Guys were shouting, and those who had remained with us, ran toward the others.

Peter grabbed my arm. "Canners!" he said in a choked voice.

"Shhhh, it's not canners. They don't take boats into the Everglades moaning and crying." My own reasoning sounded hollow to my ears. The truth was, canners were the first thing that had jumped into my mind too. They were like our boogie men, but real and alive and looking for us.

A group of indians came up the pathway from the direction of the water. At first, all we could see was a crowd, but then as they got closer to the hut we could see that in the middle of all of them was Trip, carrying someone like a baby.

A small person.

A girl.

He brought her into the hut, and laid her down on the floor. Her face was white.

I'd heard that expression before, that someone's face had gone white, but I'd never actually seen it before. Now I knew that it was no exaggeration; it was like all her color was totally gone.

I moved closer because she looked familiar to me.

Trip was furious, his face a stone mask of anger. His jaw was bulging out so far it made his face look deformed.

Her facial features clicked in my mind, reminding me of the girl with the baseball bat who'd nearly taken my head off not that long ago.

"Celia?" I asked as I moved closer.

Trip's head whipped up. "How do you know my sister?" he demanded, accusatorially.

My mouth dropped open. "I ... I met her. Before we came here. She gave me a map ..."

Her arm, or what was left of it, dropped down and thumped on the wood floor. A weak moan escaped her lips.

"Oh, my god," whisper-shrieked Peter, *"they took her arm!"*

Bodo grabbed Peter as he lost consciousness.

All I could do was stand there and stare.

Celia was lying near death on the floor of this ceremonial hut with only half an arm left on the right side of her body. It had been taken off at the elbow and the stump was wrapped in scraps of ripped up t-shirt, the end covered in blood.

CHAPTER
FIFTY-FIVE

THE CRYING AND OCCASIONAL SHRIEKING of the girls continued, while Bodo and I knelt down next to Coli and tried to help.

"She's lost too much blood. She's too pale. I know she's going into shock, but I don't know what to do about it!" Coli was crying, the words tumbling out of her mouth.

I rubbed her back. "Just make her comfortable." I pulled the cape off my head and rolled it up, putting it under Celia's head.

Trip clenched and unclenched his fists, alternately pacing behind us and coming back to stare at his sister who lay unresponsive on the ground. Every once in a while her eyelids would flutter and she'd mumble something, but then she'd disappear into unconsciousness again.

"How'd she get here?" I asked Kowi.

"She got in a boat somewhere, probably back near her parents' old vacation cabin. It's not that far from here. She must have paddled with one arm."

"Was she alone?"

"Yeah. And there's blood in the boat. I don't know how long it took her to get here."

I looked at the wrapping on her arm. "Some of that is older blood, I think."

"I'm afraid to take it off," said Coli. "What if she starts bleeding more?"

"Just leave it," I said, putting my hand on Coli's arm to let her know she wasn't alone in questioning what was right and what was wrong.

Peter was sitting off to the side, his legs pulled up to his chest, rocking himself rhythmically while he cried silently. I saw two of the girls go and sit with him. Buster laid down as close to him and he could, resting his chin on Peter's hip. Peter was oblivious to all of it.

"We needt to try and talk to her - to see if she can tell us who didt this to her," said Bodo.

Coli leaned over and tapped Celia on the cheek gently. "Celia! Celia, wake up! We need to talk to you."

Celia's head moved a little, turning to the side. Then her eyes opened and she blinked a couple times. I watched as recognition dawned.

"Bryn?"

"Yeah. It's me. You're in the Miccosukee camp. What happened?"

She turned her head and looked at the others. "Coli?"

"Yeah, babe. It's me."

"Where's Trip?"

He came striding over. "Right here, Cee. What the hell happened to you ... to your arm?" His voice broke.

"Kids. They came to the shop. They broke in ... and smashed all mom's stuff." A tear trickled out of her eye.

I felt myself start to cry too. I knew how much those stupid shell things meant to her.

"They took me and kept me at this house. It's a big one, near the water. They have lots of kids there - they use them like a ... like a ... pantry." She cried harder.

"Did she say like a pantry?" whispered Bodo. "What does dat mean?"

"Sssh, I don't know." I was afraid I knew exactly what it meant, but I needed to hear her say it. Maybe it wasn't as bad as I feared.

"What do you mean, a pantry?" asked Coli.

Celia was moaning so loud she almost couldn't get the words out. She didn't even sound human anymore. "They keep them there ... they keep them there ... for food, they keep them there." Her eyes took on a mad gleam and she whispered in a high tone, "When they need to eat ... they take a limb!"

My hands flew up to my face in horror. I felt my stomach contents churn and I had to force myself not to look at her severed arm. I knew if I did, it would be all over for me and that meal I'd just eaten.

Coli stood up, her face pale. "No!" she yelled. "That is *not* happening!"

"They ... they ...," Celia was trying to get the words out but she couldn't. She was almost hysterical now. "There were ... kids ... there were kids ... they didn't ... they were ... there were *kids without legs!*" she screamed. *"All they had left were their heads!"*

Several people backed away, many to vomit in the nearby bushes.

It was too much. Too much horror. Too much violence.

But we only had to hear it.

She had to see it and personally experience it.

She grabbed her brother's arm with her one remaining hand, staring at him with fiercely maddened eyes. "Kill me! Kill me, *please!"* she begged.

He jerked his arm away from her and stood up suddenly. *"No!"* he cried. "I can't do that, CeeCee. Don't ask me to!"

"Coli," she begged more softly now, looking at her cousin. "Please. For me. Just end this for me now. I can't do this anymore. I just can't."

Coli turned her back on Celia, sobbing, unable or unwilling to speak.

I scooted over and took Celia's hand in mine. I couldn't stand by and let this girl just lie here and beg her people to murder her.

"Celia? Listen to me. You can't ask them to do that to you."

"But I can ask you," she said in a rush, desperation in her voice. "Bryn, please kill me. If this happened to one of your friends, and they asked you, you would do it. I *know* you would."

I shook my head. "No way ... I wouldn't. We're going to get through this. *You* are going to get through this."

"I can't," she whispered, "I just can't."

"Yes, you can. You want to know why? Because we need you to show us where that house is. So we can go rescue those kids and exterminate those monsters." I squeezed her hand hard. "Do you hear me? We *have* to do this, and we can only do it with your help."

She just shook her head, her whole body trembling with anguish.

"Don't say no to me. I know you well enough to know that you value family. Those kids deserve to have a family like you have. We can't let them sit there and be slaughtered like that. Without you, Celia, they're all going to die. Slowly, painfully, and horrifically."

She tipped her head back and said, "God ... why? Why did this happen to me?" Then she whipped her head sideways to look at me. "And why did you have to put this white girl here in my face and ruin my chances of escaping this hell hole?"

She wasn't joking. She was turning her anger on me, but I was totally okay with that. Anger I could deal with - anger would keep her fighting to stay alive.

"Because you have terrible taste in art," I said. "Anyone can see that but you and your mother."

Coli nudged me, a look of shock on her face. I winked at her where Celia couldn't see me, and she visibly relaxed, nodding her head once.

"Did you just ... did you just insult my mother's shell work?"

"God, yes. Are you kidding me? Horrible stuff. Just horrible."

Celia struggled to get up.

I jumped back and got out of Coli's and Trip's way. They were holding Celia's shoulders and legs down.

"Let me up. She's gonna pay, that bitch!"

Trip looked up at me and mouthed the words, "Thank you," before turning back to his struggling sister.

I nudged Bodo and said, "Come on, let's go." Let these kids figure this one out for themselves. There'd be plenty of time later for us to weigh in with our opinions and offers of help.

We went over and pulled Peter up by his armpits, supporting his mostly limp form between us. We walked through the woods until we got to our huts, and didn't stop until we reached our mattresses.

I helped Peter lie down and put the blanket next to him on the floor with a bottle of water nearby. Bodo and I laid down on our mattresses on our sides facing each other, talking softly.

"Today wass a terrible day," said Bodo.

"Yes and no," I said.

"What do you mean? How did I miss da good parts?"

"Well, I think we can assume that the tribes will come together, now that they have a common enemy. Celia's back home and out of danger. And we've found out about a bunch of kids that need rescuing. The tribes can do this, I know they can."

"I can't belief da zombies were keeping kids like cattle. Dat's just insane."

"It is insane. But it makes sense that this would be their next level of insanity, doesn't it? Now they can settle down in one place - go out on raids to find more ... food. I hate to say it, but if I was a mentally ill but smart zombie, it's what I'd do."

"Sometimes you scare me, Bryn."

"Sometimes I scare myself, Bodo."

"So what do we do now?" he asked.

I thought about it for a second before answering. "Well ... I think we help these kids to get their act together, get them trained in combat using the krav maga and George's war journal, and then we figure out how to get those other kids to safety."

"And den?"

"And then? We figure out how to live together. We make our home here. We take care of Peter and help him get over this crisis ... I don't know. You tell me. What then?"

"I like your plan. Dare's just one thing missing."

"What's that?"

He leaned in closer to me … so close I could feel his breath on my lips, and said, "Just this." And then he kissed me.

WANT MORE?

The adventures of Bryn, Peter, Bodo and Buster continue! For more of the humor, writing style and action you enjoyed in Book 1, find the next books in the *Apocalypsis* series at your local or on-line retailer! If you don't find the books on the shelf at your local bookstore, you can order them at the front desk.

Being an independent author, I depend entirely on *you*, the reader, to get the word out about my books. If you liked this book, won't you please leave a review online and recommend it to a friend? The more you spread the word, the more books I can write, and nothing would please me more than to put a new book in your hands every single month.

I read all my reviews!

Find more Elle Casey books at the following retailers:

Amazon
iBooks
Barnes & Noble
Google Play
Kobo
Walmart
Your Local Library via the OverDrive ebook platform

Want to get an email when my next book is released?
Sign up here: www.ElleCasey.com/news

ABOUT THE AUTHOR

Elle Casey, a former attorney and teacher, is a NEW YORK TIMES, USA TODAY, *and Amazon bestselling American author who lives in France with her husband, three kids, and a number of horses, dogs, and cats. She has written more than 40 novels in less than 5 years and likes to say she offers fiction in several flavors. These flavors include romance, science fiction, urban fantasy, action adventure, suspense, and paranormal.*

A personal note from Elle …

If you enjoyed this book, please take a moment to leave a review on the site where you bought this book, Goodreads, or any book blogs you participate in, and tell your friends! I love interacting with my readers, so if you feel like shooting the breeze or talking about books or your family or pets, please visit me. You can find me at …

www.ElleCasey.com
www.Facebook.com/ellecaseytheauthor
www.Twitter.com/ellecasey
www.Instagram.com/ellecaseyauthor

Other Books by Elle Casey

CONTEMPORARY URBAN FANTASY

War of the Fae (10-book series)
Ten Things You Should Know About Dragons
(short story, The Dragon Chronicles)
My Vampire Summer
Aces High

DYSTOPIAN

Apocalypsis (4-book series)

SCIENCE FICTION

Drifters' Alliance (ongoing series)
Winner Takes All (short story prequel to Drifters' Alliance,
Dark Beyond the Stars Anthology)
The Ivory Tower (short story standalone, Beyond the Stars: A
Planet Too Far Anthology)

ROMANCE

By Degrees
Rebel Wheels (3-book series)
Just One Night (romantic serial)
Just One Week
Love in New York (3-book series)
Shine Not Burn (2-book series)
Bourbon Street Boys (4-book series)
Desperate Measures
Mismatched

ROMANTIC SUSPENSE

*All the Glory: How Jason Bradley Went from
Hero to Zero in Ten Seconds Flat*
Don't Make Me Beautiful
Wrecked (2-book series)

PARANORMAL

Duality (2-book series)
Monkey Business (short story)
Dreampath (short story standalone, The
Telepath Chronicles)
Pocket Full of Sunshine (short story & screenplay)

www.ingramcontent.com/pod-product-compliance
Lightning Source LLC
Chambersburg PA
CBHW021533250626
47154CB00006BA/2096